EYES & EARS:

The SetUp

By Kate Ayers

©Copyright January 2015
ISBN #9781503307629

Dedication

For everyone struggling with a disability:
Just believe your dreams are possible.

CHAPTER 1

"A perpetual holiday is a good working definition of Hell."
- George Bernard Shaw

Bridger Flynn had been the media darling during his years with the Portland Police Bureau. The press loved his color in this forward-thinking town; an odd combination of deep mocha skin and Irish red hair. They loved Abigail Dalton's color, too, but for a different reason. Hailing from the Oregon State Police and tending to be a Sandra Bullock look-alike, Abby's color came more in the form of unfiltered language and unsanctioned comments. So the Bureau brass were holding their breath at this morning's press conference.

In a quick briefing, the captain handling the case they were working on suggested they rely heavily on "we can't disclose that information" and "we're looking into that" types of comments. Abby had ideas of her own about what she'd like to say, but the others frowned on her richly graphic preferences and suggested that she stick with the standard protocol. In fact, everyone realized that, if Bridger had better command of his hearing, he would have been the spokesperson of choice to answer questions for the media, but there was no assurance he would not give away his disability. And wouldn't the press have a heyday with that? A deaf detective partnered up with a blind one? Best to keep that under wraps for as long as possible. Hopefully, forever. They had their fingers crossed that none of the eager Jimmy Olsens out there had done a thorough probe of Abby's past, nor of Bridger's. The reason for her retirement from the State Police supposedly remained sealed and secret. Supposedly. Everyone knew, though, that leaks happened all too often, especially when there was an ex in one's past. Or an enemy of any sort in one's present. For cops, there were usually plenty of both, Bridger and Abby being no exceptions.

- - -

One week earlier…

Bridger Flynn didn't hear the sirens coming up behind his tiny smart car. It wasn't because his mind had wandered back to last night, although it had. And it wasn't because he felt Sundays were too sacred for crime, because he damned well knew better, as Abby would say. But he didn't think twice before moving onto the shoulder, for, even though his ears were shot, his eyes were perfectly fine, thank you very much, and flashing red lights had always made his heart skip a beat, one of a few long-forgotten reasons that he had become a cop over three decades ago.

Two police cars sped by him in quick succession then turned right at the next intersection, tires squealing on the grainy asphalt. Bridger didn't know that they were headed for Tryon Creek State Park, but that's what he would have guessed if asked. He couldn't have said why; just one of those unexplainable hunches.

A short mile later, Bridger pulled into a guest slot in Abby Dalton's parking lot. Normally at this time of day, almost everyone else in the complex of chic lakefront "cottages" would be off at work, leaving a wide array of spots to choose from. However, weekends changed the whole equation, with the bulk of the residents sleeping in or, at this time of year, out motoring around Oswego Lake in their Bayliners or Chris Crafts. But a smart car measures pretty much the size of a four-year-old's tricycle, so that gave him an advantage and he tucked himself in alongside a Mercedes 560, a distant and much larger cousin to his "CON". He'd named his tiny car CON mostly because of its color scheme (black and white). Besides, C-O-N seemed a more auspicious choice for a license plate than C-O-P if he wanted to tail bad guys, although C-O-P fit the color scheme, too; it just didn't cover the stealth aspect he was going for.

Knowing that Abby was expecting him, he pushed the intercom button at the iron gate that opened into her yard. She buzzed him in without asking for identification. Bridger took his time negotiating the curving path through the miniature patch of shaded lawn bordered by herb beds. He wanted to finesse his approach. With Abby, it was best to have a strategy in place well ahead of time. Deep in thought, he flinched slightly when he looked up and saw her standing next to a mound of blue periwinkle surrounding a three-foot high bubbler gurgling to the left of her front door. Her arms were folded tightly across her chest. Although he suspected that his hearing aid needed adjustment or a new battery – almost perpetually, it seemed – nonetheless, he was surprised that her movement hadn't caught his attention. And where was Malph, her ever-present albino bulldog? Malph rarely missed an opportunity to greet Abby's guests with a deep-throated "malph, malph," which he always accompanied with an Olympic sling of saliva.

Bridger waved with a nonchalance he didn't feel. "Morning."

"Morning yourself." Abby's lean frame appeared taller than her five foot ten inches. That always seemed to happen when she was agitated. Bridger decided this might not be as easy as he'd figured. Her tone of voice over the phone had carried a definite chill, even to Bridger's flawed hearing, and she'd had time to cool it down further since hanging up. Now, as usual, she chose the direct approach. Abigail Grace Dalton never pussyfooted around. "What's this crap about a case?"

"Yeah. Exciting, isn't it?"

"Exciting? We've barely gotten to the point of forming an agency. We don't even have a name yet – or an office."

Flashing a dozen pearl white teeth, Bridger Flynn said, "Oh, yeah, that's another thing. I found the perfect space for us. It's just across the river, over in Sellwood." If he expected his soon-to-be partner to jump for joy, he had seriously misjudged.

"Without me?"

"Well, it just sort of happened." Bridger ran a hand over the thin stubble of fading orange fuzz that passed for hair on his old head. Patches of light brown skin peeked out in ever-widening spots. "Got any coffee?"

"No. I'll get you some water. Go sit on the deck and I'll bring it out."

Abruptly, Abby disappeared into the house, so Bridger headed around the side of the cottage to the lakeside deck where he discovered a very lazy Malph lounging in the autumn sun. He lowered himself carefully into a white Adirondack chair and nodded to the dog.

5

"Hey there, fella."

Malph opened his eyes, but remained motionless, looking at Bridger as though he'd better have a good reason for speaking to him, especially while he was enjoying one of his not-infrequent naps. Water from a small arm of Oswego Lake lapped at the pilings a few feet in front of the dog and muted sunlight filtering through wispy clouds made the lake's surface shimmer. The whisper of a warm wind lent the water a mesmerizing motion. With fall colors framing the shoreline, it looked like a scene from a postcard.

With a little time to kill, Bridger reflected on how much he loved water. Just about any kind of water: oceans, lakes, rivers, creeks. Even puddles. In his opinion, Portland had a truly satisfying amount of water, enough to please both him and Abby, one of the few things they actually agreed on. Water and law pretty much summed up their common ground.

A glass brimming with ice water appeared on the table beside Bridger's chair. He mumbled, "Thanks," although he really meant, "Don't expect me to drink that; it's not coffee."

Abby lowered herself into a chair near him. She could use sign language if necessary, but her deteriorating eyesight made interpreting the responses somewhat sketchy. She preferred for Bridger to read lips if his hearing aid batteries ran low, which they often did because he refused to acknowledge his impairment with any regularity. Even more so now, he tried to ignore it, like that might make it go away. Lately, Bridger had resorted to lip reading more often than even he would care to admit. So, as always when she wanted to be heard, Abby made sure her voice was loud and clear. "Okay, first things first. The office?"

Bridger rubbed his hands together like a kid anticipating a triple scoop cone of mocha gelato. "Yeah. You'll love it. It's close, it's quaint and, best of all, it's cheap." He began drawing in the air between them.

"There's an outer space, for a receptionist."

"Receptionist?"

"Sure." Bridger noticed the look of skepticism on her face. "Okay, maybe that's for down the road a bit. Anyway, then there's two inner offices that overlook Lexington Avenue."

"Lex? Good area."

"The best. The offices are just a short flight of stairs above an antiques store half a block off of the main drag." Abby leaned more toward modern, but that didn't stop Bridger from pointing it out as a plus. "Now, the coup de grace? Price is super low, and I mean super low. And it's available right now."

Abby opened her mouth to say something, but Bridger steamrolled ahead. "Oh, and it's got one of those old-fashioned doors that has frosted glass that we can have the agency name etched on. Plenty of built-in shelves. Looks like it was made for two highly successful detectives." He nodded, smiling and pointing back and forth between the both of them, in case she didn't catch his drift. "Want to go look at it?"

"Later." She sat stiffly with her arms still folded. "So what's this case?"

Bridger had hoped to delay the specifics of this next, delicate subject until he could get Abby's mood to lift. He should have known better; she never put off the direct questions. He inhaled a deep breath and plunged in, confident that his excitement would rub off on her eventually. "Okay. Remember, ten or eleven years ago, a Washington High School senior named Cory Austin was killed just before graduation? A jogger found his body on a spur trail in Forest Park?"

"Vaguely." Abby frowned. "What does that have to do with us?"

"Well, there's been a new development in the case and Shearer called to see if we would consider looking into it."

"*Captain* Shearer?"

"Uh-huh."

"Your old boss?"

"The very man."

"And why would he do that?"

Bridger sucked in his lower lip. "I sort of ran into him the other day and he said that Portland Police is farming out cold cases now."

"Cold cases. And you told him we'd be interested?" The rise in Abby's voice caught the attention of Malph. He became concerned enough that he lifted his head to look over at her and then glare at Bridger.

"Well, sure. We are, aren't we?" His "sure" still held the traces of his Bronx upbringing.

7

"Cold cases? I thought we were getting into easy stuff like tailing wayward husbands and tracking down runaways. Cold cases?"

"Sure. Bigger challenge." He beamed, showing about the broadest grin Abby had ever seen on him, although right now she remained reticent.

"Great."

From her facial expression, Bridger was well aware that she meant quite the opposite. He sat mute, giving Abby a chance to digest his news. The curve of the chair dug into his back and he had a fleeting wonder as to why anyone would pay the high price for an Adirondack chair. He figured it would take a crane to lift his 187 pounds back onto his feet once he'd managed to fold himself into one. He knew that Abby spent hours out here, reading large-print books with her magnifying glass, Malph snoozing at her feet. The rhythmic splash of the miniature waves sometimes even lulled her to sleep. An idyllic retirement plan, according to her. And Bridger was about to change all that. However, not only did he have trouble with Adirondack chairs as a seating structure, he had real trouble with a sedentary retirement as a follow-up to a career filled with gunshots and car chases.

In reality, Bridger hadn't taken to retirement all that well and had had to work long and hard to convince Abby to partner up with him in a private investigation firm. She seemed to believe that she was filling her time quite nicely and had no apparent compunction to work. Her recent grudging assent to join up with him in a PI agency had been gained by Bridger's assurances that she would be actively pursuing cases on a very part-time basis. He had left the precise percentage of time purposely vague.

Now, with the earlier sirens and screeching tires of the police cars forgotten, he suggested they go find out about their first case.

CHAPTER 2

"Everyone must row with the oars he has."
- English proverb

As Bridger piloted them north along the banks of the Willamette River, he said, his voice tinged with optimism, "Maybe we can take a look at the office space on our way back."

"Maybe." Abby's enthusiasm level remained low, but Bridger's more than made up for what hers lacked. Even the thickening clouds couldn't darken his spirits. Oregon's weather might depress some people but, if you asked Bridger Flynn, the cottony shapes of gray floating above the city only gave the sky more character. That was a good thing, too, since thick, scudding clouds came in fast and often here in the Pacific Northwest. The local weathermen often joked, "If you don't like the weather, wait five minutes."

Bridger hadn't emphasized enough the greatest thing about the office, the game changer, in his opinion, and omitted one thing he hadn't told his potential partner: The rooms had originally been leased by a friend of his who had recently been graced with a once-in-a-lifetime opportunity in Medford, a mid-sized town in the southern part of Oregon. That friend now needed to find someone ASAP to take over his lease, which had been negotiated during a glut of available space so the terms were heavily stacked in favor of the lessee. Bridger thought they would be fools if they didn't snap this office up. He crossed his fingers that he could convince Abby. Her fiscally frugal side would be her weak point here.

He shot a sideways glance at his passenger and asked, in as conversational a tone as he could manage, "So what do you think we should name the agency?"

She continued to direct her gaze out the window, attempting to make clear her lack of interest. "How about Dalton & Flynn?"

"Hm." He pretended to consider this. "I think I like Flynn & Dalton better."

That got the rise he anticipated from her. "Oh, come on. It doesn't even sound right. Besides, Dalton & Flynn is alphabetical. If we're going to use our names, that's the fairest way. Everyone does it alphabetically." Abby's graying ponytail bobbled with her quickening exasperation.

"Yeah, you're right, everyone does do it alphabetically. So why should we be like everyone?"

"Whatever." She went back to looking out at the river, although as Bridger knew, she was seeing only colors and blurred shapes. A career-ending eye disease had ensured that. Pity, really, since the Willamette, framed by a variety of lush trees along this stretch of slow-moving current, was lazily beautiful. As they approached the Sellwood Bridge, which led across to a trendy community on Portland's southeast side – the trendy community where Bridger hoped to set up their business – Abby brightened slightly. "How about Sellwood Investigations?"

"Boring."

Abby thought for a minute more. "A&B Detecting?"

"There you go putting yourself first again."

Abby's competitive nature was legendary in Oregon's law enforcement world. Most of her fellow State Police officers would swear they were surprised that she hadn't made Superintendent. Bridger believed that she would have but for the onset of the macular degeneration, a condition affecting core vision, which forced her into early retirement. True to her nature, she went out kicking and screaming, but at least she went out in one piece. Had she stayed much longer, there would have been no guarantees about that. And it wasn't just her own safety to worry about; she couldn't risk putting other cops' lives in danger. If you can't see, you have to step down, plain and simple. It devastated her, but she did it.

Now, she rolled her eyes. "B&A? Oh, come on! Talk about not sounding right."

They drove toward downtown without speaking for a mile or so before Bridger had another apparent inspiration. "How do you like River City Detective Agency?" Driving along this waterfront street, they – or at least he – could see four of the eight bridges spanning the river that cut the city through its center and gave Portland one of its nicknames, River City.

"Naw." She rubbed her face. "Let's see."

"Yeah, well, I can see, but you? Not so much."

Bridger liked to harass Abby about her limited eyesight. It was sort of a cop thing. It also served as an attempt to lighten the impact of the disease, in a warped kind of way.

"Yeah, but I can hear."

As the little car rolled to a stop at a red light, Bridger snapped his fingers. "That's it! Eyes & Ears!"

Slowly, Abby started nodding. "Pretty good. How about if Ears comes first, though?"

"Ears & Eyes? That's just plain dumb."

Even Abby would have to admit that he was right about that. It didn't have the same ring as Eyes & Ears, as the phrase goes. Begrudgingly, she said, "Yeah, okay. Eyes & Ears it is."

Bridger mouthed a silent, "Yes!" Naming the agency was one concrete step toward it becoming a reality, and he hungered for some action. Retirement had its benefits, but those didn't outweigh the detriments, in his mind. The last eight years of his career had been Hollywood dramatic, one action scene after another. Days of almost nonstop crime fighting. He'd met Abby on a task force that had been formed to catch Snowy Forbes, a serial rapist who preyed on young brunette women in the Tri-County area. Three agencies – Oregon State Police, Portland Police Bureau and Multnomah County Sheriff's office – loaned their top investigative personnel to the team, which became nationally renowned for its innovative techniques. It took them over a year and a half to catch Snowy Forbes, but the capture itself was spectacular. The local news channels had their helicopters hovering while a swarm of reporters did nonstop coverage of the many hours required for the task force members to pin Forbes down and drag him away, only a little bit bloodied. All of the major networks picked up the story. Not surprising, then, that the excitement of the chase got under Bridger's skin and he became fully addicted to the adrenaline rush. Abby had expressed happiness at just knowing the son of a bitch would be put away forever.

With her eyesight already beginning to deteriorate at that point, she had stayed on with the task force, which by then had reconfigured itself for a new purpose: the burgeoning epidemic of identity theft. The problem was in its infancy, just beginning to get recognition, and Abby found she could spend less time in a car and more time on the phone and at a computer, working with enlarged fonts and magnifying glasses. Bridger volunteered for anything that involved leg work. Once again, their opposite talents worked to their advantage on the task force.

Now, while Bridger was reminiscing about the good old days, he suggested that Abby spend some time rolling the agency name around in her head, play with the sound of it and plan a design for their business cards, letterhead and, eventually, their website. Or, more precisely, figure the best way to ask one of her artsy friends to create a killer design. Abby could come up with some good ideas, but she wasn't the one to turn those ideas into a visual masterpiece. Both of them agreed that CON's picture – or profile or silhouette – should be used to sort of make Bridger and Abby come across as friendly, real people. The little car had its own personality and the two detectives almost considered it a third partner. Of course, there would have to be enough solid, serious content to the design, too, in order to convey the professionalism they wanted their private investigative firm to portray.

Bridger interrupted their thoughts. "Nate said –"

"Nate?"

He flushed. In fact, Bridger flushed frequently and easily. Abby often wondered how he had managed to interview suspects without projecting his intentions. Maybe it was the subtleness of his reddening, since his brown skin muted the blush effect somewhat. Or maybe it so surprised people that they were momentarily disarmed by it.

Abby repeated, "'Nate'?" She would never have addressed a superior officer by his first name, despite having retired. She had learned how to get along in the department as a woman, even how to get ahead. Strict adherence to protocol, and a mouth with attitude, gave her that little edge, just enough to keep her fellow officers working to stay on their toes. While the situation has improved over time, ever so gradually, police departments are still predominately male milieus. Most of the guys tolerate women among their ranks, kind of like in the military, but tolerating is about as far as it goes. It remains a fraternity, which, by definition, excludes females.

"*Capt.* Shearer," he stressed the formal title, "said that the victim's sister found something in a closet while she was clearing out the family home after her mom died."

"What was it?"

"He didn't specify. Just said that the sister wanted someone to contact her."

"Where is she?"

"She is at her mother's house, where she is staying."

"Hm."

Bridger heard the doubt in Abby's voice as he weaved his way around a delivery van and darted back into the right lane. Half a block later, arriving at Central Precinct, he steered the car down the ramp into the underground garage. Chuckling despite herself, Abby remarked that it felt like descending a small mountain riding on a pregnant skateboard.

- - -

Capt. Shearer's office looked like a hurricane had come through it overnight. And Capt. Shearer looked like he'd been in the office at the time. Disheveled and weary, he left one with the impression of a man who had not been home since the beginning of the week. The bags under his eyes, along with the wrinkled state of his suit, went a long way toward explaining the reason that PPB had begun to farm out cold cases. Manpower was in short supply and the city government was showing no signs of changing that. The captain put his coffee mug down and shook the detectives' hands.

"Bridger. Ms. Dalton."

Abby wanted to say, "Call me Abby," but she couldn't bring herself to that level of casualness. At least, not yet. Maybe in time. Bridger, however, did not have similar qualms.

"Nate."

With the greetings out of the way, Capt. Nathan Shearer thanked them for coming as he motioned for them to follow him. While they walked, he made small talk then moved on to more personal matters.

"How's JJ?" Shearer was inquiring after Bridger's oldest child, Jessica Joie. The young woman held a special place in the captain's heart, she being his goddaughter. Shearer and Bridger had personal as well as professional history. JJ's mother Cynthia – Bridger's ex-wife – was the captain's half sister.

"Jess is in grad school, Loyola, pulling A's this semester."

Shearer beamed as though it were his grades they were discussing. "Ah, that's fantastic. Give her my best."

"I will." Bridger felt compelled to ask about his ex, Cynthia, even though they had been divorced for well over twenty years. The captain answered that he only knew what his wife told him and there had been nothing much to report lately aside from a brief spotting of Cyn at an eastside Costco. Bridger figured no news was good news.

Shearer broached the subject Bridger had been dreading: his son. "And Zach? Still couch surfing with his friends, or has he chosen a life path yet?"

A terse answer was all that Bridger offered. "He's living outside of La Pine."

"Well, that's, uh, different. What took him there? A new love?"

"Something like that." Bridger hoped Shearer would drop it now. He didn't want to go into the details. Since his son had called last night, he had tried not to dwell on his life-changing news. The kid always seemed to learn the hard way.

Zachary Taylor Flynn had been deeply affected by his parents' divorce. While Bridger had tried to maintain a visitation schedule once he and Cyn had separated, it never worked quite like intended because of his job, call-outs, vacation cancellations and the like. Zach was less understanding of his father's absences than his little sister JJ, and was just now, at age twenty-nine, starting to come to grips with it. After graduating from Grant High School, he was slow to decide what he wanted to do. So far, he'd been depending on the generosity of friends, staying with Peter for a week or two and then moving over to Paul's for the next week or so. He occasionally got employment at one of Portland's many food carts. Bridger knew that Zach loved to cook, so he'd remained hopeful that there might be a future in a restaurant on wheels.

But his hopes were dashed with the recent news that Zach had finally discovered who he was meant to be and changed his name to Moshe Akhbar. Somewhere in the center of the state, on a few hundred acres, yet another religious fervor had taken root, this one calling itself the Children of Allah, and Zachary Flynn had embraced their unconventional philosophy. Bridger had been in Portland during the rise of the Bagwan Shree Rajneesh and his zealots over in Antelope, sort of in the same area as the Children of Allah, broadly speaking. He wasn't sure whether this one was a religion or simply a scam of epic proportions.

In the 1980s, the Bagwan had attracted some very successful and very intelligent followers. But his fleet of Rolls Royces, a private jet, and lots of cash – cash that came from his followers – well, that tipped the scales toward scam in Bridger's view. At least cash wasn't what the Children of Allah were aiming at, since Zach had none. It seemed ironic, almost prophetic, that the Rajneeshees were flourishing right at the time that Zach was born. But that group had come to a bad end and Bridger figured this one would, too. In the meantime, though, he had further lost his son, for the Children of Allah required each inductee (or brain-washed prisoner if Bridger were allowed to describe it) to denounce his or her family, change his or her given name, which explained the switch to Moshe Akhbar, and become one with the Allah community.

Respecting Bridger's reticence and without breaking stride, Capt. Shearer led them to a tiny cluttered room piled high with boxes and files. He opened the door and, with a sweeping gesture of his right arm, said, "Your keys to Cory Austin."

CHAPTER 3

"The only way round is through."

- Robert Frost

The sheer volume of documents and inventoried items looked to Bridger as though the case had gone through a protracted Congressional hearing. Even with Abby's limited vision, she could see how daunting the pile was. Papers teetered in precarious stacks, every surface covered, including most of the floor. The retired detectives figured space must be at a premium, along with manpower.

Capt. Shearer noticed their deer-in-headlights expressions and hastened to reassure them. "This is not all for this case. Only about a third of it pertains to Cory Austin."

Abby and Bridger breathed out a "Whew" in unison. Both relaxed, although they realized that even that reduced amount of evidence would take some heavy wading through. It was going to be hard to know where to start. Bridger mumbled something along those lines, and Abby said, "Amen."

Before they could get discouraged, Shearer leaned against the room's only desk, smoothed his jacket and summarized for the two detectives. "Let me bring you up to speed. Maybe if I give a brief recap, it will help you focus your efforts.

"Cory Austin, if you'll recall, was a senior at Washington High School. Someone killed him just a couple of weeks before his graduation in 2002. His mom reported him missing when he didn't get up for school the morning of June 1st. This is a kid who never missed school so, when he wasn't at the breakfast table, Mrs. Austin went up to his room to see why. His bed was made, looked like it hadn't been slept in. She had no idea he had even gone out. Or when, obviously. The sister said much the same thing. No note, nothing missing from his room except the kid. Rose Austin's frantic call came into Portland Police right about the same time as we received another call, this one from an early morning jogger. The fellow had spotted a body in some shrubs beside a trail that ran through Forest Park. It hadn't been well concealed, like the killer had maybe been spooked by something. Anyway, we had bad news for the mother." The captain rifled around in a nearby file and found some color photographs of the crime scene.

Abby dug in her purse for the magnifier she carried, while Bridger moved in closer for a better view. He thought it possible that he might recognize the area since he took occasional hikes in the West Hills, but with the network of trails and the acres of forest, it seemed like a remote chance. With no landmarks to orient him, Bridger tabled the idea of trying to mentally zero in on the exact spot. Instead, he concentrated on the details demonstrated by the photos. In the first picture, a large amount of blood stained the ground and, more importantly, the boy's T shirt.

Abby flinched. Not much made Abby Dalton flinch, but she could never see blood and not flinch. She and blood had a deep-seated relationship. When she was only thirteen years old, her father had died following a vicious knife attack, an attack that became the major reason she went into police work. Even though cops see this kind of injury often – too often – most of them never get used to it. But Abby always seemed to take it personally. Blood signified life, and it signified death.

In this photo, one didn't have to look closely to see that the amount of blood was more than just disturbing. A close-up of the victim showed him lying on his stomach, one hand beneath him and the other splayed out to the side. If not for the presence of the wounds – and the blood – it might have appeared that he had simply fallen and knocked himself unconscious.

The kid's sneakers were obviously expensive – Nikes, a local company – so robbery had been ruled out as a motive. That conclusion was backed up by the presence of a BOSS Chronograph watch, which cost over $500 any day of the week, on his left wrist.

Bridger took a deep breath and said quietly, "This was a tough case. Happened a little over a year before I retired. This young man was almost the same age as my son Zach. That sort of hit too close to home."

Abby nodded. She had no children, mostly due to the short duration of her marriage, but it had something to do with the job, too. Cops don't always make the best parents. Hours are iffy.

17

Shifts change. Crooks don't work on schedules. And dealing with the dregs of society doesn't make for the sunniest of attitudes. Abby's attitude was living proof of that. Nonetheless, she had badly wanted kids and had a tough time imagining how a parent who lost a son could go on with life. It simply sounded impossible. So, during her career, any time the victim was a child, she had fought more fiercely to help find justice for him. And it wasn't just her; that was another unwritten rule among many cops.

Shearer went on, "Mm-hm, it seemed so senseless."

Abby asked who their prime suspects had been.

"Well, naturally, we looked closely at the jogger who reported it, but he was so upset he could hardly talk. And his distress came across as genuine. No sign that he was anything but an unlucky bystander. Wrong place, wrong time kind of thing. We checked his alibi anyway, and it held up, too."

"Did he see anyone else on the trail that morning?"

"He said he didn't. That trail is kind of a minor one. It's not real wide so it doesn't get as much traffic as the Wildwood that it branches off from. Probably wouldn't have mattered anyway, since we determined that the time of death was eight to ten hours before the jogger found the victim, so more like nine or ten o'clock the previous night."

Bridger glanced at Abby. She had grown quite pale. He turned back to Shearer and asked the next obvious question, "What about the parents?"

"Cory Austin's mom Rose was cleared pretty quickly. From all accounts, she was ultra-close to the boy and his sister, whom you'll meet soon. According to the mother, the father had been out of the picture for a couple years, didn't really like kids, couldn't get into the swing of going to their sports events, didn't like dealing with after-school activities or all of the time and effort that goes into maintaining a family."

Abby started to ask something, but Capt. Shearer held up a hand to stop her. "Nope, it wasn't him either. He may not have liked kids, but he was at home. Far away, in a little town called Ft. Morgan, Colorado. His girlfriend vouched for him, and gave an extremely detailed description of what they were doing when Cory went missing." He rolled his eyes, and Bridger and Abby grinned. Some color had returned to her face.

She asked, "Kid was stabbed, right? How many times?"

Shearer consulted some notes. "Eighteen."

Bridger whistled. "Did they find the murder weapon?"

"Unfortunately, no. But the coroner pegged it as a common kitchen knife probably, six-inch blade, judging from what he saw at the autopsy."

Bridger said, "Odd thing to be carrying around out in the woods."

"We thought so too. Pretty awkward. Not something a jogger would just have on him when he's out for a run. Anyway, the crime scene guys combed the undergrowth but it is very dense in that area. Even the most thorough of searches could have missed it. There's a pretty steep slope right there, as you can see from the photographs. If the knife had been tossed any distance at all, it might have landed beyond the range of the search, maybe as far away as the creek at the bottom of the ravine. And with the spring rains that year, the creek was quite swollen, pushing an unusually heavy volume of water for late May." He shrugged. "No telling where it might have ended up, if the killer even disposed of it. It's possible he took it with him."

"Are you convinced the killer was a male?" Abby asked.

"Most likely, although we couldn't be certain. The wounds were deep, suggesting the blows had been delivered with a great deal of physical force."

Bridger frowned. "Sounds like a case of rage."

Capt. Shearer agreed. "Which took the focus off of mom even more. She just didn't look capable, although I'll admit looks can be deceiving. But she was a shy, tiny thing and in pretty poor physical shape. Besides, from all accounts, she had a wonderful relationship with her son. No one we interviewed disputed that."

"How about the sister? Any animosity between the siblings?" Abby asked.

Shearer shook his head. Their investigation had revealed that Cari Austin idolized her older brother. They were both honor students, both worked on the school newspaper, and all of the other students that were around them said they always acted fond of each other, even protective of each other, got along real well. Besides, if the sister had gotten away with murder eleven years ago, why would she try to re-open the case now?

Abby acknowledged that it was a point well taken. So who did the cops put at the top of the suspect list?

"It was a short list. Pretty much everyone liked Cory. Or, if not liked him exactly, at least didn't dislike him. He was sort of a nonentity. A nerd. Kept his nose clean and out of trouble. Wasn't a contender for stealing anyone's girlfriend as far as we could tell. Wasn't a candidate for the football team, basketball team, track. No sports, really, except golf. Brainy but not obnoxious about it. Sure, a few of the kids might have razzed him, but murder? Didn't fit."

None of them liked to think of kids killing kids anyway. "Anyone on the school paper staff have it in for him?" Bridger asked.

"No. Not at all. At least, nothing came out like that. Check it if you want. He also belonged to a group called the Nerdlingers. Not sure what the purpose of the club was, but all twelve members were interviewed and eliminated as possible suspects."

"How about teachers?"

"Same answer as far as I know."

"Outside of school?"

"Didn't find much there either. He golfed a little, as I mentioned, but that didn't produce anyone to look at. He had a job at a local burger joint, worked about ten hours a week. No problems with the other employees or the managers. And no other outside activities. It almost started to look like a random killing."

Abby scratched her head and pressed her lips together. "So what was this teenager doing out late at night? Doesn't sound like it was his habit to do that."

"No, it wasn't. And if we knew what he was doing out that night, we might have a better idea of where to look for our killer, but no one seemed to know. Or if they did, they weren't sharing that knowledge with us."

Abby had one more question. "What's the new evidence the sister found?" The doubt in her voice didn't go unnoticed by the two men.

"You'll find out at 3:00 this afternoon. Cari Austin –"

"Cari?"

"Yes. I know, Cory and Cari, sort of a pattern, hm?" Shearer grinned, even though it appeared to take a lot of effort.

20

"Cari Austin is expecting you at her mom's house at 3:00. She was pretty close lipped about it when she called. Just wanted someone to come over and pick 'it' up."

Capt. Shearer had a few more photographs to show them, mostly of the body and the surroundings, from a variety of different angles. Close-ups of evidence markers and measurements added little enlightenment.

Bridger pawed through some papers in one of the files and pulled out a small picture of a young male. He looked at the captain and raised his eyebrows.

"Yeah, Cory Austin's senior picture taken for the annual."

No way to tell how tall Cory was from the photo or what he weighed, but the portrait showed a rosy-cheeked boy with an otherwise pale complexion. The face was round and covered with half a dozen or so blemishes, despite the photographer's subtle attempts at touching it up. Short hair somewhere between dishwater blonde and brown, and black framed glasses completed the classic geeky look. Bridger saw nothing remarkable about him, positive or negative. The photo clearly captured a young man with a future, though, a young man whose sister still wanted answers.

Bridger turned to Abby, "Well, let's get started, partner."

CHAPTER 4

*"Three o'clock is always too late or too early for anything
you want to do."*

- Sartre

After Capt. Shearer left them to fend for themselves, Bridger made sure that Abby was doing okay. Her pallor had lessened, but he knew that savaged and/or brutalized bodies would upset anyone, even though police types become more accustomed to them than the average guy on the street. Bridger himself could never look at a victim of violent death without being overcome by a sick feeling. Despite two and a half decades as a police officer for the City of Portland, he found it hard to accept that people actually do that kind of violence to other people. Of those twenty-five years, he had spent fifteen as a detective and had seen plenty of homicides in his career.

And, of course, he was familiar with the facts surrounding the murder of Abby's dad. Bridger had still been living in New York at the time that it happened, but he had done some research into the case after he met Abby and she had later filled him in on some of the other particulars. Barely in her teens, the resultant trauma had sent her into a catatonic state for months afterward. It took a lot of counseling and struggling to put the raw pain behind her. That incident was a big part of what led her into law enforcement. And a huge factor in her inability to form lasting relationships.

Teddie Dalton had owned a charter fishing business in Astoria on the northern Oregon coast, where Abby grew up. Each day, when the other kids hopped on the bus after school, Abby would walk down to the docks to see her dad. She loved the misty salt air, the mournful cries of the gulls, even the coarse roughness of the ropes which tethered the boats to the dock. More than all of that, Abby loved helping her father.

One bleak March day, she arrived within minutes of what appeared to be a robbery gone wrong and found her dad crumpled in a spreading pool of blood. One of Teddie's employees, hearing her panicked shrieks, ran to help. Of course, it was too late. The employee led the little girl away from the scene and held her in a tight bear hug until the police arrived. They took over from there. Abby remembers nothing of the days immediately following the one that took her father away forever. She retreated to a safe place inside her head and stayed there until she felt comfortable coming out.

Abby's mother, Grace Dalton, didn't hesitate to quit her long-time job as receptionist at an Astoria law firm to spend all of her time working to heal Abby. A large payout from a life insurance policy, along with the sale of Teddie's fleet of fishing vessels, allowed Grace to focus every last effort on helping Abby get well. Plus, Grace had another daughter, Abby's older sister Lorna, to comfort as well. Recovery hadn't come easy, but the Daltons were a strong and determined lot. They carried on, even with a piece of themselves missing.

Now, Abby appreciated Bridger's concern and told him so, but assured him she was coping just fine.

For the next couple of hours, the two detectives sifted through several files from the box that Shearer had opened. A little after noon, the captain checked in to see whether they wanted some sandwiches or maybe salads; one of the guys was making a run to a deli down the street. They thanked him and shelled out two ten dollar bills to pay for a pair of pastramis on rye and went back to studying the files.

By 1:15, with their lunch over, Abby yawned, stretched and put her magnifier down. This was the part of the job she had once hated. Even when she could see well, combing through paperwork had bored her. That is, until the task force had nabbed Snowy Forbes. Something within Abby opened up then, leaving her with an almost unquenchable lust for research. If there was a piece of the puzzle buried deep, Abigail Dalton would fish it out. Bridger, on the other hand, didn't have the patience for it. Give him action any day.

"Find anything interesting?"

Bridger looked up and cupped his ear. Abby raised her voice a notch and repeated the question.

"Not really. You?"

"No, but it's early. Reading through reports doesn't always pay off for me. I imagine you're anxious to talk to the jogger, get started finding Cory's classmates and get their stories firsthand. Maybe one of them will give us a valuable clue, whether they know it or not."

Bridger nodded. "I hope so." He looked down at his watch. "Hey, why don't we take a break? Nate said Cari Austin is expecting us at 3:00. That gives us plenty of time. Want to run out and see the office?"

Abby rubbed the back of her neck. "What I really want to do is curl up on my deck with a good book and my dog Malph."

Bridger had wondered when she would get around to saying something like that. He supposed he couldn't blame her, but he also knew she wouldn't be able to give up now. Not with a young man dead and all but forgotten. Abby had sunk her teeth in far enough that she'd see the case through to a conclusion. Then all Bridger would have to worry about was whether he could keep her around for the next case. Setting up an office seemed like another concrete step toward ensuring that would happen. They had already settled on a name and landed their first case. That felt like a pretty good start. Maybe he should give her another little nudge.

"Aw, come on, Abs. We need a break."

"I'm not arguing that we don't need a break, just what kind of break I'd like. And don't call me Abs."

"Okay." Bridger headed toward the door. Abby hesitated before following. Indeed, she welcomed a break, even one that involved scoping out a potential office for Eyes & Ears. Begrudgingly, she was warming to the idea of an agency with Bridger. She had always liked working with him. This case, though, looked like way more work than she had signed on for. She'd begun to suspect that her new partner had pulled his famous bait and switch trick and she told him so. He just shrugged and said, "Pffft," before leading the way back downstairs to the car.

- - -

CON sat hidden by a large, black, unmarked SUV in a corner of the garage. If Abby had gone down there alone, she'd have never found it. They hopped in and fired up the little car. Going back up the ramp made Abby laugh again. The smart had a tendency to lurch on the ascent, which sort of tickled her as a mechanical idiosyncrasy that added to its already quirky personality.

Back outside, the skies had brightened, and Abby put on her sunglasses. She wore dark glasses frequently, including indoors, to aid in reducing glare, so Bridger wasn't surprised to see her pull them out. She adjusted them on her nose before swiveling toward him. "You've never told me much about your ex. What's the story there?"

"Cynthia?"

"You have more than one ex?"

"What do you want to know?" Bridger gripped the steering wheel like maybe he would rather not explore that particular topic.

Abby wasn't about to let him off the hook. After all, he'd roped her into a major project with this Cory Austin murder when she would be far happier lounging by Oswego Lake. If talking about his one-time wife made him uncomfortable, that felt like fair payback.

He sighed in resignation as he braked for a red light. "Well, we met my first year on the job, at a nightclub called Le Bonne Chance."

"I used to love that place."

"Did I hear right? Abigail Dalton has been to Le Bonne Chance?"

"Sure. It was one of my three favorite hangouts in Portland."

"Huh. Small world. Well, anyway, I loved to dance and she did, too. Cyn could dance all night, and we were good." He drew out the word "good" to emphasize it. "Like a lot of young and naïve couples, we thought that was all we needed. So we got married, soon had two kids and then tried to settle into domestic life. Turned out we weren't too good at the mom and dad thing though. After seven miserable years of trying to make it work, we admitted defeat and split up. That was about a week before Christmas of 1988. Sums it up in a nutshell."

The light turned green and Bridger started forward again.

Abby contemplated what he'd said for a few more minutes. It wasn't an uncommon story among cops. Not only do they not always make good parents, but they don't always make good spouses either. If anyone recognized that, it was Abby. She'd tried marriage once. Hers hadn't lasted as long as Bridger's even. In fact, it hadn't even lasted an entire year.

Naturally, Bridger knew about Jay, the Oregon State Police detective Abby had hooked up with. After something like nine months, she and Jay called it quits. Her competitive nature killed any seed of romance that might have tried to grow. She knew it. Hell, everybody knew it. She didn't try that again. Oh, there were relationships, but Abby never allowed them to "advance to the next level". Once, she had briefly considered a fling with Bridger, but their connection started as a friendship and remained a friendship. Neither of them wished to change that.

Now Abby believed Bridger seemed sort of directionless, bored, possibly full-blown lonely. That could be the reason he was pushing so hard to start this agency. Sure, he was fairly close to his kids, but they had their own, busy lives. She wished he would find a more satisfying diversion than solving cold cases, particularly when he insisted on taking her along for the ride. Out of the blue, she said, "You need a woman."

"Look who's talking, lady who sits on her deck and reads to her dog."

"No, really, you need a woman."

Bridger replied with a straight face and just a hint of impishness, "I'm thinking about getting a cat."

Abby sighed and shook her head.

- - -

In less than fifteen minutes, Bridger eased CON to the curb outside of 1313½ Southeast Lexington Avenue. A narrow two-story stone façade hid a boxy building dating from the 1950s. In the front, it had a security door with six numbered buttons. Bridger pressed #203. Someone buzzed them through. Inside, they faced a tiny foyer with a staircase straight ahead and an ancient elevator to the right. They chose the stairs.

A man greeted them at the top of the flight and Bridger introduced Abby to Reggie Preston, explaining that he was the guy who held the lease to the office space, and a fellow musician. In fact, music was how they knew each other. Reggie looked as eager as a dog urging its owner to throw the ball, come on, throw the ball. He motioned them into #203 with a wave and a smile stretching across his broad face.

Abby took in the arrangement of the furniture, thinking it was just where she would have put it. And just the type she would have chosen. When Reggie proclaimed that he was leaving the office furnished, Abby began to suspect Bridger had a hand in that as well. Maybe more of his bait and switch. The setup was too good to be true, unless it had had a little help.

The two men were catching up on old times as Abby toured the three rooms comprising the space. In the office that she decided would be hers, mahogany bookshelves against one long wall nestled up against two file cabinets and an escritoire. She had always wanted an escritoire. Reggie was planning to leave it here? How convenient was that? It smelled of Bridger again.

Oh, well, she thought, *the place is almost ideal, plus close to both my home and Bridger's.* His houseboat at Oaks Park couldn't be more than a five-minute drive, and her lakefront cottage might be about double that. She thought, *What's not to like?* But she decided to ask anyway, "So, Reggie, why are you leaving?"

He looked a little nervous as he answered, "Well, you see, I got an opportunity in Medford."

"Why not take the furniture?"

"Well, it's a really good opportunity."

Abby's peripheral vision was pretty fair, and she could see Bridger grinning. What was up his sleeve?

"So you're just going to leave it here. Give it to us." Unbelievable.

"Um, yeah. I mean, it's a really, really good opportunity. As in everything is supplied, including a car."

"You leaving your car here for us as well?"

He laughed. "That's a good one, Ms. Dalton."

Bridger jumped in. "Abby, he inherited a winery in the Applegate Valley. It's got sixty-five acres planted in chardonnay and forty-five more in cabernet. The tasting room is 3500 square feet and looks like a French mansion. Then there's the French mansion. Furnished in French baroque." He winked at Reggie. "Okay?"

Reggie smiled sheepishly. "Yeah, see, I really don't need the furniture. It would cost more to hire a mover than it would be worth to take this stuff. I'm just going to pack up the files and books and put them in storage. Then I'm going to go make some wine."

"His lifelong dream."

Abby sighed and said, "Where do we sign?"

CHAPTER 5

"A man's most valuable trait is a judicious
sense of what not to believe."

- Euripides

Now that they had the office situation sewed up, Bridger and Abby each pocketed their own set of keys and left Reggie to finish packing up. He said he'd be out by the end of the day; he didn't have much more to do. They wished him the best of luck in his new venture. He'd need it. Wine-making isn't exactly lucrative for the majority of small producers. It comes with other benefits, though. Like wine.

Outside, in the car, Bridger was punching Cari Austin's address into the GPS when his cell phone rang.

"Bridger Flynn here."

For a second, Abby sat there baffled before she realized he wasn't talking to her. She'd never gotten used to Bluetooth and now Bridger wanted her to get used to his hearing-aid-compatible phone. He considered himself lucky that there even was such a thing, while Abby cursed the new technology with a vengeance. When a phone rang, damn it, she should be able to hear it. And it shouldn't sound like The Dance of the Valkyries or Hotel California. Phones ring; that's just the way it is.

Bridger listened a second, then said, "Oh, hi, Nate. We were just on our way. We might be a little bit early if that's all right." He listened a moment longer. "Great. It should take us about twenty minutes. Tell her we'll see her then."

Their route took them back through downtown, passing on the southern edges of the core, avoiding much of the heaviest traffic, which meant that they made good time. The Austin home was in a neighborhood called Goose Hollow, at the base of the West Hills. The house looked a little rundown to Abby, but she supposed exterior upkeep hadn't been a priority for its occupants during the past year or so. She didn't recall if anyone had said when Mrs. Austin had died nor whether she'd been sick for a long time, but that could account for at least some of the deterioration.

The doorbell had that old-fashioned, rich tone that Abby always associated with her grandmother Maddie's house. It emanated from somewhere deep within the Tudor-style home. Almost an entire minute passed before Cari Austin opened the heavily-carved front door.

Bridger had about four inches in height advantage over her, which would mean that Abby had five except that Abby's heels would add another two inches to that.

The young woman standing before them could hardly have been less robust, rather shapeless in loose brown slacks and a tan shirt. And it was hard to see how her blonde hair could be more nondescript: shoulder length, limp, lusterless, and the color of dead corn husks. It would be nearly impossible to picture her as their killer.

"Ms. Austin?"

She nodded several times as though nervous, before clearing her throat to squeak out a timid, "Yes. Come in."

The detectives introduced themselves as they stepped into the cramped entry. There was a long, uncomfortable moment while they stood looking at each other. Bridger almost thought that Ms. Austin wanted him to take the lead. After a couple of false starts, she finally managed to head off down a dingy hall covered with a floor runner. Bridger and Abby followed, noticing the multitude of pictures hanging on the walls, which were in need of a wallpaper makeover.

The hall opened onto a large kitchen at the back of the house. It had a trio of windows overlooking a tiered, mature garden of fairly good size. A glass and chrome table stood in an area featuring a bay window. Ms. Austin pointed to a cardboard shoebox sitting on the table, then backed away and wrapped her arms tightly around herself. She seemed to have trouble figuring out where to look as Bridger stepped toward the box.

He glanced around, then turned and clasped his hands in front of him. "Do you mind giving us a little background, Ms. Austin?"

"Cari, please." She cleared her throat again. "Um, where should I start?"

Bridger explained that they had spent a couple hours at police headquarters coming up to speed on the case and filled her in on the few facts they knew. But they needed every detail she could remember and he urged her to jump in whenever something occurred to her. Then he asked some conversational questions to put her at ease, mostly centering on her life eleven years ago. This had the intended effect, and she relaxed as she remembered some of the good times. When her brother had died, Cari was a sophomore, an honor student, and worked on the school paper with her big brother. By then, she had her life already mapped out.

"I wanted to be a special ed. teacher. There are so many children that need one-on-one attention and too few people who go into that side of teaching." She smiled regretfully at the memory of where she had hoped to be. Her eyes took on a misty look. "Unfortunately, Cory's death kind of upset those plans. I couldn't concentrate, fell off the honor roll. Just sort of didn't care anymore. I guess it was lucky I even finished school. Then I moved to Boise and away from all of the reminders of Cory. I found work as an aide in a nursing home. Older people suited me a lot better. I couldn't stand to be around kids anymore."

Cari had shrunk about two inches in height since she started this conversation. She finished with a description of her return home to Portland to help her mother, Rose, who had been suffering from Alzheimer's for six years.

"We understand your mother was ill for a period of time," Bridger said.

"Yes." She looked up at him, her eyes blinking rapidly. "At least six years. The last year, though, she deteriorated quickly."

"I see."

Abby wanted to know when Ms. Austin – Cari – had come back to Portland, and whether she stayed in the family home or somewhere else.

"A little over eleven months ago. Yes, I moved in with mom here."

Made sense. Otherwise, how could she cover all of her mother's needs? Still, it must have been a difficult situation. The young woman had made an admirable sacrifice, although it sounded like Cari Austin didn't have much else going on.

"Anyway, I just got around to cleaning out some of her stuff." She looked down again. "She died ten days ago. I've been avoiding her bedroom, so I decided to start in Cory's, with the closet. That's when I found…that!"

As she said this, she thrust an arm toward the box, then quickly hugged herself again.

Bridger pushed opened the lid with the tip of a pen, and winced. Cari wrinkled her nose, turning away. Abby craned her neck to see the contents.

"Damn. What kind of sick f–" Abby bit her lip, then took a deep breath before continuing. "Geez, who would do something like this? Any idea whether your mom knew about it?"

Ms. Austin shook her head, looking at the floor.

"You said you found it in Cory's closet. Was it stuck behind something or right out where you could get to it easily?"

"Just up on the shelf. I think there could have been another box in front of it."

"You think? How sure are you?" Abby might have grown more impatient if Cari weren't so mousy and apprehensive. The energy emitting from the young woman cried out for understanding. Abby still had a job to do, although for now she would dial back her usually aggressive approach.

Cari Austin cupped her hands in front of her face, a gesture of deep concentration. When she finally answered, she seemed close to tears. "I'm sorry. I just can't – I don't – I'm not sure."

"That's okay," Bridger said, his voice as smooth as velvet.

"Why would anyone keep this?" Abby wondered aloud.

Bridger ventured, "Well, it's sure not a lucky charm. The, uh, condition is pretty rough." He looked at Cari. "Do you know what it is?"

She did indeed. "It's a cat's paw. Our cat's, Frizz."

"I see."

His tone must have conveyed reservations, because Cari's eyes suddenly grew as big as dinner plates. "You don't think my mom did this! Oh, no, no, no. I don't know why it was up there, but mom didn't do this." She looked at the severed cat's foot lying on a soiled dish cloth stiff with what appeared to be dried blood. "This is Frizz's paw. My mother would never have hurt Frizz. No, it's connected to Cory's death somehow. Don't you see?"

They didn't see, actually. It appeared to be the work of a deranged mind, and hadn't Mrs. Austin suffered from some form of dementia? Alzheimer's? Something mental? But Cari looked more than frantic to convince them.

"How do you know it's Frizz's paw?" asked Bridger.

"Who else's would it be? Frizz was gone. Disappeared. He was orange, like this. And he had this little funny shaped dew claw." She still couldn't bring herself to look in the box again. The dew claw she spoke of might or might not have been there, but the paw had become so desiccated in the intervening eleven years that it had withered to a malformed oval with tufts of hair and four or five tiny brittle claws. Specific attributes were hard to define.

Abby asked, "Do you know when Frizz, um, died?"

"That's the thing, see. We never found Frizz, but he went missing a couple weeks before Cory was killed."

This new fact changed things somewhat. The paw did look quite old, but neither Bridger nor Abby would have laid odds that it belonged to a cat that had last walked this earth eleven years ago. Why would someone do this?

Every community has a spate of animal cruelty that pops up on occasion. Some disturbed individual, usually an abused child, takes to torturing small animals, most especially house cats. This might have been one such time, which begged the question, "Did Cory like Frizz?"

Cari slumped, as though Abby's insinuation was too heavy a load to bear.

"I'm sorry, Cari. We have to ask. Is it possible your brother cut off Frizz's paw?"

Her face fell, like she had no hope of conveying her point in a way that they would understand. "No. He loved that cat even more than mom did. And before you ask, I did, too. Someone did this to Frizz. They killed him, just like they killed my brother. I don't know who and I don't know where this came from, but it wasn't any of us." Cari Austin's face had grown bright red and she stood shaking with what seemed to have morphed into anger. She looked genuinely pissed off, so they figured she might be telling the truth. Her newfound ardor showed just the kind of backbone that Abby admired. Maybe this mouse could roar after all.

"Okay, Cari. Thanks."

Bridger changed the subject slightly. "You said you don't know who did this to Frizz. Were any kids at school giving Cory trouble?"

Cari Austin calmed down a smidgen, but it took an effort. "No."

"Anyone bullying him? Threatening him? Did you ever see him backed into a corner or, say, see him trying to get away from anyone?"

"No. My brother – well, he wasn't popular, but everyone left him alone."

Except for the killer, Abby wanted to say.

Coming from a different angle, Abby took over the questioning. "Did you hear any rumors about other cats being mutilated around that time? Other students' pets missing or turning up hurt?"

Cari looked out the window. The detectives wondered whether she had any idea or whether her answer would have any meaning whatsoever anyway. Capt. Shearer had said the investigators reported that Cari Austin looked up to her big brother. Idolized him, is how they put it. Could she be subjective at all with those kinds of feelings?

She stared at the backyard for about a minute, then shook her head. "I really don't remember anything like that. We thought Frizz ran off, or maybe got eaten by a coyote or something." Packs of coyotes roamed the urban hills, often subsisting on domestic pets. Posters pleading for their return appeared on telephone poles and lamp posts with sickening frequency.

"So you never saw your cat again, and you never saw this foot before today," said Bridger.

Cari Austin's gaze still angled toward the floor.

The detectives found the young woman's reluctance to make eye contact troubling, yet they understood that some people had difficulty with it, particularly around police types.

She shrugged. "No. When we realized he was gone, we were super upset. But then Cory was killed and, well, it was too much to deal with. We kind of forgot about Frizz for a while. Then it just didn't matter anymore."

Abby thought about how she would handle the loss of Malph. The idea made her shudder. That bulldog had only been part of her life for a little over two and a half years, yet she loved him with all her heart. (That was more than she could say for her ex-husband, Jay. But then, Malph didn't argue with her, or if he did, she usually tuned him out.) She had never been a cat person, but those who were seemed to be as smitten with their pets as she was with her dog. She shook her head at the notion of Bridger getting a cat. How had she ever become such close friends with a man so different from herself?

All of that flashed through her mind in an instant before she decided it was quite plausible that she would forget about even Malph if her sister Lorna had been murdered shortly after the dog disappeared. That would be a lot to handle all at once. She knew too well how it felt to lose a loved one to violence, so she could sympathize with this young woman. Sometimes she didn't show it, though.

Abby asked about Cory's room, whether it was substantially different than when he died or what Rose Austin had done with it. If little had been touched, the likelihood of discovering something new was much higher, although both detectives knew the investigators would have covered it pretty thoroughly at the time of the kid's death. Still, Bridger had developed a sixth sense for finding things that others overlooked.

Cari's voice came out somewhat nervous, unsteady. "Mom hardly ever went in there. At first, she couldn't face it. Then it seemed to comfort her somehow to simply leave it alone. Not that she kept it like a shrine or anything," she added, hastily. "Lately, she'd been getting confused often. Sometimes I'd find her just standing in there, with a blank look. I don't think she had any idea where she was."

Maybe, maybe not. Nonetheless, the detectives wanted to see Cory's room next. And the closet that had housed the severed cat's paw for what must have stretched into over a decade. How had no one smelled something rank? And how had the police missed it in the first go-around? Some tough questions now needing some straightforward answers.

CHAPTER 6

*"It is not necessary to understand things
in order to argue about them."*

- Beaumarchais

Cari Austin had led them to believe that her mother hadn't kept Cory's room as a monument to her dead son. However, now, when they walked in, it looked like the high schooler might have just stepped out for a quick run to the mall. Maybe Mrs. Austin had ventured in occasionally to dust, but otherwise the room felt eerily normal: bed still made, clothes hung up except for a light sweatshirt tossed over a chair and a pair of shoes discarded carelessly to one side of the single tall dresser. The kid's textbooks were neatly stacked on a small desk nestled against the wall beneath the room's sole window. Somebody must have been in denial to claim that this wasn't a shrine.

Bridger gazed over the desk, down to the yard eighteen feet below and observed, "He certainly didn't leave the house this way."

Abby carefully picked her way across the room to join him, more out of habit than any actual ability to judge distance to the ground, then turned toward Cari Austin, who remained in the doorway. "How did your brother get out that night? Did everyone think that he simply walked out the front door?"

"I'm – I'm not sure. Does it matter?"

"Probably not a lot. He must have had his own key anyway."

"Uh-huh. He did." She bobbed her head.

Bridger moved closer to both women in order to better catch the conversation.

Abby switched gears again. "So for some unknown reason, he left the house without telling anyone. Did Cory have a girlfriend?"

36

Cari snorted. "Hardly."

Abby cocked her head and asked, "Why 'hardly'?"

The young woman blushed. "Oh, sorry. I didn't mean anything by that. Just that…well, just that all the girls thought they were too good for him. They didn't really go for my brother's type."

Abby wondered what type that might be. In her experience, beauty – or handsomeness – was indeed in the eye of the beholder. Look at Bill Gates. He wasn't bad looking, just not in the same league as, say, George Clooney when it came to gorgeousness. But Melinda had fallen for him and Abby didn't believe it had everything to do with Gates' money. Or take Donald Trump. Well, maybe it did have everything to do with *his* money. Despite her indisputable lack of romanticism, Abby still believed there was someone for everyone in this world.

While she was mentally pondering the mysteries of love, her partner followed up with a question of his own. "How about Cory; did he have a type he liked?"

Cari looked at Bridger as if trying to gauge his angle. Often, whether he meant to be ambiguous or not, most times people couldn't tell from his face. As usual, his expression remained neutral, bland and guileless, characteristics Abby had trouble achieving, and she wasn't alone. Bridger's colleagues called this the Flynn Effect. Many tried to copy it; none were successful.

Cari finally answered, "Um, yeah, he had a type he liked. He sort of went for tall girls with dark hair and dark eyes. He always said they were mysterious. If you ask me, they were just different from him and I think that intrigued him."

"Anyone in particular?" Bridger asked.

She nodded with the nervous vigor the two detectives were beginning to identify as her norm. "Um, yeah, a Portuguese foreign exchange student, but she left after just one semester."

"That kind of rules her out."

"Yeah. Oh, and – I almost forgot. There was a junior named Amanda Ferguson. She was on the newspaper staff with him. Cory liked her all right, but I think she hoped for more than just collaborating on a story."

Abby took notes. "Did you know Amanda?"

Cari shook her head as she walked hesitantly over to join the detectives. "Not well. I was just a sophomore," she said, in explanation. They all understood how the separation of grades worked. Juniors rarely hung out with sophomores or, heaven forbid, freshmen. Sometimes, maybe, if they were dating, but mere friendships didn't often extend to underclassmen. There was an odd sort of superiority that came with being older, as though age brought with it wisdom. In some cases it did, if only a little bit, especially in teenagers, where wisdom tended to diminish with the introduction of hormones into the mix.

Cari explained, "Amanda came to the house a few times, to work on some news story or idea. Cory said how much he liked her writing. They laughed a lot together. I thought he might ask her out or something, but he never did. Then, after awhile, she sort of stopped coming around anymore."

"Anyone else?"

"No." Cari ran her hand along the desk, like she might be able to connect with her dead brother by touching it. "Oh, wait. I did notice he got kind of tongue tied around a senior cheerleader, Vanessa Hoyt. I could read him well enough to know he had a humongo crush on her. Who didn't? But Vanessa was untouchable."

"How so?"

"I mean, she was like a goddess. Blonde, tall, perfect body, expensive clothes, dating the most popular guy at Washington."

Everybody remembered a Vanessa from their high school days. Of course, they weren't all named Vanessa. For Abby, it was a girl called Cecilia Brookes. If you asked Bridger, he'd reply Gloria, but couldn't remember her last name. It didn't matter. The Vanessas of this world attract the envy of everyone around them. They always seem to have the best anyone could ask for and not a care in the world, when, in reality, they usually don't. Even the most fortunate-appearing among us have problems, sometimes bigger and deeper than the rest. If they were lucky, maybe Abby and Bridger would get a chance to find out what Vanessa Hoyt's problems were. First, though, they'd have to find her.

"So what happened to Vanessa Hoyt?"

Cari shrugged. "Um, I'm not sure. I heard that she and her boyfriend got married. My memory is a little fuzzy on that, but I think she was pregnant."

"Do you remember the boyfriend's name?" Abby crossed her fingers.

"Oh, yeah. Christopher Reilly."

"Wow, that came easy."

"Everybody remembers Chris Reilly." She blushed again. "He was totally incredible. Tall and blonde like Vanessa, really well built. They were a natural couple. She was head cheerleader and he was a big football star. Had a scholarship to U of O, to play for the Ducks."

Abby always rooted for the Beavers, the rival Oregon college team, while Bridger followed the Ducks. He had for years because, as he said, they were a team that generally kicked butt, particularly with their rapid pace of play, and he commented on that every game. But neither detective could recall a U of O player named Christopher Reilly. Cari had a vague impression of something about an injury, a leg or a foot, but the details eluded her. Abby moved on to another subject.

"The police talked to you the day your brother was discovered, right?" She purposely tried to word the question in as delicate a way as possible. The image that was seared into her mind from just seeing the photographs was not something she wished to dredge up for this young woman. Assuming the officers had spared the family the worst of the gore eleven years ago, neither Abby nor Bridger had any desire to open old wounds unless absolutely necessary. Despite their best efforts, tears threatened Cari's eyes.

"Sorry." She wiped at her cheek.

Abby put a light hand on her shoulder and said, in an uncharacteristically kind voice, "No problem. But anything you can tell us could help. New eyes and ears, you know."

Cari took a deep, shuddering breath. "Yes, they talked to me. Mom didn't want them to, but I did. I had to. It was Cory, after all. I just don't think I said anything that did much good."

Abby tended to agree, after reading the officers' notes from that time. "Think back, Cari. Are you positive Cory didn't tell you something that might help us figure out where he was going, and why?"

Attempting to relive that night clearly took its toll on her, judging by her weakening posture. "Sorry. I wish I could remember. Sometimes, his club, the Nerdlingers had meetings, but never late at night."

"The Nerdlingers?" Bridger asked, remembering that name from their briefing with Capt. Shearer.

"Yes, the Nerdlingers. It was a computer club at Washington High. Kind of geeky, but I thought it was pretty cool. Anyway, they sometimes met in the evenings."

"How late?"

"Um, maybe eight?"

"Are you sure he was home at eight that night?" Abby asked.

Cari looked startled. "What?"

Abby repeated the question. "How do you know he was home at eight? Was he hanging around with you and your mom? Was he studying in his room? Did he have a nightly habit, like did he always come downstairs before going to bed or just turn his lights out and go to sleep?"

The detectives could see Cari struggling to reconstruct evenings in this house from more than a decade before. From the young woman's description, Bridger and Abby gathered that the Austins were a close-knit family. According to Cari, Rose Austin insisted they all sit down to dinner together, with few exceptions. However, once the meal was over, Cory usually went up to his room to read, work on homework or write articles for the school paper. Cari liked to watch TV with her mom, curled up on the sofa, until around 9:00. If Cory had sneaked out before they went to bed, he would have had to tiptoe downstairs, then down the hall and out the front door, a difficult but not impossible feat to accomplish unnoticed. Although, if it were a meeting of the computer club, why would he need to sneak out?

Bridger swept his eyes around the room and said, "So, if Cory was a member of the Nerdlingers, where is his computer?"

Cari appeared confused for a moment, then her face brightened. "Oh! I'm pretty sure the cops took it."

The detectives exchanged looks. They hadn't seen anything about the kid's computer on the evidence list. Abby made a note to check that out.

Next, Bridger asked another question he hadn't seen the answer to in any of the reports. "Did Cory have a cell phone?"

"Sure."

"Do you know where it is?"

Ms. Austin shook her head. "No."

"Have you seen it since that night?"

Her eyelids fluttered in quick bursts and she appeared to retreat to another time for a moment. "Oh. Um, no, I don't think so." This thought seemed to worry her.

Darn, Bridger thought, but said, "That's okay. Do you think maybe the cops took that, too?"

"Um, maybe." She blinked several times more. "Sorry, I just can't remember."

"Don't worry about it. We will look into it."

They turned Cari's attention to the school newspaper. Was there any friction between Cory and the journalistic staff? They already knew about Amanda, so they exempted her.

Cari started to shake her head in that exaggerated way she had, but stopped. Her face lit up. "Wow, I'd forgotten, but, yes. There was one guy. Let's see, what was his name?" Her eyes roved the room as though the answer might be hiding behind something. "Toby Meyer. That's it, Toby Meyer. He was always fighting Cory's ideas and leadership. You could tell he really wanted to be the editor." Her excitement quickly faded. "But I don't think he'd do anything to hurt Cory. I mean, that would just be weird."

Had that name been in the police file? Abby made another note, and a mental one to put Toby Meyer toward the top of their list of people to interview. Then she asked about articles Cory had been working on around the time of his death. She wondered whether any of them fell into the category of expose', such that he might have really pissed off someone or revealed a horrible secret that got him killed.

Cari didn't remember anything embarrassing or lurid, but they could look for themselves. Cory kept copies of every issue of the newsletter he wrote articles for until he became editor and then all of the issues after that.

"Your brother worked at Burger World, too, right?"

"Uh-huh."

"Any problems there?"

"He never mentioned any. I mean, sometimes his manager would do something super stupid, which bugged Cory, but that was just because the manager wasn't very good. I don't think they argued ever, though."

They thanked her, gathered up several of the newsletters and Cory's yearbooks, and motioned for Cari to lead them back downstairs. The past hour had been an emotional one for her. It was time for Bridger and Abby to leave and let Cari get back to picking up the pieces of her life. She had been through a lot in her few years and still had a lot to face, especially with clearing out the family home. And now, long before the age of thirty, here she was, all but alone in the world. As they reached the hallway below, Bridger stopped to gaze at a black and white portrait.

"What a lovely picture. Who is that?"

"Oh, that's my mom."

Abby squinted at the photograph and moved in close. Sometimes she could make out a few details without any aid if she did that and angled her head just right. This one was large enough that the magnifier wouldn't be of much help anyway.

Bridger looked from the portrait to Cari Austin and back, before asking, "Your mother was Asian?"

Cari's smile widened and she nodded with even greater than usual enthusiasm. "Uh-huh. Japanese."

A closer inspection of the young woman showed some Eastern characteristics they had missed until then. Bridger could scarcely hide his astonishment. In actuality, the Portland area had a large contingent of Asian residents, and the city didn't seem to have what the police would consider hate crimes aimed at them, but it might still be an avenue to explore, especially if the detectives on the case back in 2002 hadn't gone down that particular road. Another mental note. That list was growing longer by the minute.

CHAPTER 7

"It is impossible to enjoy idling thoroughly unless one has
plenty of work to do."
— Jerome K. Jerome

Once they had dropped off the shoe box with its repulsive contents at the forensics lab, Bridger and Abby traveled south along the Willamette River once again, except this time winding down the eastside bank. They ended up at the Leipzig Tavern, their longtime hangout, an old Sellwood neighborhood spot they had discovered during their Snowy Forbes task force years. Now, to at least Bridger's delight, it was mere blocks from the brand-new offices of Eyes & Ears Detective Agency. Bridger could barely conceal his enthusiasm. Private investigations may not carry the same panache as city police work, but it ran a close second for him. If he had to be retired, at least he could still solve cases.

Now, at the end of their first day as partners of Eyes & Ears Detective Agency, they settled into a scarred wooden booth and each ordered their usual. For Bridger, Knob Creek bourbon. Abby selected a local chardonnay from a wide range of white wines. Both sighed in relief as the waitress ambled off, grateful for the darkness inside the bar after what they'd seen. For several minutes, they sat without speaking, until the alcohol smoothed out the rough edges of their day. They understood that they were going to eventually need to hash things over in order to plot their next step. But for just a little while longer, they wanted to put reality off.

Snatches of some song teased Abby's ears. It might have been "Light My Fire" by The Doors or any one of several German drinking songs. Hard to tell over the constant din in the fair-sized bar. Of course, asking Bridger would be no help. He couldn't hear her, much less the background music. If he could, he'd have told her it was "Three Little Words" by jazz great Doc Cheatham. Bridger loved good jazz. In fact, several times a month, you would find him playing piano late nights at a tiny watering hole called The Woodstocker, hammering out a Dave Brubeck riff or some Chick Corea composition. That's where he'd met Reggie Preston, the fellow they subleased the office from. The Woodstocker's owner was always pleased to see the old detective drop in for a spontaneous jam session.

Tonight probably wouldn't be one of those nights, though. In fact, it might not happen again until the Cory Austin case was solved. Bridger only had sleepless nights when his mind wasn't occupied. And sleepless nights were what took him to The Woodstocker for what he called music therapy. But now, he and Abby would spend more time at the Leipzig in the coming days. They could blend in there and talk about anything without attracting unwanted attention. The largest hurdle was hearing each other over the crowd.

The Leipzig drew an eclectic mix of customers, from thirty-somethings meeting their friends before heading into downtown Portland to neighborhood regulars on their way home from work to old timers like Bridger and Abby. The place had an unpretentious feeling of comfort and walls that could tell more stories than a volume of Mother Goose.

Bridger leaned forward on his elbows and finally broke their reveries. "Well, Ears, what do you think?"

"About what?" She spoke extra loudly, although no one around them took any notice.

"Oh, the day in general, the office, the agency, the case. Our first case."

Abby waved him off, like shooing a pesky fly.

"You liked the office, didn't you?" He sported a boyish grin that normally would charm the most stoic of people, although rarely Abby. Not much charmed Abby Dalton.

She looked up at the ceiling, a gesture Bridger knew as her coping mechanism, one she usually employed when she didn't want to explain the cause of her massive frustration. Especially *to* the cause of her massive frustration. "Yes, I liked the office. How could I not? Everything was just exactly as I would have done it. The style of furniture, the placement of the furniture, the location of the building. It's all perfect. Our first case?" She dropped her head into her hands. "Oh, hell, I wish we were just trying to find out who Mrs. Smith is boinking on the side."

Bridger sucked in a deep breath. "Yeah, I know. Sorry about that. We really don't have to sign on for this one, Abs. I probably overstepped when I committed to it."

"You sure as hell did." Abby sat up and took a deep drink of her wine, then slowly put her glass back on the table. "Damn it, Bridger."

He released the breath he'd been holding. "No worries. I'll call Nate in the morning." Not the answer he'd hoped for, but not one he would have bet good money against either. Maybe tailing wayward wives would be more fun than he thought. At least they had an office now. Who knew what interesting cases might come through their door? He sighed again. He shouldn't have pushed her so hard, should have eased her into the idea of cold cases.

Abby swallowed another mouthful of the chardonnay. "And don't call me Abs."

"Right."

"Okay." She pinched the bridge of her nose between two fingers, hard. "Son of a bitch. Okay, if you do talk to the captain, ask him if he has Amanda Ferguson's phone number."

Bridger glanced at her and arched his brows in a silent question. Even a fully sighted person would likely not see that in the Leipzig's dim light, but Abby could sense his incredulity.

"Oh, stop it. You know I won't quit now."

Bridger smiled and reached over to pat her hand. "That's my Abs."

She snatched her hand out of reach, saying, "Don't call me Abs."

"Right. No problem."

"We should talk to this Vanessa Hoyt or whatever her name is now, too."

"I'll get on it first thing tomorrow."

"And where the hell did Cory's computer go?"

Bridger nodded. "That's the $64,000 question, isn't it? It sure would be nice to find that out. Let's make it a priority to track that down."

They sat there, each mulling over their own thoughts while the bar bustled around them.

The song reaching Abby's ears now was Taylor Swift's "We Are Never, Ever, Ever Getting Back Together". She looked across at her new partner and the irony wasn't lost on her. She didn't want to work cold cases, but Cory Austin deserved justice so she would see to it that they solved this one and then it would be their last cold case. Shearer would have to find someone else to farm them out to, simple as that.

As long as they were talking about the Cory Austin case again, though, Abby mused aloud, "I don't recall seeing the name Toby Meyer on any interview sheet." Cari Austin had mentioned him briefly as a student working on the newspaper staff who acted jealous of her brother's position as editor of the *Washington Post*.

"There wasn't one. I did a pretty thorough search of those sheets and the catalogue of witnesses. It was a pretty exhaustive list, too, focused mostly on the school, but that makes sense. After all, the kid spent the bulk of his time there and on activities related to school in the evenings. But no one named Toby Meyer was in the file." Bridger had considered the possibility that the detectives eleven years ago had formed preconceived ideas about what happened; thus, a witness or two went overlooked. He decided to play devil's advocate now. "The encounter in the woods really could have been random, a crime of opportunity. That might be why the officers never found a viable suspect."

"Pretty damned violent for a crime of opportunity. Eighteen stab wounds?"

"Yeah."

"You don't really think it was random."

"No."

"Speaking of the officers, I read a few reports by a Derek Moss. I don't have the best eyes, but I'd say he really could use a refresher course in writing."

Bridger hung his head and smiled down into his bourbon. "Derek Moss. He's a genuine piece of work." He said "genuine" with a long "U" and a long "I" and stretched out each syllable. "Yep, genuine. I tried to avoid him whenever I could. I hadn't remembered that he had worked this case when I agreed to take it on. There weren't many cops at PPB that I actively disliked, but Moss was one of them."

"I imagine that's got to do with something other than poor language skills. So what was it?" Abby asked.

"Uh-huh. Well, for starters, he had an inflated opinion of himself. Add to that that he didn't take criticism well, wasn't a team player, pranced around like he was Indiana Jones. You name something you don't want a cop to be and you've got Derek Moss."

"Well, then, I look forward to chatting with Officer Moss."

Bridger chuckled at that. Abby's reputation as a canny interviewer was well known in the police world. Putting her in a room with Derek Moss would certainly produce an interesting drama if not an outright brawl. He wouldn't miss it for all the money in his retirement account.

"And I look forward to watching that little scene."

Bridger signaled the waitress for another Knob Creek. When Abby frowned, he wondered whether she was concerned about his sobriety or the case, but Bridger never indulged to the point of perceptible inebriation. After the briefest of intervals, Abby nodded that she'd take another white wine. Bridger gave her a thumbs-up. "That's my Abs."

"Oh, hell, might as well."

CHAPTER 8

"A woman may very well form a friendship with a man, but
for this to endure, it must be assisted by a
little physical antipathy."

- Nietzsche

Abby and Bridger hadn't spoken about it at Leipzig Tavern but now, at home, she thought back over the day's events. Something bothered her. Partially due to her diminished eyesight, she could hear the subtlest of changes in everyday voice inflection – often giving her a peek into a person's degree of veracity – while Bridger watched for telltale signs in body language. That's part of what made them such a good team.

Now, Abby felt a nagging doubt. Maybe it was nothing. Maybe she was reading too much into the hesitation that came before Cari Austin's answer to Bridger's final question. Maybe Cari was a slow thinker. Or maybe Abby should trust her instincts.

Shortly after the sun set, which was now just shy of 7:30, Abby sat on her deck, like she did most mild evenings, listening to Malph snore – he did a brilliant job of that – and to the water's mesmerizing rhythm in the fading light. To her, the colors of the sky could not be any more beautiful to a person with no sight impairment. And here, in late September, with the trees turning to warm corals and bright ochers which somehow were more vivid for Abby, she found that tonight she did not miss her once-perfect vision after this day of looking at photographs of a broken and bloodied body.

Once darkness fell in earnest, the breeze dropped off and a pleasant peace settled over the lake, and over Abby's mood. Lights on the far shore reflected off of the gentle waves. An occasional warm puff of air ruffled her shoulder length hair. Malph stirred at her feet. She sighed, with both resignation at having an unwelcome job to do and contentment at a day well spent. Or at least an evening well spent. She hadn't yet fully embraced the idea of being one half of Eyes & Ears Detective Agency.

But Bridger is so excited, she thought. *Damn, that man needs a hobby.* And while she would have preferred that he channel that energy into his fondness for birdhouse building, she realized the mystique of wood carving didn't quite measure up to the thrill of solving a mystery. In fact, the promise of untangling a thorny mystery was what had drawn her in this far. Besides, even though she promised herself not to take on another one, she had to admit that cold cases were actually more intriguing than fresh ones. Finding that clue everyone else overlooked, wow, what a rush!

The direction of Abby's thinking got her up out of the deck chair and into the desk chair in front of her computer. Despite her visual limitations, Abby was exceptional at online research. With font size easily manipulated, the Internet proved far faster and far more productive than poring through books (large print for her nowadays) or, worse, agonizing over tiny typeset with her magnifier.

Thinking back, the last thing that she and Bridger had seen as they left Cari at her door was the picture of Rose Austin, exhibiting her distinctive Japanese features. Looking at the children, few people would have guessed that the mother was Asian, but there was no mistaking it. Abby recalled Bridger mentioning an angle not investigated by the original detectives. Could this be a hate crime case? Was Cory Austin killed because of his Japanese blood? Or did someone go after Rose's son in order to send her a message? Trying to run her out of town? That sounded kind of Old West, but this was Oregon, after all.

Abby's fingers flew over the keyboard like tiny dancers as she typed "Portland Asian discrimination" and waited for Google's results, and there were a surprising number. Several blogs led the list. At the time Cory Austin died, blogging hadn't really taken off yet, although a young man like Cory, with his Nerdlingers Club leanings, might have known about it. But in this age of electronic wizardry, there were hundreds of entries. Damn, they really needed to see that kid's computer.

Reading the bloggers' comments, Abby noticed a tendency of some writers to imply that Portland had a growing issue with hate crimes aimed at Asians. Yet, those appeared to be somewhat sparse. There was one in particular, and Abby wondered whether the blogger's ethnicity might be a coincidence. Maybe he was simply hypersensitive to what other people said. Or maybe he was so annoying that other people couldn't resist verbally attacking him. Whatever the reason for the fellow's hurt feelings, there weren't a plenitude of complaints suggesting that the city had a big problem. Still, it was possible that certain individuals might have been targeted. Was Rose Austin one of those?

Abby spent a couple of hours testing different theories and using various keywords. A lot depended on phrasing and wording. Abby knew how to maximize the information she uncovered and which hits would produce the most relevant results. She had plenty of experience at it. Wikipedia had several articles, as did archives of some newspapers from around the Metro area. Nothing earth-shattering though.

By midnight, weary but still somewhat stoked, she awoke Malph and shooed him into his crate, where he resumed his snoring while Abby lay in her bed wondering about Cory Austin's killer. It had always gone like this. Abby was never a halfway sort of woman. A case invaded her core fiber, totally took over her consciousness and ate at her until she chased down the resolution. She would eventually become exhausted and her mind would give itself up to sleep, but that usually didn't happen any earlier than 2:00 a.m., if she were lucky. Her last thought before drifting off had to do with Bridger, though. What was he thinking about?

- - -

Bridger had taken half of the *Washington Post* newsletters home with him to look over. After enjoying the container of soup he'd picked up from the New York style deli next to Leipzig Tavern, he made his way over to a plush leather chair as old as his houseboat. It had been re-cushioned and re-covered twice, but still hugged Bridger's bulky frame and looked extraordinarily homey. He picked up one of the newsletters and smiled as he read the masthead, realizing how much he liked the school paper's name. *Washington Post* made it sound important, like its big brother, the, well, *Washington Post.* He figured that Abby had spent some time on her deck, reading the six issues that she'd taken with her. Hopefully, she had found something in one of them that could help reveal their killer.

As he looked out over the top of the last edition that Cory Austin had worked on, to the city skyline beyond his position on the river, he tried to envision the kid's final few days. What had it been like those last two weeks before graduation? Bridger found that he had trouble venturing a good guess. Hell, he had trouble even remembering what high school had been like. That was a long time ago for Bridger, and the width of a very large continent away. How different was Walton High in The Bronx, New York, from Washington High in Portland, Oregon? Besides being on opposite coasts, there was a gap of over forty years. Man, how had that happened? He had packed a lot into those four decades, but still, the time had flown. His once robust head of hair now sported only a little red fuzz, faded red fuzz if he were to be completely honest. And his once-well-muscled body had grown a bit soft. Maybe more than a bit.

He shook his head and refocused on the paper before him. Even though printed on cheap stock, it had a semi-professional look about it. The particular edition Bridger held in his hand had stories from various contributors and student reporters, covering all sorts of subjects. The September 11th attacks earned at least a mention in one or two of the articles. For the students, the memory of the Twin Towers belching toxic, sooty smoke, before – unbelievably – crumbling and taking thousands of lives down with them hadn't yet faded enough to bring back the apathy rampant before the terrorists hit. As always, young people handled the trauma in their own ways, yet they were no less dramatically affected by it than adults. This particular trauma heralded a new reality for them, an incontrovertible change in their world and its future.

Cory's final edition signaled the end of his time at Washington High, its publication date just two weeks before graduation ceremonies. He missed seeing it in print by a single day. Too bad, for he had done his best work as his swan song. The entire senior class was pictured on the front page, mugging for the camera as they stood on the 50-yard line of the Washington High Coyotes' football field. Of course, none of the faces was remotely recognizable in the sea of 194 students. Cory's photo as editor held a place of honor in the upper right-hand corner and the names of the rest of the staff were listed beneath. Amanda Ferguson's name showed up as a roving reporter. Cari had mentioned her as a person of interest in her brother's life. Maybe she had stuck around the metro area. Bridger hoped so. That would significantly boost their chances of setting up a quick interview with her. He was curious what she might have to say about Cory after eleven years. Would she even remember him?

As Bridger was thinking of Amanda Ferguson, a boat sped by, using a weak spotlight and barely slowing to reduce its wake, contrary to the warnings of numerous signs in the area. What was wrong with these folks? It was long after dark, making hidden hazards nearly impossible to see. And, besides safety, apparently courtesy was also far from their minds. *Probably drunk,* Bridger grumbled, and gathered up the file.

On the way to his bedroom, the image of the cat's severed paw slammed into his mind again. What a gruesome discovery for young Ms. Austin. Had Rose found it, too, long ago? Had she run across it recently and then not remembered? Had Cory seen it? Did it really have any connection to the boy's death? Bridger had a hunch that it did, just not quite how. Tomorrow, he and Abby would go back to the precinct and pick up witness lists and contact info and find out what happened to that computer. For now, though, he needed some rest. He locked up and went to bed. Unlike Abby, he fell into a deep sleep before his head even touched the pillow.

CHAPTER 9

*"The task of the real intellectual consists of analyzing
illusions in order to discover their causes."*

- Arthur Miller

Early the next morning, Bridger sat in the car outside Abby's cottage, listening to his voice mail. A call had come in while he was driving over to pick her up. He hadn't yet gotten used to wearing his earpiece as a matter of habit so he had been unable to answer his cell phone. When he'd been working, he never forgot his equipment, but his attitude had relaxed during the intervening years of retirement. Another reason to get back to some kind of useful occupation. He was afraid of losing his edge.

Cari Austin said in her message that she had remembered something that might be helpful. That sounded vague, but they could use any leads at all. Any seasoned detective knew that sometimes the smallest thing turned out to be the biggest clue. Bridger punched in Cari's number and leaned his head against CON's window, relishing the feel of the sun shining in on his balding old head.

She answered right away in a voice quivering with exhilaration. Apparently, while she had been straightening up Cory's room after Bridger and Abby left the day before, she'd moved the textbooks piled on his desk. A test paper fell out of "Advanced Trigonometry" and it sparked a memory of an incident at school she figured the detectives would like to know about. Bridger thanked her, explaining that even the most minor detail helped tell the story.

"Okay. Um, well, see, Cory was really good at math. I mean, really super good. About a month before he died, he was taking a test and found an error on one of Mr. Shin's trig exams. That was his math teacher," she added, unnecessarily. "But, when

Cory pointed it out, Mr. Shin went ballistic. I mean, he just got really super crazy. That was totally out of character for him."

"Did you see this happen?"

"No, huh-uh. I wasn't in advanced trig. But I had Mr. Shin for sophomore algebra." She seemed to think Bridger was questioning how she knew the teacher's customary manner. "He was always so cool in class."

Now Bridger had to wonder whether she meant cool as in calm affect or cool as in someone worthy of her admiration. Was that even a term kids used these days? "So you liked him?" He didn't add "as a teacher," giving Cari the chance to decide for herself what he might be getting at.

"Um, yeah. He was okay."

Cari's answer struck Bridger as genuine, if a bit uncertain, so he got off the subject of Mr. Shin's coolness and asked, "If you weren't in that class, how did you find out about him going ballistic?" He emphasized the phrase as she had. "Did Cory tell you?"

She took some time before answering. "Hm, I don't think it was my brother that told me, but I can't remember. I may have just overheard some kids talking."

Bridger didn't think it was important where she'd heard it, but he always liked to stockpile as many details as he could. Over the years, he'd learned that you just never knew when one of them might break the case. As someone famous had once said, you can't have too many facts. Maybe it was Jack Webb from *Dragnet*, pretty much his favorite TV series when he was about seven.

"Do you know if Mr. Shin took it out on Cory in any way?"

This time, when she answered, Cari sounded surprised by Bridger's question. "Oh. Um, no, I don't think so. He just got all mad and exploded, and then that was it."

Unless he took it one step further, like with a knife, Bridger wanted to say. Instead, he thanked Cari and ended the call.

While he'd been on the phone, Abby had come through the gate and over to the car. Startled, Bridger wondered how long she'd been standing there. He had been engrossed in his conversation with Ms. Austin. To be frank, he wouldn't have heard Abby's approach anyway; those days were long gone. She slid in beside him, smiled and said, "Good morning."

Bridger braced for a facetious comment, figuring that Abby was still smoldering over being blindsided by his deal with Capt. Shearer to investigate cold cases for PPB. But he was braced for a comment that didn't come. He relaxed while keeping a wary eye on her and recapped what Cari Austin had told him.

"Well, then, that's another avenue that needs to be explored. Let's get down to the precinct and pick up that contact info. We're still beginning with the jogger this morning, right?"

"Right." Bridger decided not to question Abby's good mood. It was bound to turn soon enough. It always did. Abby Dalton could be as mercurial as a smoldering fire. You just never knew what would set her off. He did know, though, that it would be judicious to get her some coffee. Immediately. Coffee was the magic liquid that equalized Abby's volatility.

There was a Human Bean kiosk just six blocks down the street, Bridger's number one choice. He often started his day with a visit to the Bean whether he had business in Lake Oswego or not. Marla, the young woman who worked there six out of seven days a week, had been a street kid back when he and Abby were working on the Snowy Forbes serial rape case. At the time, Marla hadn't managed to form a tough crust like the bulk of the city's homeless kids and Bridger worried that she might trust the wrong person. It was all too easy to do. She had survived her share of scrapes, robberies and minor assaults, but she had survived. For that alone, he considered her one of the lucky ones. Five years ago, after more than a year and a half on the streets of downtown Portland, Marla had moved the six long miles out to Lake Oswego with a power-driven boyfriend who didn't take care of her in a way that Bridger thought he should and he let the young man know.

Normally, Bridger Flynn came across as an affable guy with an easy smile and a self-effacing manner. But he could transform himself into a vision of dark anger, when his hooded eyes would shine with a deadly calm, and the potential for violence would be evident in his deep brown face. During one of those rare times, Bridger's dangerous side emerged and he lapsed into a cocky gang swagger that he'd learned in his youth and reverted to his Bronx slang and vernacular. So, on that long-ago day, confronting Marla's boyfriend, his terms were quite explicit and delivered in words the boyfriend understood well.

55

Therefore, with not even a brief glance over his shoulder, the pimple faced kid pulled up stakes and left. Marla stayed, but only because Bridger pleaded with her and ultimately promised he would put in a good word for her with the owner of the nearby Human Bean. Because of Bridger Flynn and his instinct about her, one-time street girl Marla found a steady job and the ability to support herself without relying on anyone else. He remained faithful to the Bean because he liked to take his business where it would matter, and here it would.

Sunday night, Bridger and Abby had agreed that they should start their investigation on Monday with the unfortunate jogger who found Cory's body, a man named Randall Cross, and hear his story firsthand. Their first stop, however, would have to be Central Precinct, where they could make copies of the interview sheets and get the addresses of pertinent witnesses, and maybe even some overlooked ones. So early that morning, Bridger motored tiny CON up Macadam Avenue and into the heart of downtown Portland.

At Central, if anything Capt. Shearer looked wearier and more disheveled than the previous day, with his tie hanging loose and his shirt sleeves rolled up beyond his elbows. The crease in his pants was now only a distant memory. Bridger made an offhanded comment about the dangers of overworking.

Shearer ran a hand down his face, as though that might chase away the exhaustion that had taken up residence there. "Thanks, Bridger. Haven't actually been home since I last saw you."

"What's going on?"

"Baby snatching."

Abby moaned. In her opinion, not a lot could be worse than losing a child, even if there was a chance of getting it back, unlike Cory Austin who was never coming back. "Shit. What happened?"

Shearer motioned for them to follow him and started off down a hall, speaking over his shoulder as he walked. "The mother was pretty badly beat up. Whoever grabbed the kid attacked her in Tryon Park. Lots of people wandering around in there, but apparently no one saw or heard anything. The docs think she'll pull through, but they can't be sure. Her baby's just eleven months old. Little girl."

Bridger whistled. "Tough one, Captain."

"Yeah." He stopped abruptly and rubbed his eyes. "In answer to your question earlier, Bridger, I've put in a call to Evidence about Cory Austin's computer. We should have an answer soon."

"Thanks. It could be very helpful."

"I'll let you know when we find something out." Shearer began walking again. "Well, you said you needed some contact info on the case. You realize, though, that since it's a cold case, the last known addresses are pretty old."

"Right. We'll start with what the files say and take it from there. Abby is a whiz at locating folks, even ones who don't want to be found."

She smiled self-consciously when the two men looked her way. While it might be true, Abby didn't take compliments well. Criticism was far easier for her to deal with.

- - -

Tracking down Randall Cross took little effort. His address was in the initial report the officers took and had remained the same over the last eleven years. That fact surprised both of the detectives. Most people moved at least once and usually twice in that length of time. They figured Mr. Cross must be that rare individual who was happy with what he had.

It took only fourteen minutes to get to Cross's place from Central Precinct. The apartment building appeared old but well maintained, a light brown brick, two stories high with the ground units opening onto a courtyard that boasted a couple dozen camellia bushes and small ribbons of lawn. Although Randall Cross wasn't home at that time on a Monday morning, his landlady was. She was also eager to know why the police wanted to talk to him. Her interest didn't appear to be anything less than bald-faced nosiness.

"Is Mr. Cross in any trouble, officers?" The glee that shone in her eyes made it clear she hoped for something juicy, probably so that she'd have some gossip to share with her Bunco group.

Bridger flashed his most disarming smile. "No, ma'am, we just want to ask Mr. Cross a few questions."

Abby added, in a more surly tone, "Following up on an old case."

The landlady's face fell but she volunteered to help by giving them the address of her tenant's place of employment.

Randall Cross worked at the City of Portland Water Bureau and, on Mondays, he got a later than usual start due to team meetings and weekly planning sessions. They caught up with him as he was heading out to his car. Cross stood about equal in height to Abby, which made Bridger look up just slightly. From the man's lean build, they could surmise that he still jogged. He had a pleasant face, oval with a cleft chin, thick ginger hair cut short and a runner's lanky body. Bridger called out his name as they walked toward him, his hand extended in greeting. Cross took it with a firm grip. Bridger and Abby displayed their credentials, and Cross nodded, as if he'd been expecting something like this.

Abby told him they had come about Cory Austin. She began to refresh his memory but he held a hand up before she got three words out. "I remember. How could I forget? That was a horrible thing. They never caught the guy who did it, right? Is there a new lead?"

"There might be some new evidence. We're not sure whether it's related to Cory's death though."

"Can you tell me what it is?" He looked from Abby to Bridger and back.

Bridger studied his feet before answering. "His sister found a cat's paw, apparently cut off and put in a shoe box, in a closet at home."

"Oh, God. How awful. Poor girl."

This time, Abby answered. "Yeah, she was pretty upset about it, although she's a young woman now. She thinks it belonged to their cat and that whoever cut off the paw may have been the one who stabbed her brother. We're looking into that theory, and other possibilities, too. Did you hear of any animal mutilations going on back then?"

Cross frowned. "No. Of course, I probably wouldn't have paid a lot of attention, since my landlady doesn't allow pets." He grinned, a little lopsidedly. "Unless you consider fish to be pets."

Abby didn't. But then she also didn't consider cats to be pets. At least not the kind of pets worth spending time and money on. She took Cross through his original testimony, asking how often he jogged on that specific trail, time of day he normally went, people he encountered. Were there any regulars? Were there any persons that looked out of place, like someone not dressed for a walk in the woods? His responses didn't deviate from what the detectives had read in the reports. With the easy questions out of the way, Abby signaled Bridger to take over. That puzzled him, as she ordinarily enjoyed the down and dirty stuff. Maybe she was losing her grit.

Nonetheless, Bridger picked up the thread. "So you found the body between 6:00 and 6:30 a.m.?"

Cross cringed at the word "body".

Bridger noticed and apologized, "Sorry, but can you describe what you remember about that morning?"

"Unfortunately, I remember everything about that morning." A faraway look clouded his eyes. "It was such a beautiful day, the first of June. That's about my favorite time of year. Or it used to be. The forest smelled fresh with the early sun drying the late spring dew. Birds were singing. The rhodies were in bloom. It was invigorating just being out there."

Bridger glanced at Abby, knowing that she scoffed at descriptions that included words like "invigorating". She preferred something more earthy, like "damned fine."

Cross sucked in his lower lip. "I'd been running for about thirty-five minutes, mostly on the Wildwood Trail, as usual, but I like to mix it up now and then so I take side trails, too, but only the ones that loop back. I'd just veered off onto this little path a few hundred feet before. That's when I came across the kid. I almost stumbled over him. At first, I thought it was a red scarf or somebody's jacket." He took a moment to compose himself. "So much blood. Geez. I – I'm ashamed to say I got sick."

Bridger said, "Don't be." He himself had had trouble keeping his breakfast down more times than he cared to admit, especially at a particularly brutal scene. Abby, though, had an iron stomach. No one had ever seen Abigail Dalton lose her cookies like that.

Cross continued, "When I recovered enough to talk, I called 9-1-1 and sat down on a rock to wait for the cops."

"Did you touch anything? Move anything?" They could always hope he had found the knife and would be ready to turn it over to them after all this time, but of course, that was wishful thinking.

59

"No. I didn't see anything but the – the body. And I didn't go near him. It was obvious that the kid was dead."

"Could you tell that it was a kid?" Abby asked. She rued the fact that she couldn't see Cross's facial expressions.

He chewed on his lip again. "Not really. He was – I mean, the body was lying on its stomach. Oh, I did see a watch on his arm. It was big, definitely looked like a guy's watch. And the arm looked like a guy's. But it was covered in so much blood." He hesitated and shook his head. "I found out later that he was just a kid. Geez."

"Anyone else around that morning?"

"Naw. I told the cops this before. Didn't see anyone out there. That's how it normally was. Just me." He snapped his fingers. "Oh, wait. Sometimes I'd run into this guy walking his dog, but that didn't happen more than two or three times, and definitely not that day."

Abby asked what the guy walking his dog looked like.

"Probably late fifties. Slight build, tallish. Muttered to himself some. I mostly noticed the dog. It was huge." He shrugged. "They seemed harmless though."

The detectives looked at each other and Abby wrote a note to check that out. People who seemed harmless weren't necessarily so. Look at Ted Bundy. A lot of women trusted him, probably because of his earnest good looks, and they paid dearly for that trust. And muttering to oneself wasn't a characteristic normally associated with a mentally stable person. It might be nothing, but it would definitely bear looking into.

CHAPTER 10

"You shall judge of a man by his foes
as well as by his friends."

-Joseph Conrad

On Sunday, Bridger had found the name of Alan Garfield in one file. He figured Garfield was the fellow the jogger mentioned encountering a few times on the forest trails, as his interview sheet talked about his walks in the woods and a dog. Back in 2002, Garfield told the investigating officers that he saw Cory Austin approximately once every two or three weeks walking in Forest Park. He took his dog out at the same time every day, sometimes twice, and they occasionally would run into the teenager. An odd sort of friendship had sprung up.

The detectives parked directly in front of Alan Garfield's Northwest Portland house, noting it had a tidiness that looked as though in recent years it might have fallen on hard times. The paint around the windows of the little bungalow was peeling and the front door had a three-inch scrape just below the handle. The doorbell worked, though, and Abby soon heard footsteps approaching, along with a deep throated bark. She put her hand on Bridger's arm to warn him.

A thin face peered through a screen when the front door opened. It had a friendly quality, with genial eyes and brows that appeared as though they expected a pleasant surprise. The bark had come from what appeared to be a piebald pony, although it soon became clear that it was merely a very large dog. Randall Cross hadn't exaggerated when he described the enormity of the creature.

Bridger held up his license, which he had encased in a rich brown leather badge holder, and introduced himself and Abby before inquiring, "Mr. Garfield?"

"Yes." The man reached down to take hold of the dog's collar. He addressed the animal as Duke while instructing him to sit. Duke planted his sizable haunches right next to Garfield's feet as his owner motioned the detectives inside. "Come on in."

Abby had called ahead to make sure Alan Garfield would be home after Bridger showed her the interview sheet again that morning, and the man had been most cooperative. Now, entering the tiny house, Bridger took the lead while wondering, *How does one live with a dog that large in such a small space?* To its credit, though, the home had a decent sized yard with plenty of grass and a pair of giant oak trees which provided a nice amount of shade. Duke followed the three humans into a cozy living room and sat beside his owner's chair. Abby and Bridger perched on a worn loveseat, waving off the idea of coffee or tea. Garfield reached over and patted Duke's head with gentle affection.

"As I told you over the phone, yes, I met the young man the police were asking about back then. Cory, was it?"

Abby answered, "Yes."

"Yes, uh-huh. Well, I walked my dog in the park pretty much every day. That would have been Duke here's granddaddy." He stroked the animal's back fondly. "This guy is barely a year old, aren't you, boy?" Duke's vibrant pink tongue flicked an impressive four inches out of his mouth as he tried to kiss Garfield's face. "Yes." He looked back at his guests. "Anyway, like I told the policemen, what, ten, twelve years ago, apparently Cory would occasionally walk that same path on his way to some school activity, mostly a club he belonged to. It was kind of a shortcut for him." He stopped, a pained expression clouding his face. "What a nice kid. Tried to discourage him from walking in there alone."

Abby couldn't tell how old Alan Garfield was but she'd have guessed probably between fifty-five and sixty, judging by his gait and strength of voice. She would ask Bridger later for a fuller description, try to get a better mental picture of the man. The dog, she could tell, was a Great Dane, if only because of his distinctive profile and his colossal size. Her eyes weren't great, but she made out that much. Listening carefully, what she heard from Garfield didn't set off any major alarm bells. Most people hid something when questioned, however small or inconsequential, and this man was likely no exception. Abby simply took it as a challenge to find out what.

Beside her, Bridger urged him to go on with his recollection of Cory Austin.

Alan Garfield sighed. "Yeah, sure sorry about what happened to him. Such a nice kid. He loved Jake. Duke's granddad," he repeated, in case they had missed it the first time. "Always carried treats in his pockets just to give to Jake. Odd, too, because he said he didn't have a dog. I guess the family owned a cat though. Didn't matter, he still carried those treats. Quite the animal lover. He talked a lot about his cat. Loved him like I love Duke here. And Duke's daddy and granddaddy." He rubbed his chin, thinking. "Let's see now. Cat had a funny name."

Abby wasn't sure that Bridger had heard Garfield; the man had begun speaking almost as though to himself. She helped him out. "Frizz."

"Yeah, Frizz." He broke into a huge grin. "Frizz, yeah. Funny name. Anyway, he loved that cat."

"Did he talk about any of his friends? The human ones?" This last question sounded harsher than Abby had intended. She sometimes grew impatient with too much sentimentality and her voice betrayed her.

Garfield didn't appear to notice. He looked at the ceiling for a few seconds, eyes darting from corner to corner, clearly trying hard to remember. "Yeah, he did. There was a girl. Can't remember..."

"Amanda?" Abby asked.

"Amanda? Hm."

"Vanessa?"

He shook his head. "It's been too long." The crease between his brows deepened. "Maybe she worked at the school newspaper with him. Did she? That sounds right. Yeah, I think she did."

That would have been Amanda Ferguson.

Alan Garfield had little more to add, although Abby got the distinct impression that now he was holding something back. A faulty memory or omission by design? She decided that it might behoove them to revisit Mr. Garfield when they had a handle on a lot more information.

Back in the car, Abby recapped for Bridger what he had missed of Garfield's answers. Garfield had a tendency to mumble and the timbre of his voice fell into a range not easily picked up by Bridger's hearing aids. Both of them, though, felt that he had been honest with them, if not entirely open. Bridger had watched where the man kept his gaze as well as how stiffly he held his body. Abby, naturally, listened for inconsistencies and subtle changes in tone. The detectives ended up on the same page. Garfield had only told them part of the story, whether he knew it or not.

- - -

The next person on their list was Lincoln Shin, the math teacher that Cari Austin called about. They had obtained his address, but before visiting Shin, the detectives wanted to see for themselves the test paper Cari had found. She'd said it spurred a memory, not that it was the actual test paper in question. Nevertheless, it might hold some clues.

Her mother's house – now her house, they supposed, as sole surviving relative – was only a few blocks from the Goose Hollow Inn, a classic Portland eatery and a place Bridger had fond memories of. They had to pass by it anyway so, being just a half hour shy of noon, they decided to stop in for an early lunch. The usual midday crowd hadn't yet materialized, making it easy to find a somewhat isolated table, and they sat down to work out their strategy for questioning educator Shin.

Abby ordered a Reuben with fries; Bridger, a Caesar salad, although the aroma of the split pea soup wafting out of the kitchen made it hard for him to stick to his diet. Despite working out three days every week – except for this one, which demanded every minute of his time pursuing a killer – Bridger tended to retain an extra fifteen pounds that stubbornly refused all of his efforts to rid himself of them, while Abby remained slim with only her occasional paddles around Oswego Lake in her kayak, and just look at the woman's nutritional intake.

While they waited for their meals, they laid out their ideas. Unless it was one of the school district's in-service days, the teacher should not be home from work for several more hours, so that gave them plenty of time to polish their plan.

Once their entrees had come and gone, they lingered over coffee and shared a slice of apple pie, another gastronomic pleasure not on Bridger's diet but irresistible nonetheless. Then, finished at Goose Hollow, they drove over to the Austin house.

Cari answered the door as though she had been standing right next to it, this time wearing a different pair of drab baggy pants and a look of bemusement. "You must have read my mind! I was just about to call you. Again."

Abby asked why, even without seeing the young woman's expression.

Cari nodded enthusiastically, a nervous habit the detectives were growing accustomed to. "The mail arrived a few minutes ago, and this was in it." She produced an envelope and held it out to Abby, who handed it over to Bridger.

He said, "It's from someone named Amanda Shaw." His expression was blank for a moment, then he snapped his fingers. "Oh, *Amanda*. Amanda Ferguson?"

"Uh-huh." Cari continued to nod and grin broadly.

They had worried that it might take hours of tracking in order to find Amanda's current whereabouts, but this saved them a whole lot of effort. The return addressee was Amanda *Shaw*, but the sympathy card inside left no doubt that this was the Amanda they were seeking.

Bridger groaned when he read the rest of the return address. "Tumwater. She lives in Tumwater."

Abby said, "Hell."

A pretty little suburb of Washington State's capitol, Tumwater was a couple of hours up Interstate 5 from Portland. Neither of the detectives wished to take a road trip. Not yet, at any rate. For now, they figured, Amanda could wait.

Bridger reminded Cari of their reason for coming over: the math test. She led them back to the kitchen, where the paper lay on the island counter. Scrutinizing the questions, Bridger emitted a low whistle. Cory definitely excelled in the subject, as evidenced by a large A+++ at the top of the page, but Bridger had no idea if the paper contained problems of algebra, trig, calculus or a set of formulas for a new spaceship. Aside from confirming that the kid was brilliant, the test was disappointing in its revelations. The detectives thanked Cari and left, promising to stay in touch when anything new came up.

- - -

They figured that Lincoln Shin would still not be home for another hour or so, assuming his teaching duties kept him at the school for at least a short while after the students left at the end of their day. Believing they could use this opportunity to their advantage, Bridger and Abby decided that a little advance reconnoitering was in order.

Shin's name had come up as the only teacher Cory had ever had the slightest hint of trouble with, according to Cari Austin, and she'd emphasized *ever*. She said that her brother had pointed out a mistake on one of Mr. Shin's trigonometry exams and the teacher went ballistic. Apparently, Linc Shin prided himself on being God's right-hand man when it came to mathematics, so having a student correct him didn't sit at all well. Nonetheless, it seemed like a long stretch going from an embarrassed teacher to an enraged killer.

Abby said, "Well, those math types can be pretty fiery."

Bridger laughed, then grew serious. "If nothing else, we might learn something new about our victim through Mr. Shin's eyes."

Even though Shin taught at Washington High School in downtown Portland, he lived on the Beaverton side of the West Hills, in a uniquely rural pocket of acreage and seedy homes. Driving along, they noted that some of the area residences featured overstuffed chairs as porch furniture and appeared to be competing for the title of most inspiring display of dead cars, if only judged by the sheer quantity. Weeds had edged out lawn as the ground cover of choice.

Bridger missed the turn onto the property the first pass by, as the overgrown driveway was difficult to see coming at it from that direction. He turned CON around at a chained-off fire lane with a thick patch of Queen Anne's lace towering almost two feet high and eased back onto the street. At the instant they got back to the driveway leading to Shin's house, an ancient Gremlin careened out and took off westbound in their eastbound lane. Bridger swerved, jostling Abby roughly, who bumped up against the passenger side door.

"Shit."

"Looks as though we just missed our Mr. Shin," said Bridger, watching the car fade away in his rearview mirror. The vehicle appeared to have the original paint, which is to say that it now was mostly rust with a few patches of dull gray showing through. The middle-aged man behind the wheel had been much the same color as his car. "I think that was him in that old Gremlin."

"A Gremlin? Really? Hell, I didn't know any of those still existed."

"Hard to believe, isn't it?"

"Actually, it's hard to believe anyone ever bought one. This guy kept one? What a nut job."

"Yeah. I wonder what he was doing home in the middle of a school day," Bridger said, almost under his breath. "Well, let's drive on down to the house, just to be sure it was Shin."

The rutted dirt lane proved almost too much for the smart car, and for Abby's back. They bounced along for about seven hundred feet before the canopy of branches overhead opened onto a clearing littered with garden implements and broken clay pots surrounding a brown lump of a house with paint in the same condition as the Gremlin's.

Abby exited the car first, while Bridger fumbled to release his seat belt. The cloying odor of a nearby honeysuckle struck Abby with a vengeance in the mid-afternoon warmth. They approached the front door together and Abby pounded her fist on the pitted old wood. Bridger peeked through the windows to either side of the tiny porch but the panes had almost certainly not been cleaned since the house was built sometime in the early 1960s. They waited a full minute, knocking two or three more times. No one came to answer.

The setting would have been extraordinarily pretty had it not been a repository for discarded car parts and lawn mowers. An oval pond with a weeping willow at one end of it occupied a prominent position to one side of an unkempt yard. A miniature dock jutted a couple feet out over the water, a few of its boards missing. Half a dozen ducks swam along at a snail's pace, bobbing for invisible insects and quacking at each other nonstop. The serenity of the scene served to lull Bridger and Abby into an ungrounded sense of security. Naturally, Abby heard it before Bridger.

"Son of a bitch!" She grabbed her partner's arm and yanked him forcefully toward the car. Bridger sprinted, not waiting for an explanation. They had worked together long enough for him to take the presence of danger on faith. That may have been what saved them both from serious injury. Abby reached her door first, cursing as she missed the handle and scrambled for a handhold. Bridger slipped on a damp patch of moss, but righted himself with little delay, hurtling for his door. Abby slammed hers at about the same time Bridger opened his. Fortunately, the dog was intent on getting at Abby, providing Bridger with the slimmest margin of time to reach safety.

Abby said, "Shit," then thanked God she had left the window rolled up. The animal barked and lunged in a frenzy of frustration. Gnashing teeth left a smear of foam on the glass. The dog's weight, along with its fury, rocked CON with each hit of its muscular body.

Bridger puffed out his cheeks and exhaled noisily. "There's another reason to own a cat."

"What?"

"Have you ever had one chase you to a car?"

"Cats don't care enough to bother," Abby replied, her voice shaky.

Bridger looked out his window at the dog, which had now come around to the driver's side as though he wanted to make sure he got his point across to both of the trespassers. "We might want to call ahead the next time we visit Mr. Lincoln Shin."

"Oh, hell, yeah." Abby swallowed. Not a lot of things scared her, but an animal protecting its territory doesn't play by any discernible rules, so she preferred to steer clear of anything guarding its home turf, if for no other reason than to avoid any painful misunderstandings.

"So, where to now?" The tremor in Bridger's voice belied his otherwise confident tone.

"I think maybe I'm done for the day. How about you take me to my place?"

CHAPTER 11

"A dog reflects the family life. Whoever saw a frisky dog in a gloomy family, or a sad dog in a happy one? Snarling people have snarling dogs; dangerous people have dangerous ones."

- Arthur Conan Doyle

The afternoon had ended badly, so now Bridger held out little hope that there would be a chance to ruminate over the day's events with his new partner. Abby's hands trembled most of the way back to her house, although she stared straight ahead with her jaw set. Bridger would have loved to know what was going on inside her head, and he'd bet that she was hard at work on a new scheme for approaching the math teacher. He guessed the next trip to Lincoln Shin's house wouldn't go the same way as today's had. Abby would see to that. She learned from her mistakes. And from the mistakes of others. And she made them pay.

When CON pulled into the parking lot at Abby's cottage, she busied herself with digging through her purse. "Aha!" She'd scored her keys. Bridger put the car in "Park" and looked over at her. She reached for the door handle.

"Might as well come in." She didn't see his look of surprise but probably knew it was there. After all, they had been partners for a long time, even if the agency was new. "We've got a hell of a lot of stuff to talk about and a shit pot full of strategizing to do."

He waited while she opened the gate and then followed her to the house. Malph came around the side, announcing his presence with a hearty "malph, malph." Bridger responded with Daffy Duck noises, as he always did, in a lame attempt to prove to the dog how silly his own barking sounded. Malph seemed not to care. In fact, if anything, he acted as if he kind of liked Bridger's goofy antics.

Even though it was early, Abby poured herself a glass of wine while Bridger searched through her liquor cabinet for some bourbon. Drinks in hand, they arranged themselves outside on the deck. It was nearing the fall solstice, so the sunshine had weakened somewhat, but the temperatures remained pleasant in the afternoon and evening hours and would for about three more weeks, if they were lucky, when it would turn crisp as darkness descended a few minutes earlier every day. Come December, it would be pitch black not long after 4:00 p.m.

Malph came over and put his head in Abby's lap, possibly sensing her lingering distress. She ran a hand down his short, white fur half a dozen times before observing, "You know, we should find out if Rose Austin had a housekeeper."

Bridger reached up to adjust his hearing aid, causing Abby to sense that he hadn't heard. When she repeated her suggestion, he nodded. "Good idea." After a short pause, he went on, "Who do you want to talk to next?"

They both nursed their drinks, in no rush. Finally, she said, "Lincoln Shin. Let's just make sure the son of a bitch is expecting us. He obviously isn't the kind of guy to sneak up on."

"Really glad you heard that dog today. It could have gotten pretty ugly."

"Damn straight. Next time, I'll be armed." Whether she felt Bridger raise his eyebrows or not, she waited just long enough to make him a little jumpy, then added, "With mace." He relaxed somewhat, but didn't know whether to believe her.

The next day, being Tuesday, would also be a school day. Bridger put forward the possibility of confronting Shin at work, rendering moot any need to equip themselves with mace or any other form of weaponry. They kicked that idea around and, finding nothing to dissuade them, agreed to give it a shot.

"Do we need to check out Burger World? Cory worked there, after all."

Abby considered that only briefly. "I don't see how it would help. Eleven years have passed. No one who worked with him will still be there."

"Probably not."

"If we run out of other leads, then maybe. Meanwhile, let's concentrate on more likely scenarios."

Abby polished off the last of her chardonnay, stood and stretched before announcing, "I'm going for a spin in the kayak.

Won't be more than about half an hour. Make yourself at home." Malph heard the magic word "kayak" and trotted behind his mistress, sticking close so that he wouldn't miss out on the trip. She routinely invited him to go along, but if he hesitated she left without him.

Bridger watched her as she donned her safety vest and wrestled the seventeen-foot sea kayak into the water, then balanced with her paddle to ease herself into the double cockpit. Malph hopped clumsily into the seat in front of her and they glided out onto the sparkling waters of the small lake.

Not yet six o'clock, the shadows on the far shore had already begun to grow long with the inevitable approach of autumn. As he sat on Abby's deck, Bridger reflected that Cory Austin had experienced too few autumns. Someone – he and Abby, if Bridger had any say in the matter – needed to find justice for the boy and bring what some called closure to Cari, although Bridger didn't believe in the concept, especially when applied to emotions.

Fifteen minutes later, he went inside to pour himself another drink and spied the *Washington Post*s on the coffee table. He picked them up and returned to the deck to keep an eye on Abby while scanning an issue or two of the school newspaper.

The first one had a story about Chris Reilly's crippling injury. It was front-page news. Did Cory make the decision to feature it in that prominent spot? If he had, was it so that Reilly's career-ending mishap would not be missed by anyone? Could Cory have thought it might win over the girl of his dreams, if he had one, by emphasizing the sports star's newfound physical imperfection? That sounded like skewed logic if Bridger had ever heard any, but teenagers aren't known for their good judgment, even the super brainy ones. Their social skills leave a lot to be desired, too. One could view the article as a cruel attempt to knock the jock down a notch. Did Cory Austin have that kind of spiteful cunning inside of him?

Bridger realized that he and his partner had little enough idea of Cory Austin's true nature. What they knew about their victim came mostly from his sister, who admittedly had a positively slanted view of her brother. His peers, the majority being the Washington High students, could probably shed a truer light on what the kid was really like and help form a more rounded picture of him. Kind of A Day in the Life of Cory Austin. Thinking

71

about that, Bridger looked out on the lake, watching Abby's graceful strokes and wishing she would come back in soon.

- - -

Abby and Malph cut through the placid water with ease. She knew that Bridger would wait; he had that restlessness he always got when something weighed on his mind. They would talk, but right now she needed some time to calm herself. Shin's dog had unnerved her more than anything had in a long while. She relied heavily on her ears, compensating for the loss of her sight, but more and more she missed the aid of her eyes, especially in this line of work. Damn the macular degeneration. It left her feeling helpless at times and wanting to scream in frustration.

Today, hearing the gnashing of teeth and the pounding of paws on the car window had made her feel vulnerable in a way she rarely did. This whole case was bringing back bad memories. Abby had seen some terrible crime scenes in her career, but the photos of the Austin boy's body, with so much blood and so many stab wounds, provoked a flashback to the day she found her father on the docks mere moments after he died. Even the lapping of the water now against the side of the kayak reminded her of the sound of waves hitting the pier pilings forty-some years ago. She would give almost anything to turn back time and change the outcome of that awful day.

Malph sniffed the air and sneezed, then looked over his shoulder at his mistress. She smiled. Dogs have a way of knowing exactly when their owners need comfort. Malph's timing was perfect. Not just then, but always. *He's one hell of a dog,* she thought, with swelling fondness. At that point, Abby realized she had worked out the day's kinks and was ready to head back to her cottage.

- - -

By the time Abby and Malph returned, Bridger hadn't yet figured out the reason for the story about Reilly's injury being on the newsletter's front page, but he had decided it was time to talk to the fallen football player. And he reminded himself, too, that he needed to check with Capt. Shearer again on the status of Cory's computer. Had the PPB located it yet? Maybe he and his partner ought to drop by the Evidence room and expedite things a bit.

Abby refilled her glass and came out to sit with Bridger, feeling the effects of the recent exercise in her arms. He brought up the idea of fleshing out their victim through talking with his classmates. And the sooner, the better. Abby agreed without argument.

Bridger had another area to discuss. "Okay. So here's what I'm curious about. I know your sense of hearing is heightened to nuances of inflection, most especially tinges of deception. You may not be able to see the flash of guilt on someone's face, but you can hear it in their voice. So did anyone today say something that tells you we need to delve deeper into their story?"

Abby considered his question for a few moments before looking at him directly. "No. Well, maybe Garfield." Over the course of working this case, Bridger would trust Abby's instinct on this and query her at the end of each day. Abby, likewise, would depend on Bridger's readings of body language.

They spent the next hour exchanging thoughts, laughing a little and trying to feel better. Tomorrow might be a tough day, but Cory Austin deserved no less than their full effort. So it was that they called it an early night.

- - -

Abby's mind still reeled after Bridger had left. She wanted a chance to grill Lincoln Shin, so polishing her theory tonight about how to approach the math teacher might yield better results in the morning. Even more than that, she buzzed with anticipation over dissecting Cory Austin's personality. Finding out what made the kid tick could help guide them through the upcoming interviews. She made a list of questions for Cari and for Cory's classmates, then she perched in front of the computer and went surfing.

Abby's research that evening took a turn that she hadn't expected. Googling different keywords led her to articles she hadn't uncovered the previous evening. Why she even revisited the idea of an Asian hate angle was a mystery in itself. But she needed a direction and little they had learned from the interviewees had made her suspicious so far. Oh, there were deceptions, but she hadn't heard what she considered a major lie. So that stirred her to look elsewhere, although she hadn't ruled anyone out entirely. Now, in her searching, she had found links to gangs and cults with origins in China and Japan, even some from Tibet. Portland, it seemed, had once been a hotbed – albeit a small one – of activity for several secret societies, and not all that long ago.

CHAPTER 12

*"It is often easier to fight for principles
than to live up to them."*

- Adlai Stevenson

First thing the next morning, they found Chris Reilly at a jobsite in outer southeast Portland. While they had planned to start with Lincoln Shin, the teacher's awkward schedule made it more convenient to talk to him shortly before noon. Meanwhile, they had no time to waste. When they had phoned, Reilly's wife told them that Chris worked as a house framer, which raised a few questions about the wisdom of his choices, considering the downturn in home starts over the past four years due to the economic recession. Construction didn't stop entirely, though, so maybe that spoke to Reilly's abilities. Still, it was a long way from his previous life as a budding football star.

As they climbed out of CON, Abby heard someone yelling to a man balancing precariously on a roof joist. He didn't sound angry, exactly, but not happy either.

On closer inspection, Bridger recognized Christopher Reilly immediately, partly by his bulk. Abby had relayed to him that, in her call to Mrs. Reilly earlier that morning, she had been told that Chris Reilly had put on thirty pounds since high school. Or, rather, since his injury. At six three, he also towered over the other framers on his crew. But it was his platinum blonde hair, lush and shiny on his head, and nearly transparent eyelashes that set him apart from the rest. He may have gained weight but he still looked good.

Mr. Reilly noticed them and came right over. At least he wasn't a man to avoid confrontation. Walking toward them, an easy smile lit up his face. Maybe he thought they were potential customers coming to check out the quality of his building.

After introducing himself and Abby, Bridger glanced around and commented, "Nice."

"Thank you." Reilly's smile wavered only slightly when the detectives displayed their PI licenses. "How can I help you?"

It was Abby who answered. "We'd like to speak with you about Cory Austin."

"Who?"

She rolled her eyes. He had to be joking. How many high school seniors lost one of their classmates to a vicious murder? She said, with measured patience, "Cory Austin. You know, the kid from your school who was stabbed to death a couple weeks before graduation."

"Oh, yeah. Sorry, the name didn't click. So what can I tell you about him?"

Bridger stepped in closer, so that he could hear better, and to give Abby a chance to cool off a bit. She had a tendency to flare with little provocation. "We're looking into his murder."

"Huh. After all this time?"

Nodding, Bridger went on, "Yes. It was never solved and some new evidence has surfaced. A cat's paw was found in a shoe box in his closet."

Reilly winced. Abby would have thought that an odd response, if she'd seen it. It might have come across as a guilty reaction. The man lowered his head, shook it, and then closed his eyes.

Bridger noticed and asked, "Do you know something about that?"

Abby listened closely to the answer.

Chris Reilly looked up and sighed. "Sort of." He swiped a hand down the side of his face. "Cory Austin was this really geeky guy, see, but he kept hitting on my girlfriend."

"Vanessa Hoyt?"

"Uh-huh, Vannie. Well, Vannie liked attention. She sort of led him on. It was kind of a game with her. That didn't make me very happy either. Finally, it just got old, him following her around all the time. I sort of lost it one day and said some things to him, sort of threatening things." He hung his head again, losing a full inch in height. "I'm so sorry. Anyway, soon after that, his cat disappeared and naturally he blamed me for it."

The three of them stood there in silence for a minute. Abby simmered. She hated animal abusers. They rated well below slugs in her book. But they weren't trying to catch a cat torturer. They were trying to catch a murderer. Nevertheless, she let herself vent a little.

"You know that the cat died, right? Bled to death. It wasn't quick and it wasn't easy." She didn't know any of that, but she really wanted to hammer home the cruelty of the act. Chris Reilly should suffer for what he did. She just wished she could see his face clearly.

Bridger could, though, and he saw Reilly's eyes grow as big as saucers. "Hold on. No, no, no, you don't understand. He *thought* I did something to his cat, but I didn't."

Abby folded her arms, tilted her head to one side and said, "What?"

"No, no, no. I threatened the guy and I'm not proud of that, but I didn't touch his cat. No way. I'd never hurt a thing, especially a cat. No, huh-uh. My little girls would never forgive me if they thought I did something like that. They have a cat, and they'd be crushed if anything happened to Mr. Puss." He grinned with an expression that made him look like he was eight years old again. "Me, too."

Reilly's expression was pleading for them to believe him. Bridger did, but he knew it would take more to convince his partner. She couldn't see the raw pain on the man's face when he talked of the injured animal, nor the fondness when he spoke of his "Mr. Puss".

Chris Reilly continued, "The kid thought he had it figured out, thought for sure I'd done it, and he got even." A humorless laugh issued from him almost like a bark. "Damn, did he get even."

"How so?" Abby asked.

Chris Reilly took a few steps, demonstrating his limp. Even though Bridger had read about his injury, somehow they had both missed his gimpiness before now, probably because of his impressive height and hair. "He did this to me."

"Cory Austin crippled you?" Abby couldn't mask the doubt that hit her like a slap upside the head.

He nodded. "Oh, yeah. He rigged my locker so that this concrete block fell on my foot and crushed it."

Now Bridger looked skeptical. Had he heard right? It was all too easy to doubt his ears. Reilly smiled. "I know what you're thinking. Not possible. But the guy was a damn whiz at angles and fulcrums, if that's the right word. He knew exactly what he was doing. And it worked just like he planned." The smile had vanished, replaced by a tight jaw and a faraway look. "Yep, worked damn good. He ruined my football career."

So that's why Bridger and Abby had never heard of an Oregon Duck named Chris Reilly. He had been eliminated before he even had a chance to start. His GPA must have been marginal then, too, since he didn't attend U of O at all after his injury. All of his talents likely came in physical form rather than cerebral. They asked him what he did after his sports plans collapsed with his fractured foot.

He shook his head again. "I was the golden boy, with the pros ahead of me: big bucks, fame, the whole nine yards. Then this. Shattered something like six bones in twenty-three places. My foot couldn't be reconstructed, but they did their best. Plus it took forever to heal. I never played again, not even just a friendly game with my boy Dexter. I'll always have this limp. And pain. Fortunately, my uncle had this construction company and I'm pretty good with a hammer. It's not my first love, but it pays the bills."

"Must have been tough," Abby said, still thinking Reilly had to have retaliated somehow.

He snickered, a bit of ugliness mingling with the laugh. "You don't know how tough. Those were some bad times. Vannie broke up with me, started going out with Tony Jacobs. He was our star quarterback, ended up at UCLA."

"So what did you do, Chris?" By now, Abby sounded almost maternal, a sneaky trick she liked to employ instead of working the good cop/bad cop routine.

He looked at her straight on before answering. "Yeah, well, things weren't going too good between us. Vannie liked glamour, couldn't stand being out of the spotlight. That's why she dumped me for Jacobs. That lasted a couple weeks and then Vannie told me she was pregnant." He glanced away. "That would be Dexter. He can be kind of a pill, but he's mostly a good boy."

"What happened to Tony Jacobs?"

Reilly laughed. "He washed his hands of Vannie right away. Didn't want nothing to do with a damn baby."

Neither of the detectives followed UCLA, but Tony Jacobs' name was somewhat familiar. Chris Reilly had to have been royally pissed off. Not only did Jacobs steal his girl but he stole his career, too. All because of Cory Austin. Abby tried to imagine how she'd have reacted if someone had done that to her. She guessed Bridger was asking himself the same question.

She posed the natural follow-up. "So what did you do?"

"Nothing."

"Really? Nothing? He ends your career and you do nothing?"

"You think I killed him?"

"He was stabbed eighteen times. That's the work of a very angry person."

"Yeah, I was angry, but I couldn't even walk for weeks. No way could I hike the trails in Forest Park. You can check with my doctors."

"We will." And, of course, they would, but the guy had a valid point. The murder had been committed deep in the woods. How would Chris Reilly have been able to negotiate those trails? Maybe he hired someone, but that wasn't usually how high school jocks took care of business. It didn't ring true.

"Okay. I won't say I didn't want to hurt the guy. He was like a pesky rodent, following around after Vannie like a damn lovesick puppy, tongue hanging out at the sight of her. Then he snaps and turns into this monster."

They stood there, waiting for Chris Reilly to finish his thought.

"Yeah, well, maybe I am a damn coward, but I didn't do anything. I had enough to worry about."

Reilly offered his hand. "Look, I got to get back to work. I hope you find who did kill Cory. I honestly do." He gestured at his foot. "Maybe he did me a favor. I mean, I'm blessed with a great job, three great kids – I'm doing okay. Who knows what my life would be like otherwise? For lots of players, the fame and fortune goes to their heads. They get into drugs or worse. I'm doing okay."

Abby noticed that Reilly hadn't included Vanessa in his list of great blessings.

The two detectives watched Chris Reilly fall back into his foreman role, already barking out orders as they left the jobsite.

- - -

Twenty minutes later, they walked up the steps to the Reilly house. The woman who answered the door wore heels even higher than Abby's, forcing Bridger to look up at both of them. He had gotten used to that over the years, that and a lot of other things about women. He had never gotten used to facial piercings, though, and this otherwise stunning creature had defiled her ski jump of a nose with a large, shiny gold bead. Bridger forced himself to focus on something else: Her platinum blonde hair. That couldn't be natural, he thought. And did she wear contacts? Those eyes couldn't be natural either. They were the color of the polar seas, and they looked about as cold and unfriendly.

He noticed Abby introducing herself so he reached out his hand to shake the woman's. She hesitated before responding with a limp grip. Two miniature versions of Vanessa Hoyt Reilly appeared behind their mother. All three of the Reilly females wore several shades of purple and multiple layers of makeup. These little girls couldn't be nine yet, but they had on more eye shadow than Kiss on show nights and hair as bleached as Christina Aguilera's.

Before them was the beauty queen of Washington High School in 2002. It appeared that she had acquired a taste for pasta in the meantime, in addition to three children. The intervening years had left her body well on its way to what one would kindly call pudgy, although she dressed like she must have dressed twenty pounds and ten years ago. She had obviously never seen the inside of a gym and allowed mirrors to lie to her. Vanessa and her daughters stood blocking the doorway and chewing gum.   A yellow tabby cat came up onto the stoop and weaved its way inside the house as it meowed out a steady string of feline complaints.

Abby glanced at Bridger, clearly as unimpressed with what she could see of Vanessa Reilly as he was. Finally, they asked if they could come in. It would only take a few minutes of her time.

Mrs. Reilly hesitated before sending the twins, whom she introduced as Sophie and Sonia, into the kitchen, and offering the detectives chairs in a cluttered living room. She sat down across from them with a scowl.

"I don't have long. The girls need to be somewhere in half an hour."

"Sure," said Abby, not believing her. "We won't take much of your time."

Bridger said, "They're lovely young ladies." His comment had the exact effect he'd intended. Vanessa puffed up like a peacock at the mention of her daughters.

"Thank you."

Abby brought her up to speed on the new evidence that had reopened the case. What the detectives considered more than repugnant had little visible effect on Vanessa. She simply stared at them, apparently waiting for a question to respond to or maybe more talk about her pretty children.

"I imagine the news of Cory Austin's murder must have been quite a shock at school."

A shrug.

"They usually bring in counselors to help students work through their loss."

"Uh-huh."

Her lack of emotion gave Bridger the impression that they were boring her. His partner was doing a commendable job of holding her temper in check. She had little tolerance for idiots and even less for self-centered brats.

"It sounds like you didn't need any help dealing with it."

As if suddenly realizing her demeanor might be inappropriate, Vanessa sat up straighter and cleared her throat. "No, I, um, am pretty private about things."

"I see."

They regarded her without speaking for a few moments, noting her increasing uneasiness.

Abby switched subjects abruptly. "Your husband told us about Cory Austin rigging his locker."

"Yeah, right?" She made a face. "If not for him, we wouldn't be living like this." Her voice gained in volume, enough so that Bridger heard clearly and followed the sweep of her arm as she indicated their surroundings. Aside from clutter owing to slovenly housekeeping, the place had potential.

Abby couldn't work up any sympathy for this spoiled woman. "Apparently, Cory flirted with you sometimes."

"Yeah."

"And you encouraged him."

Looking up from under her brows, Vanessa said, "Yeah, but it wasn't really like that."

"No? So what was it like?"

Vanessa glanced toward the closed door, where Abby heard Sophie and Sonia quarreling in the back of the house. She prayed that their mother would ignore them. It wouldn't do to give her time to think over how to answer. Vanessa glanced toward the kitchen once more, and then tossed her hair back over her shoulder. "I mean, come on, he couldn't have thought I was serious."

Bridger stared with distaste at what Abby couldn't see: a narcissistic female who had toyed with a young man she considered too far beneath her to worry about hurting his feelings. The expression she wore said, *How stupid could he be to think that I would look twice at him? I mean, duh!*

The cooing of a mourning dove wafted in through the open window. It caused Abby to think of a young Cory Austin walking through Forest Park on a late May evening. Had the birds known something was up? Had they gone silent just before Cory was permanently silenced?

"So you were just playing with him?"

"Well, yeah. I mean, it was just too easy. I know I shouldn't have, but I couldn't resist." She twirled a long strand of hair as she said this.

Abby had known girls like Vanessa. Everyone had, in fact. They thought only of themselves: what *I* like to do, what makes *me* happy, how do *I* look. Me, me, me. If attention turned toward someone else, they did whatever it took to bring it back around to themselves. They couldn't stand not being the center of everyone's admiration and constant focus. The two eight-year-olds in the kitchen were well on their way to becoming their mother. Just what the world needed: more children growing up caring only about their own personal gratification, with the shallowest outlook on life, an outlook that would nag at them when people quit noticing them and started turning away. And people would. It's an incontrovertible fact: Beauty fades. And the power that comes with it leaches away with each passing year and each new wrinkle on a once-pretty face. Vanessa Hoyt Reilly might never grow ugly, but she already was needing to invent new ways to demand women's envy and draw men's stares. Lines had formed at the corners of her eyes and her chin had begun to sag. Without the money to buy her looks back, she would find herself viewed as just an everyday housewife and mother. Abby doubted she would take it well. No, not well at all.

Abby smiled indulgently now. "So he dashed your dreams and Chris's career. That must have made you pretty angry."

Vanessa's head came up in defiance, exhibiting her misplaced passion. "Yeah, it did. Chris was awesome. He was going to be a huge star, play football for U of O, and I was going to be the head cheerleader. We had huge plans."

"Head cheerleader? I thought you were pregnant."

"Well, yeah, but…" she let the rest of that thought dangle. "Anyway, here we are. In *Gresham*." She made another face, as though smelling rotten eggs.

As Portland suburbs went, Gresham didn't rate real high on the scale of chic places to live. The best one could say was that, for skiers, it provided excellent access to Mt. Hood. Otherwise, its location actually made getting anywhere difficult. It had its good points, though. Abby just couldn't think of any right off.

"So you got back at him." Bridger had been sitting by, quietly observing the conversation between the two women. The calm with which he asked the question startled Vanessa.

"What? No!"

"He was stabbed eighteen times. Someone was very angry with him."

"It wasn't me!"

Mrs. Reilly had gone pale. Was that due to the thought of eighteen strikes with a knife or due to something else, like guilt?

CHAPTER 13

*"A teacher affects eternity; he can never
tell where his influence stops."*

— Henry Adams

Vanessa Reilly had clammed up at the mention of eighteen stab wounds. Whether that was due to shock or fear or for an entirely different reason, Bridger and Abby knew well enough that their time would be better spent elsewhere, but their professional investigative strategy had them already promising themselves to return in a day or so. In the meantime, maybe Mrs. Reilly would stew about the savageness of Cory's death, think about his agonizing last moments and wonder what he'd felt. Probably not. They didn't think Vanessa had that kind of emotional depth within her. And, while she may not have wielded the knife, she had most certainly and most cruelly slashed the young man's heart to shreds, and that made her a despicable example of humanity in Abby's eyes.

She wondered why society placed so much more emphasis on appearance and less on character. Why would this blonde bombshell with nothing going for her but great hair and long, perfect legs have been looked up to at Washington High when her classmate, Cari Austin, sweet and caring albeit short, plain and tending toward homeliness, went unnoticed day in and day out? Why put empty good looks on a pedestal, without at least peeking below the surface to see if there was anything worth idolizing there?

It wasn't like Abby was envious. She had never had trouble with popularity. Even now, with the unmistakable charm of Sandra Bullock's smile and rosy cheekbones, she attracted the opposite sex easily. But it never crossed her mind to use her good physical fortune as a way to entertain herself at another's expense.

As they walked out to the car, Abby was remembering a news story she had watched on TV recently with intense admiration. It concerned a beauty pageant winner who escorted a Down 's syndrome boy to his school prom. The young fellow was a human treasure but he didn't have coolness and physical looks going for him. Not by a long shot. Yet the tall, dazzling woman beside him walked proudly into the dance with her arm linked in his as though he were the image of Adonis. Appearances were overrated, if you asked Abby. She grumbled and made a comment to that effect, but said it quietly enough that Bridger didn't pick it up. His mind was elsewhere anyway.

He wanted to stop for a pastrami on rye at Kornblatt's for lunch. It was something of a throw-back from his New York days. He didn't often eat sandwiches – trying to minimize his bread intake – but Kornblatt's pastrami wedged between two pieces of marbled rye slathered with a tangy Thousand Island sauce could change his tune without a second thought.

Today, though, his partner had a craving for doughnuts, one of the few things Abby claimed to have a soft spot for. Bridger didn't believe Abby Dalton had any soft spots. Besides, he tried to avoid cop clichés, like eating doughnuts. At least, he had until she introduced him to Voodoo Doughnut. Unique to Portland, the funky business had gained an almost cult following because of their evilly genius bakers who were always thinking outside the box. The menu read like a Harry Potter book gone culinary. No one could resist Voodoo's over-the-top offerings, like the bacon maple bar. Or an extreme little something called the Memphis Mafia, Bridger's latest favorite, which featured chunks of bananas and peanuts and chocolate chips. For some reason baffling to Bridger, women seemed to claim chocolate as their personal province, but the Memphis Mafia threw in peanut butter – no argument, a manly condiment – and plenty of peanuts, so Bridger believed that made it masculine by default.

Abby wouldn't have given Bridger's Mafia a second thought, sticking with her preference, the Dirt Doughnut, a yeasty piece covered with vanilla frosting and crumbled Oreo cookies. Like her choice of chardonnay when it came to wine, she rarely deviated in her choice of the Dirt when it came to Voodoo. And since the shop had several locations, all of them on the way back from Gresham, it didn't even take a coin toss. Kornblatt's simply lost out.

Fortunately, the line at Voodoo wasn't too long, considering there would usually be a half block of bodies to wade through. They got their food in less than twenty minutes and found a street-side bench to sit on. While the midday sun posed a weak threat to Abby's icing, the late summer warmth went a long way toward enhancing the eating experience.

"Washington High next?" Bridger asked, between bites.

Abby wiped her mouth with a thumb. "Yep. I'm ready for the math teacher."

- - -

At the school parking lot, Lincoln Shin's gray Gremlin sat squeezed between two shiny Chevrolets, like it was embarrassed to be seen out in the open. Bridger nosed CON into a spot which didn't really exist. Abby said nothing if she noticed. They probably wouldn't be long, anyway, and Bridger's temporary business card with an embossed badge logo on the little car's dashboard might carry some weight if anybody bothered to look.

The administrative offices sat directly inside of the front entrance, off of the foyer to the left, so that's where the two of them headed. The way in which schools scheduled their days, with classes starting at odd times like 9:10 or 11:50, made it hard for the detectives to gauge when they might be able to catch Mr. Shin for a quick interview. They hadn't exactly called for an appointment, but that never deterred them. They had a fair idea of Shin's schedule from a little misleading phone conversation Abby had had with a school secretary earlier.

The woman behind the counter which separated the public and/or students from the staff wore clothes and a hairstyle that would make her difficult to distinguish from the kids. Looking around, the manner of dress shocked Bridger. Back in the day, he'd had to wear a uniform. Much of the attire he saw now bordered on the hideous and reminded him of the shabby threads Welfare cases had no choice but to wear when he was growing up. These kids voluntarily dressed this way?

Abby, standing beside him, heard snippets of conversations from students mingling in the hall and shook her head. She had heard and used most of those colorful words herself

– almost daily, in fact – but thought they should be reserved for adults. Maybe adults in a certain sort of environment. These were the hallowed halls of education? Whatever happened to respect and a sense of propriety?

Apparently the woman at the desk wasn't the person who handled visitors, for she remained seated and entirely ignored them. A girl appearing to be about fifteen years old stood leaning against one wall and another slouched beside Bridger at the counter. A man came out of an office and handed the sloucher a form, which she snatched with impatience, then huffed out of the room. Abby cleared her throat. The man did a double-take like he was startled to see them.

"May I help you?"

Abby displayed her license and told him they were there to see Lincoln Shin.

"Is he expecting you?"

"I don't think so," Abby replied.

The woman at the desk spoke up then, as she consulted some papers. "He's in class until 12:40. Then he has a break until 1:10."

Bridger looked at Abby, who said, "We can wait ten minutes. Would you please summon him to the office here then?" Without pausing for a reply, she added, "Thank you," and motioned for Bridger to follow her.

Standing just outside the door, Abby passed the time making some phone calls to set up further appointments while Bridger fiddled with his earpiece.

Exactly twelve minutes later, Lincoln Shin strode down the hall, confidence oozing from every pore. At least he dressed like a teacher, or sort of, with chinos and a collared shirt. Gone were the days of suits and ties, apparently.

Bridger caught sight of him first, naturally, and intercepted him before he got to the administrative offices. Neither detective got out their licenses, trying to make their presence seem as friendly as possible. No reason to cause problems for the teacher in front of his students.

Shin seemed wary, but his bravado wavered for only a second. He suggested they step into an empty classroom a few doors down. He could spare them exactly ten minutes.

Frankly, the detectives had been surprised when they found out that Shin was still teaching at Washington High. Eleven years ago, he already had put in the required time with the district. Abby made a comment along those lines.

Leaning against a desk, arms folded across his chest, Shin said to Bridger. "I retire at the end of this year."

Abby said, "Makes for a long career. That's like, what, thirty years?"

"Thirty-one," he said, keeping his focus on Bridger, who turned toward Abby.

"You must love your work."

"The kids are fantastic," he said, glancing out the window and then checking his watch.

Abby hadn't seen any "fantastic" kids in the hallway, but maybe they were around somewhere, or maybe it was due to her diminished eyesight. Whatever, she decided to quit with the small talk and get down to business and set herself a goal of getting Shin to respond to her face. "We're here investigating the murder of Cory Austin."

Goal accomplished. Lincoln Shin couldn't resist turning toward her. Bridger watched carefully, thinking he noticed a break in the teacher's façade. But what did it mean?

Shin recovered himself quickly, folding his arms again and leaning back against the desk. "Wow. That happened a long time ago. Boy, I haven't thought about that in years. Cory was one of my best students."

"Really?" Abby asked.

"One of my best ever." He held her gaze with an expression that Bridger would have described as impudent. She stood up taller, making it necessary to angle her head down toward the teacher as she spoke.

"Hm. Because we got the impression that he pissed you off."

"Really?" Shin mimicked Abby's earlier question and straightened his back in a move clearly meant to one-up her.

"Something about a trigonometry test and an error on it. Your error." She emphasized the word "your".

Shin's mouth tightened and he cleared his throat. Then he visibly relaxed, but Bridger thought it took some effort. "Just a little misunderstanding. A small matter of interpretation."

A matter of interpretation? In math? Abby almost laughed. "I had no idea there was such a thing as a matter of interpretation in math."

Shin didn't rise to the bait, but returned his gaze to Bridger and shook his head. "Cory's death was a tragedy. A horrible tragedy. Is there some new evidence?"

They told him about the cat's paw. He made a face but said nothing.

Abby asked, "Did Cory have trouble with any of his other teachers?"

"He didn't have trouble with me, if that's what you're implying."

"I'm not implying anything. Just wondering if he had problems with any other teacher. I'm not sure how to phrase that so I don't offend you," she said, knowing quite well what she meant by her wording.

Lincoln Shin drew in a deep breath and replied, "Not that I ever heard. You might ask Linda Short. She's the school secretary. Been here longer than I have."

"Were any of the other administrative staff here back when Cory was in school?"

"No. Eleven years? A lot's happened in that time. You're lucky that Linda was here. And me," he winked at Abby, who didn't consider herself lucky in the least.

She asked, "Did you notice any of the other students ever giving Cory a hard time?"

"No." His head slowly inclined to a spot over Abby's head. "Well, one of the cheerleaders kind of flirted with him, but I thought that she was doing it as a joke, not because she actually liked him. She wasn't exactly giving him a hard time. Just one of those things kids do."

Yeah, right, she thought, *let's make fun of the nerd.* "Do you remember who that was?"

The teacher rubbed his chin as he appeared to think back. "Yeah. Yeah, it was a senior named Vanessa Hoyt."

"You have a good memory."

"You haven't seen her." He rolled his eyes and fanned himself, which made Bridger frown and wonder, like his partner had earlier, what had happened to propriety. It certainly seemed to be in short supply at Washington High.

"Ah." The detectives didn't feel the need to inform Shin that they actually had seen her. Instead, they chose to let him remain in the dark about that.

"Yeah. Whew!"

"I assume this cheerleader had a boyfriend."

"Yes."

"And I assume he didn't take kindly to her flirtations."

Shin rolled his eyes again in dramatic fashion, enough so that even Abby noticed. "Naw, he knew she wasn't serious. No concerns there."

"Actually, there were concerns. The boyfriend threatened Cory, and then, when Cory's cat went missing, Cory blamed the boyfriend, rigged his locker and caused a rather nasty foot injury."

"Really?"

It was Abby's turn to mimic Shin. "Really? You mean to say you never heard about that?"

Shin did a remarkable job of putting on an innocent face. Or did he really not know what had happened? "Nope, never heard a thing about that."

Bridger couldn't say whether he believed the teacher. But he had been watching this exchange quietly and decided that they were getting nowhere. He didn't want to run out of time before they ran out of questions. So now he wanted to know about Cory's interactions with the school newspaper staff and the other members of the Nerdlingers.

Shin shook his head. "Never heard a thing about problems with either of them. The kid got along with everyone, even though he wasn't real popular."

Abby broke in, "He was real *unpopular* with someone."

Shin ignored her, and Bridger said to him, "Can you tell us who his friends were? Who he hung out with?"

The teacher shook his head. "Sorry."

Abby came at him again. "Do you remember an Amanda Ferguson?"

He shook his head again, then said to Bridger, "Are we done here?"

"If you think of anything," Abby fished out one of her business cards and handed it over to Shin, who shoved it deep into a pocket without a solitary glance at it.

CHAPTER 14

*"Never forget what a man says to you
        when he is angry."*

— *Henry Ward Beecher*

Not many years ago, Abby would have stormed out to the car steaming and cursing after an encounter like the one they just had with Lincoln Shin. Time and maturity had taught her that it didn't help one little bit. Assholes were assholes and there was no changing them, so why bother getting all worked up over it? Lincoln Shin had proven himself a Class A asshole but she would find a way to come out on top. She always did. How he had managed to retain his teaching position for three decades with his attitude Abby couldn't fathom. Maybe it was a little something called tenure, which sometimes made for a crippling requirement that a school district keep a teacher who should have been let go a long time before. But he was still there, as was Linda Short, school secretary. Her status was another thing Shin helped them with; Linda was currently out sick, he told them. She had barely started the school year before the flu bug struck her hard, knocking her down like she'd smacked into a concrete wall. Interviewing her would be delayed a few more days, but at least they had another name.

All fired up, Abby suggested that they drop by Headquarters and do a quick perusal of a few more reports, pick up an address or two for the victim's classmates, and see if they could snatch a couple more interviews. She was geared up to tear someone apart. Toby Meyer, for example. Cory's sister had told the detectives that Meyer strongly resented Cory's position as editor of the *Washington Post* and had made it clear that he, Meyer, was a better choice for the post. Jealousy was historically a prime motive for murder, which should put Meyer high on their list of suspects. The detectives hadn't seen an interview sheet, though, with his name on it, so they could only hope that an address had been entered into the file somewhere. Either way, he seemed like a logical next step. One o'clock had just come and gone. The guy was probably at work, if they could find out where *work* was.

The trip into the deep center of the city from Washington High School took just nine minutes. Within fifteen, Bridger and Abby found themselves in the cluttered little room Capt. Shearer had first ushered them into back on Sunday.

Abby was growing more pumped and began rifling through files and papers with little regard for order or tidiness. She didn't need perfect eyesight for the task at hand; she had seen enough reports in her career to know which forms would have the information they were seeking. Even though most of the pages were a blur to her, their format was so familiar that her magnifier would not be necessary.

Three minutes later, she found a page that had potential and signaled to Bridger, who seemed distracted. In the elevator on the way up from the parking garage, Abby had heard a sound that she had come to recognize as a text message being sent to Bridger's fancy phone. When he glanced at the screen, what was written there had audibly shaken him and left him in a subdued mood. Several attempts to draw him out thereafter failed. Abby knew he would take her into his confidence if and when he felt like it. She let it slide, for now.

"Aha!" An address leapt up from the report before her. She pointed at it as she slid it over to Bridger. He confirmed that it related to Toby Meyer.

"Let's go." They were both up and out of their chairs in an instant, headed for the door. Having a lead gave them the energy that the earlier stall in the case had sapped them of.

It had taken them less than twenty minutes inside Headquarters to find Toby Meyer's address. Abby wondered out loud why Meyer had not been interviewed during the active investigation eleven years ago.

"We should ask that question of Derek Moss. It would have been his responsibility at the time."

"Well, then, let's do that."

Bridger checked a schedule with one of the department secretaries, then said to Abby, "We might just have gotten lucky."

The pair made a detour down a side hall and looked into what Portland Police Bureau officers called "the den," a euphemism meant to transform a dingy room of plastic chairs and scuffed tables into an inviting space, at least in name. The den would gain in population the closer they came to shift change. Now, though, only three officers spread themselves out across the expanse of cheap furniture.

Bridger wasn't surprised to see Derek Moss lounging by himself at a table in one corner, reading the Metro section of *The Oregonian*. Bridger had dealt with Moss when the young man was just a recruit. He hadn't liked him then and he didn't like him any better now. The kid was a hot shot, or thought of himself that way. Apparently, he hadn't changed much in the intervening years since Bridger had retired, at least when it came to ambition. Some people – like Moss – had a talent for doing nothing and not getting caught at it. Yet he had made sergeant in record time and was on track for another promotion, if the rumors could be trusted. The Peter Principle at work.

Bridger led the way over and they stopped six inches from Moss's seat. Abby cleared her throat loudly rather than wait to be noticed.

Sgt. Moss looked up. "Help you?"

Bridger handed him his card. Moss's expression remained bored but at least they had his attention. Or part of it.

"Yeah, Bridger Flynn. I remember you. What do you want?"

Bridger gave him a quick summary of their reason for being there, emphasizing Shearer's role in it. Moss sat up a little straighter at the mention of the captain.

"So what do you want with me?"

Abby's eagerness to get on with it wouldn't allow her to keep quiet. "We're looking over the files and re-interviewing witnesses to see if we can find a missing piece. And I think maybe we just did. One of the victim's schoolmates who held a bit of a grudge. Just one thing: There's no indication that anyone ever talked to him."

"So?"

"'So'? Wow, good answer."

"Listen, lady –"

Bridger stepped a few inches closer. "The lady's name is Ms. Dalton. She's my partner. Now, let's start again. There was a kid named Toby Meyer. He worked with the victim on the school newspaper. The vic's sister thought he was jealous of her brother, to the point of wanting his position."

"So?"

Bridger hurried on before Abby had a chance to intervene again, this time maybe by grabbing a handful of Sgt. Moss's shirt. "So we thought someone might have interviewed him."

"Did you see an interview sheet in the file?"

With measured patience, Bridger said, "No. That's why we're talking to you. We were wondering why not."

"Don't ask me. I wasn't the lead detective."

You weren't any *kind of detective,* Bridger wanted to say, but instead he asked, "Was there any attempt made to find Toby Meyer?"

Moss shrugged. "Beats me."

Everything beats you, thought Bridger, while he figured Abby was thinking, *What a useless piece of shit. Figures they want to move him up in the ranks. That's how the bureaucracy does things.*

Before they turned to leave, Abby said, "So when you searched Cory Austin's home, how did you miss the box with a bloody cat's paw in it?"

"What?"

"I think you heard me, but just in case you didn't, I'll repeat myself. How did you miss a bloody cat's paw?"

He answered, with a steely edge to his voice, "Because it wasn't there."

"What do you mean, 'It wasn't there'?"

Moss stood abruptly, a move that didn't go unnoticed by the other two officers in the room. "Just what I said. It. Wasn't. There." He stared at Abby, as though daring her to challenge him one more time.

"Then how do you explain it being there now?" Bridger asked, keeping his tone even as he subtly positioned himself in front of Abby. Anyone overhearing the conversation would have described Bridger as the proverbial cool cucumber: No frown, no voice tremor, no raised volume, and wearing a neutral expression. That was another example of what his fellow PPB officers had called the Flynn Effect. Aside from blushing easily, Bridger Flynn had no faults when it came to interviewing techniques.

Moss just shook his head and walked away. Bridger didn't stop him, but he wasn't done with the subject quite yet. He would bide his time and catch the officer unaware when it suited him. He just hoped he got there before Abby.

As he was thinking that, Abby landed a punch on his right arm.

"Ouch! Why did you do that?"

"Damn it, Bridger, never step in front of me like that again." Knowing that he was about to make an excuse, she cut him off. "I can take care of myself. And I can handle a piece of shit snotrag like Moss."

Rubbing his arm, Bridger apologized. "Sorry, Abs."

"Damn straight." She took a couple of deep breaths, getting herself under control. "Now...Toby Meyer?"

"Uh, yeah."

"And don't call me Abs."

"Sure."

"What's going on with you?"

"What do you mean?"

"Come on, Bridger. You haven't been yourself since you got that text earlier."

"It's nothing."

"Don't give me that 'It's nothing' shit. Spill it." Abby planted herself squarely in front of her partner and stood her ground. He may have wanted to tell her in his own way and in his own time but Abigail Grace Dalton lived by her time table. She'd given him almost an hour to tell her. That pretty much expended her cache of patience.

Bridger wiped his hand down his face and looked at the floor. "The text was from my son Zach. Or Moshe as he's now called."

"Moshe?"

"Long story. I'll tell you all about it later." His almost pleading tone kept Abby from pursuing the matter. "Let's concentrate on Toby Meyer for now." He added, "Let's hope he hasn't changed *his* name."

- - -

As it turned out, Toby Meyer had changed his name. He now went by Chester Bono. At least during working hours. Toby, aka Chet Bono, was one of the headliners at Darcelle's, a long-time local favorite showplace – or dance club, or gay bar, take your pick. All of Darcelle's employees were male, although some presented as pretty convincing women. The club featured male strippers, provocative dancers and cross-dressing female impersonators. It was into this last category that Chester Bono fell. Chet did a killer imitation of Cher.

If the detectives hadn't made that side trip to talk to Officer Moss, they might have caught Toby Meyer at his apartment in a renovated Old Town brickfront. According to the manager, though, they'd just missed him.

"Hold on a sec." She left them at the door and disappeared down a darkened hallway, a faint odor of musk and cedar replacing the Chanel No. 5 that surrounded her like a cloud. When she returned, the manager was strutting like the hen who laid the golden egg. She carried with her a flyer for Toby's current show. She smiled in the way a proud mother would when showing off her son's acceptance letter from Harvard.

Bridger looked the flyer over and said to Abby, "The show doesn't start until 8:00."

While they both suspected it would take quite a bit of preparation and makeup for Chet to become Cher, they bet it wouldn't take four and a half hours, so Toby/Chet likely had plans to stop somewhere between home and his place of employment. It now came down to a choice between whether to try catching Toby back at his apartment the next morning or hit Darcelle's later on that evening. The problem with waiting was that they had appointments scheduled and an upcoming trip to Tumwater planned. In the end, they opted to come back later in the evening. Abby figured that, whether he knew it or not, Bridger needed to not be alone for a while. Solitude would only give him a chance to brood over whatever his son had gotten into, which clearly was upsetting her partner. Darcelle's would certainly take his mind off of those problems. She had been to several of the shows and knew they were not only outrageous but hilarious, too. Judging from the front of the house, back stage there could only be massive amounts of shocking and uproarious activity. It sounded like a fine way to pass at least part of an evening.

In the meantime, some paperwork beckoned. Bridger pointed CON toward their office. "Their office," he liked the sound of that. Eyes & Ears was now official. They had filed their business name with the Secretary of State and he had little doubt the license would be granted. He wanted to walk through the rooms, breathe in the mustiness of the few books on the shelves, gaze out the window to the left of his desk and try to instill some sense of adventure in Abby Dalton. He also wanted to send some emails. Just as he felt he was catching up with technology, email had become passé, replaced by texting, instant messaging, something called Skype, and who knew what else? Something that had probably been designed that afternoon as they were chasing leads, for all he knew.

After typing up a brief summary of their day's work, they locked the door of Suite 203, 1313½ SE Lexington and drove to Abby's cottage to feed Malph. She said something along the lines of being thankful they didn't have to stop and take care of that cat Bridger kept threatening to adopt. He needed a woman, not a fur-covered feline. She added, too low for him to hear, *If only he understood that.*

CHAPTER 15

"One man in his time plays many parts."
- Shakespeare, As You Like It

Even in the trendiest parts of downtown Portland, Tuesday nights don't draw the larger crowds that throng to the theaters and clubs on the evenings toward the end of the week. Nonetheless, Bridger and Abby arrived at Darcelle's just shy of 7:00 o'clock, a full hour before show time. Neither of them wished to hang around too long after the stage acts started. Their hope was to get in, catch Toby Meyer/Chet Bono for a few pointed questions, and get out before total pandemonium set in. Of course, it didn't go quite like that. It never does.

First off, Toby/Chet hadn't yet gotten to the theater, which had Guy, the back stage manager, in a hand-wringing snit. The detectives had been able to get inside without a hitch and were now amazed at the chaotic atmosphere, even though they had expected it. Somehow, the performers were going to control, harness and organize all of the seemingly random madness into a couple hours of entertainment an audience would be willing to pay good money for.

Abby heard the manager cry, "He's supposed to be here no later than 6:45. His act begins at 8:10." The man paced some more and flailed his hands, which gave the appearance of a couple of angry birds that had gotten loose.

One of the male strippers who was already in costume patted his shoulder in a gesture of sympathy. "He'll be here, Guy. There won't be any problem. Mr. Geoffrey can get his makeup on in twenty minutes. Or less! Don't worry." His hand rubbed a little lower on Guy's back.

While Bridger caught about every third word, he nonetheless deduced the reason for the two men's histrionics. Hoping to get some information before either one had a complete meltdown, he asked, "Does Chet have a dressing room we could look at?"

The manager shook his head as he turned to yell at a man in a glittering swan costume. "Not really. It's just a cubicle. Mr. Geoffrey only needs a teensy bit of privacy so he can concentrate when he's doing the makeup, but this place isn't big enough for everyone who thinks he's a star to have his own room, so they're all sort of in the middle back there." He waved vaguely off in the distance while consulting his clipboard again. When he looked up again, a groan escaped him.

Abby tapped Bridger's shoulder to signal that she had a question about what she'd heard. Bridger turned in the direction of the manager's gaze and noticed a tallish man strolling toward them, stridently if a bit unsteadily.

Bridger chuckled and said to Abby, "I'm guessing this might be the tardy Toby Meyer." He also guessed he might have a fair idea of what the man had been doing since he'd left his apartment well over three hours before.

Guy grabbed the man's hand and pulled him over to a chair, which the newcomer fell into like all of his bones had gone missing. "Oh, geez, Toby. Not again."

Toby/Chet looked a little under the weather and, from Guy's comment, the detectives gathered that it wasn't the first time this had happened. Hopefully, Mr. Geoffrey could work wonders with lipstick, eye shadow and face powders. Glancing around at some of the other dancers, it looked as though Mr. Geoffrey could indeed work wonders. Lady Gaga walked by arm in arm with Beyonce, who almost ran head-long into Madonna. Bridger's jaw dropped. How could they do that? Every one of the guys in costume was a dead ringer for the personality he was imitating.

Once the manager had scrutinized Toby's face and decreed him fit for night duty, albeit marginally, he got him up and shoved him toward his station. Bridger led Abby after them, deflecting much of the line of befeathered and besparkled entertainers. Even though she was no stranger to disorderly scenes, the theater lighting and general unrealness was causing her more than a little discomfort. It had as much to do with the missing pieces of her vision as with the general melee going on around them.

In less than a minute, Toby sat before a mirror with Mr. Geoffrey already hard at work applying a liberal quantity of foundation in the first stage of transforming Toby/Chet into Cher. Bridger promised they would stay out of the way and explained to Toby what they were doing there. The entertainer appeared unfazed, sat with his arms limp and relaxed. Whatever his substance of choice had been earlier in the evening had clearly left him mellow. In under an hour, this fellow was supposed to be prancing around the stage with Cher's boundless energy? Good luck, Guy. Mr. Geoffrey could only do so much.

With the preliminaries out of the way, Abby started in on the harder questioning. "We heard you worked on the school newspaper with Cory Austin."

"Uh-huh."

"How did you get along with him?"

"If you heard I worked on the paper with him, darling, you probably also heard I wanted to be the editor." Toby had turned to look up at Abby. Mr. Geoffrey grabbed his chin and guided it back into position.

"Did you?"

"Oh, my, yes." He turned again.

Mr. Geoffrey pushed Toby's head back around and hissed, "Stay still."

Keeping his eyes on Abby in the mirror, he continued, "Yes, dear one, I did want to be editor. And, in reality, I would have done a smash-up job of it." Toby smiled at his reflection. "Besides, I wanted the notoriety, too."

"You thought you'd have been a good editor? Why? Did you ever have a chance to prove it?"

Toby turned fully around, eliciting an exasperated curse from Mr. Geoffrey. "Have you seen any of the *Washington Posts*?"

Bridger answered, "Yes, I looked over the last six issues that Cory Austin did."

Toby shook his head. "No, darling, you saw the last *five* issues he did. The sixth was mine."

Abby could only imagine the smug expression he wore on his face, but pride oozed from him in hot waves. Nonetheless, she had trouble believing him. "How do you figure that?"

Despite the challenge in her voice, Toby answered without acrimony. "Because, dear one, Cory dropped the ball. For some reason, he just quit doing what he was supposed to do. Half the time those last few weeks, he didn't even show up to work on the paper. It was obvious to everyone that something was bothering him, and big time. Fine by me. I saw an opportunity and ran with it. Too bad it was just that one issue, though."

The one issue Cory never got to see. And it hadn't been Cory Austin's swan song after all. Toby Meyer had been the person to produce the bombshell last issue of *The Washington Post* for the Class of '02. Maybe his confidence wasn't unfounded after all.

Abby asked the obvious. "Did you ever find out what was bothering him?"

Toby/Chet had turned back to face the mirror, garnering a grateful smile from Mr. Geoffrey. "Well, darling, he didn't confide in me, uh, us not being the best of friends." He rolled his eyes. "Yeah, I know, total understatement. Still, the newspaper staff did work as a team most of the time. Eventually, I heard a rumor that he was upset about something to do with his cat." He rolled his eyes again. "I mean, really?"

"Had something happened to his cat?"

"I guess. The rumor was that it lost an ear or maybe a foot. Tail? Hm. Oh, hell, can't remember precisely."

"Did you hear how it happened?"

When he opened his mouth to answer, Mr. Geoffrey shushed him while he painted a coral gloss onto Cher's lips. Already finished, the eyes had taken on the shape of the famous singer. Even the cheekbones had been shaded and rouged to make Chet's cheeks look like Cher's. With a wig of long, black hair, the illusion would be fantastic. Then, once zipped into a slinky, sequined gown – pow! – he would *be* Cher.

While the makeup man put on the finishing touches, Toby said, "Huh-uh," with his mouth clamped shut.

Abby tried another tack. "Who all knew about the cat?" Obviously, not Cari, as the mummified remains of the paw in her dead brother's closet had shocked and deeply distressed her.

A shrug left them hanging.

"Did Cory know who hurt his cat?"

Another shrug. Mr. Geoffrey was exerting his will upon Toby/Chet and, since the detectives had promised not to interfere, they could hardly complain. Still, they needed answers.

"Let me ask it this way: Did you have anything to do with it?"

The room was becoming rowdier the closer it got to the opening act, so Bridger was having difficulty hearing. The lights were bothering Abby's eyes, as she'd forgotten her dark glasses. Toby sat still as a statue for about two heartbeats. "Look, I was a confused kid."

Abby had to stifle a laugh. *Was confused?* He was currently undergoing a change from Toby Meyer, aka Chet Bono, to Cher. How much more confused could a person be? Bridger had probably not caught the comment, because he remained silent. Abby hoped he was paying attention to Toby's expressions and eye contact. As she had this thought, a question about his last comment occurred to her and she almost forgot her current question.

"Did you covet more than Cory's position as editor? Maybe Cory's affection?"

Cher ceased grinning. Before he could answer, Mr. Geoffrey pronounced him ready for show time and urged him to get dressed. There was no trace of a stagger as he disappeared behind the stage. The interview had ended. But the detectives weren't done with Toby Meyer. Not by a long shot.

- - -

Outside the club, a small line had formed, with customers anxious to get into their seats milling around and chattering. Their energy nearly matched that of the performers. Several glanced at Bridger and Abby as they left, probably wondering whether they were anybody famous, or at least famous enough to merit attention. Despite Abby's almost celebrity demeanor and general haughtiness, the crowd came to the conclusion that she and Bridger weren't worth their time.

Bridger had parked CON two blocks away, praying that there would be less hassle with traffic than closer to the theater. He had missed much of the second half of the interview, with the decibels inside Darcelle's ramping up to a fever pitch, so he asked Abby to sum it up for him as they walked.

When she had finished, he asked, "So do you believe him?"

"Hell, I don't know. I mean, it's tough to believe a man who earns a living by dressing up like a woman and pretending to be a famous singer."

Laughing softly, Bridger said, "Yeah, I can see that. But, occupation aside, what did you think of his answers?"

"Well, I was surprised he knew about the cat, but it sounded like it wasn't much of a secret, at least among the newspaper staff. So why didn't Cari hear about it?"

"Good question, Abs. Could he be making it sound like common knowledge, even though it wasn't, to cover up his part in it?"

"Shit, Bridger, I guess anything's possible. He didn't exactly answer my question about that directly." Abby held onto Bridger's arm in the dwindling light, unsure precisely where the curb ended. She hated the feeling of dependency, but she hated the possibility of turning an ankle even more, so she chose the lesser of two evils. "He was pretty straightforward about his desire to be editor, and about seizing the chance when he got it."

"Yes, but does that point to his innocence or to his cunning?"

Abby started to answer but her words were drowned out by a siren as a Portland Police car whizzed by.

CHAPTER 16

"There is nothing so useless as doing efficiently
that which should not be done at all."
- Peter F. Drucker

By Wednesday, they felt like they were spinning their wheels. Abby suspected that the homicide detectives over a decade earlier had experienced much the same feeling. A young man had been maliciously attacked on a beautiful spring day in the midst of Portland's most scenic urban park, yet the killer had never been caught. For eleven years now, he'd remained free. That was unacceptable to Abby. So now she believed that they needed to start thinking outside the box and find a new approach in order to solve the case. She decided to toss around some creative ideas.

Her partner arrived carrying coffee and bagels with herbal schmear, and they sat down at the bar-height table she had mapped out as her dining area. A light fog had crept in overnight, shrouding the lakeshore in a swirling chill.

Abby took a sip of her dark roast blend and ran a hand through her hair, which fell loosely to her shoulders this morning. Without realizing it, she inhaled a nervous breath and expelled it. She usually stuck to the tried and true route or, put another way, she generally remained less open to more out-of-the-ordinary avenues. As she'd grown older, though, she found herself not as averse to coming at things in different ways, which was part of what had led to a lack of sleep lately. This was still an area that she ventured into with caution. But Abigail Dalton rarely showed any trepidation, and now her voice belied her lack of confidence with its volume and strength.

"Okay. Here's a little food for thought. I've spent some time the last couple of evenings exploring Asian hate crimes in Portland."

Bridger cocked his head, a gesture which acknowledged that he'd heard her words yet might not agree with their content.

"I'm not saying it's necessarily the direction we should go, but I felt it needed to be looked at."

"Uh-huh."

"I mean, if we're going to believe that the cat's paw Cari found is connected to her brother's death – and I'm not sure I do, but if we're going to go with that, why not check out whether it could be a warning from an Asian gang, say, or – here's an even crazier idea – the son of a Pearl Harbor victim?" As she spoke these words out loud, she acknowledged to herself the unlikeliness of them, even the absurdity.

"Uh-huh."

"Well, it could be," she said, in a petulant tone, not sure what Bridger meant by his noncommittal comment, but figuring he lent about as much credence to these new ideas as she did, which added to her crankiness. "Hell, you're the one who brought it up."

Bridger arched his brows, but Abby kept her eyes lowered, not that it mattered. "After we left the Austin house the other day" – Was that the first visit or the next? She couldn't remember. "Anyway, we agreed that the original investigators didn't look into this angle."

"There was probably a reason for that," Bridger suggested, as he chewed slowly.

Abby frowned at him. "Whatever. Okay. So maybe it wasn't a hate crime. Try this on then. I found out about some secret societies in Japan that did really gruesome things to keep their members in line. They even brutalized non-members occasionally if they knew those people had heard sensitive stories about them. Rose Austin was Japanese. It's not really a giant leap. Maybe she got involved with one of these groups, or ran afoul of one of them and they decided to get even."

"Hm."

"Damn it, Bridger, you come up with something then. Did another kid do this? Is that better?"

Abby didn't see the grin that crept across Bridger's face. It came from frustration more than amusement. In fact, he was at a loss to explain any of what they had learned so far, which admittedly wasn't much, but in reality it was early yet. Very early.

What he did believe was that they needed to get to know their victim better in order to find his killer. The more they understood of the kid's character, the better chance they had of finding out what happened and why, which made him suggest that they take that drive up I-5 to talk to Amanda Ferguson. Amanda Ferguson Shaw as she was now known.

Before they did that, Abby said she wanted to spend a little time leafing through Cory's yearbooks. Maybe tomorrow would be a good day for the road trip. Today looked like the kind of day to wrap up in a sweater and do some reading. Malph lumbered his way over to the door, so Abby let him outside and followed, pausing to gauge the temperature. Fall sunshine worked hard at burning the fog away, leaving behind columns of steam rising from the lake's surface. Borderline for comfort, but good enough. Too soon, they would be forced to stay inside or switch to storm clothing and their winter constitutions.

She motioned to Bridger, who picked up a trio of annuals and carried them out to the patio. On her back way inside to top off her coffee, Abby glanced over at her partner and smiled. He had already opened one yearbook and, from his statue-like stillness, appeared deeply engrossed in its initial pages. He'd gone off into his own little world, just like he always had done. He lived a case as much as she did. Hopefully, the school annuals would give them clues that would lead them somewhere useful.

As September was drawing to a close, the shadows were growing longer and the days shorter. A chill tinged the late morning air now. The detectives sat next to each other on Abby's deck, Malph sleeping at her feet and occasionally disturbing the peace with a muted "yip" as he chased a dream rabbit. Abby pulled her sweater tighter around her arms. Oregonians don't go inside just because of weather or a dip in the temperature. The natives are died-in-the-wool outdoorsmen. While Abby fell into the category of native Oregonian, Bridger hailed from New York, where outside can be a troublesome, even deadly, place. From what he'd said, the neighborhood he'd grown up in had been relatively safe. Relatively. Still, his background differed wildly from hers.

Abby was raised in a small coastal community, where murders were extremely rare, yet she lost her father at an early age to one of the town's extraordinarily few homicides. Bridger, on the other hand, grew up in one of the world's largest cities, with danger lurking on every street corner. When he wasn't trying to set up musical gigs, his father worked as a firefighter, probably doubling his danger factor over Teddie Dalton's reasonably sedate occupation as a commercial fisherman. Yet, while Teddie was dead before Abby graduated from high school, Willie Flynn went on to complete an inglorious career – inglorious according to Bridger, who was not his father's biggest fan – and continued to live back East in The Bronx. Alternatively, Bridger's glamorous French mother Joie had died of breast cancer five years ago while Abby's mother Grace still enjoyed robust good health. One just never knew what life would throw one's way.

Abby sipped her coffee and suggested to Bridger she could brew a pot. He declined as he turned another page and read the comments some of Cory's friends had written in his senior annual. Neither of them expected a confession to jump off the page. The best they hoped for was to find the names of close friends so they could better personalize the murdered boy by talking to those who had known him best.

Bridger tapped his finger on the inside back cover. "Here's a comment by a kid named Seth. Not too common a name back then, so we might be able to find him in the index pretty easily. Sounds like he worked on the paper with Cory, although I don't remember a Seth listed on the masthead. We can look at that."

"So what does he say?"

"Oh, you know, just the normal kind of stuff kids write. 'It's been a great four years. Really enjoyed working with you. Blah blah blah.' But maybe he can help us with Cory's character a bit more. Let's see," Bridger said as he began to leaf through the senior index. "Yep, here we go. Seth Bonebrake."

Abby typed the name into her iPhone, scoring a phone number on Google with ease. After going through several more entries and some phone calls later, they had set up appointments, two for Friday, one for late that afternoon. They reserved Thursday for the trip to Tumwater.

The fog had completely dissipated by the time Abby brought out three containers of cold leftover Chinese take-out and a couple of forks. They ate lunch in contemplation of the lake, ignoring Malph's sudden, insistent attention, which was brought on by his penchant for potstickers.

Finally, Bridger wiped his mouth with a napkin, finished chewing, and said, "Back to Toby Meyer. Did you seriously believe he had a crush on Cory?"

Abby put her fork down and ripped open the sack of fortune cookies. "Maybe."

Bridger frowned. "Maybe? Come on, Abs, that's a cop-out. Your ears were on high alert. What did they tell you?"

"What did your eyes tell you?" She countered.

"Okay, this is my take on Toby Meyer. I saw a drugged-out kid who craves the limelight but knows he's small potatoes. I saw an unhappy guy who gets high so he can make it through each night parading around onstage in women's clothing. I saw a scared little boy hiding behind Cher's façade. I saw a young man abandoned by love, the faded-by-time kind of love; no happiness, just confused desperation. There. Your turn, Abs."

"Don't call me Abs," she said, without any conviction behind it. "Maybe it was wishful thinking, the idea that he was attracted to Cory. It would be a good motive behind the murder. In reality, I can't say that I really heard anything that confirmed my suspicion. Toby did seem to have a chip on his shoulder though."

"Who wouldn't have, in his shoes?" He laughed.

"Groan."

"They were great shoes, by the way. Shiny black stilettos, with an ankle strap. Maybe Bruno Maglis."

Abby's jaw dropped. "What did you say?"

"Oh, come on. I know a little about style." He regarded his khakis and Izod shirt. "Well, I *know* about it. I don't necessarily consider myself an icon."

Abby nearly choked on her last bite. "Good, because no one else does either." She coughed twice before recovering her composure. "Seriously, though, how do you know about Bruno Maglis?"

"Cyn loved expensive shoes. Bruno Maglis were her favorite. Said they made her legs look long and slender. Part of why we split up."

"Long, good-looking legs?"

"Her obsession with things we couldn't afford on a cop's salary."

Abby understood that, although she never had felt the financial pinch like most of her fellow officers did. Her mother had made sure she would forever be comfortable, if not exactly rich, by setting up a trust fund early on. Not a big one, but a big enough one. And Abby was a woman of simple pleasures, so it would last awhile. "Hm. Anyway, back to Toby Meyer."

"Yeah. Well, I'd bet that not many of his male classmates traded hoodies and jeans for sequined gowns and a collection of wigs. That's enough to put a chip on anyone's shoulder."

"It was his choice," said Abby, in a voice so quiet that she wondered how Bridger heard it.

"Maybe not."

Their eyes met, and Abby had the feeling that they were no longer talking about Toby Meyer, but had segued into the present life of Zachary Taylor Flynn. On their drive back to Lake Oswego from Darcelle's the night before, Bridger had filled Abby in on what little he knew of his son's new life as Moshe Akhbar and his recent enthusiastic connection with the philosophies of something called the Children of Allah.

After Bridger dropped her off, Abby had done a rudimentary Google search of the group and found that she didn't like what she read any more than Bridger did, but the Children had not broken the law. Not yet. It did appear to be heavily weighted toward male members, but did that mean anything? Did Bridger suspect his son had gender confusion? Nothing he had said last night would lead her to that conclusion. She decided he was probably questioning Zach's ability to make wise choices rather than his sexual orientation. Did the Children of Allah have some hold over Zach that inhibited his power of independent thinking? While Abby's heart ached at seeing her partner in such apparent pain, right now she needed to make sure their concentration remained on Cory Austin. As soon as they solved the mystery surrounding that young man's death, they could tackle the question of how to save Zach.

She said, "So we're in agreement that Toby probably didn't have anything to do with Cory's murder? Does that put us back to Asian gangs or random encounter?"

"Did Toby have an alibi?"

"There was no interview sheet, remember? And we didn't ask him."

How could they have skipped that question? Had they been so focused on the cat's paw that they forgot about the basics? Or had the years away from police work dulled their skills that much? Abby replayed the previous night's interview over in her head. Nope, they had not established an alibi with Mr. Meyer. Another good reason to talk to Toby again. She dreaded the idea of returning to Darcelle's though. Where once it had been fun, now it only served to accentuate her broken vision.

Even though they hadn't asked Toby his whereabouts on the night of Cory Austin's death, they had gained something valuable from their visit. They had fleshed out their victim quite a bit through the eyes of Toby Meyer. He was a good source of reference, being a classmate, albeit a somewhat jealous, petty one. Unfortunately, Cher's curtain call had come before the detectives had concluded their questions. Next time, the man's alibi would be at the top of their need-to-know list.

CHAPTER 17

*"Everyone is a moon and has a dark side
which he never shows to anybody."*

– Mark Twain

At ten minutes to 4:00 that Wednesday afternoon, Bridger and Abby exited CON and walked toward the pro shop at Red Tail Golf Course, known originally as Progress Downs. To Abby, it always would be remembered that way. She had good memories of taking lessons at Progress with her ex-husband, Jay, during which she had proven herself a very bad player but an uncommonly good sport about it. Who would have thought that Abigail Dalton, the most competitive woman the Oregon State Police had ever hired, would be so humble about failing at something?

Today, their appointment with Seth Bonebrake had been easy to set up. They simply explained their purpose over the phone and Cory Austin's old classmate seemed eager to help in any way he could. His shift started within the hour of receiving their call, so would they mind coming out to Progress late in the afternoon? They could hardly believe their luck. Finally, a contact that promised to be pleasant.

Dressed in tan pants and a pastel aqua and yellow plaid shirt, Bonebrake met Abby and Bridger with a genial "Hello" and a firm handshake. He towered over both of them, but probably weighed less than half of their combined weight. And he smiled enough for the entire roomful of people.

Yes, he had worked on the *Washington Post* with Cory Austin, at least for a few months. He covered sports. Looking around at where he currently worked, that made sense to the detectives.

According to Seth Bonebrake, Cory was a serious kid with a wicked sense of humor that would kick in at odd times. He loved his family, would fiercely protect his mother and sister from any and all verbal assaults, although he left a lot to be desired when it came to physical protection; not really the type of fellow who worked out or flexed muscles, unless you counted his brain as a muscle. He was brilliant. Bonebrake had never met anyone who could measure up to Cory Austin's intelligence. That certainly explained Lincoln Shin's inability to keep stride with his student.

Knowing that Amanda Ferguson had worked on the school newspaper along with Seth, the detectives next broached the subject of whether she had a "thing" for Cory.

Bonebrake cringed, yet continued to smile. "Yeah. It was pretty obvious. She was always hanging around Cory, making up reasons to talk to him, asking him questions anyone would know the answer to. Always acting like she was his closest friend."

"How about Cory? Did he act like they were close friends?" Abby asked.

"Oh, he acted like it didn't bother him, but he didn't really seem all that comfortable around her. Might have just been that she was a girl. He didn't have much experience with girls. I mean, yeah, he had a sister, but not, you know, anyone like a girlfriend."

"So it was kind of a one-sided relationship."

"Exactly."

Abby switched to another subject. "Did Cory have any enemies that you can remember?"

"Naw. He wasn't that kind of a guy. He didn't really make enemies. Cory sort of blended into the background, if you know what I mean. Except for his test scores, no one would have paid any attention to him."

"Did you notice any animosity between Cory Austin and Toby Meyer?"

Bonebrake blinked a few times, a response not lost on Bridger, although he realized Abby must have missed it. He asked, "Do you remember Toby Meyer?" He began to describe Meyer, but Bonebrake snapped out of his daze.

"No, no, I remember Toby Meyer. Um, animosity? I don't think so, but Toby was a tough one to figure. He sort of danced to a different drummer, if you know what I mean."

Bridger knew what he would mean by that, but wondered what Seth Bonebrake meant.

"Oh, you know, he didn't play well with others. Had a tendency to stir things up. Like he always wanted attention – good or bad, he didn't care."

"How did that manifest itself with Cory?"

"See, that's why I said I didn't think there was animosity. They clashed, yeah, but nothing really came of it. Cory seemed to dismiss Toby as though he was a pesky fly." He spread his arms in a "what can I tell you" fashion.

"That can't have gone over well with someone wanting constant attention," Abby said.

Bonebrake laughed. "Yeah, I can see why you'd think that. But I never noticed any obvious anger between them. Just more of an arm poke kind of thing. A little jab and then move on."

Abby changed subjects again. "What were Cory's hobbies; do you know? Did he ski, snowboard, surf? Play checkers, chess, video games, D&D? Race RC cars?"

Bonebrake thought for a few seconds before replying. "Naw, nothing real physical. Except golf. And he only did that for the mental challenge, really. Yeah, some chess, but mostly he liked the types of things that he could do alone."

"Do you know if he liked music? Did he have a favorite band? Go to any dances?"

"No, Cory didn't go to dances. Never saw him at one, anyway. I think he read a lot. Used to see him hanging around the library all the time. But music? I don't recall him ever talking about popular songs or wearing ear buds or anything like that."

Abby and Bridger wanted to broaden their picture of Cory's nature, see him in 3-D, but he had been maddeningly private. Abby asked, without really caring about the answer, "So, how about favorite authors? What genre did he like?"

Bonebrake shrugged again. "Anything classic. Nothing contemporary, really, unless it involved history. Memoirs. Languages."

Bridger had some questions on more relevant topics. "Did Cory have any new friends he'd made, say, shortly before he died?"

"Not that I know of."

"How about a personality change, even a subtle one?"

Seth Bonebrake just shook his head. "Cory could be moody."

"How so?"

"Oh, I don't know. Let's just say he got sulky sometimes. He wasn't the sort to go postal or anything. But he would go quiet, do a brooding sort of thing."

"Was this brought on by any particular reason? Do you have an example?"

"Let's see. Yeah, I remember once when a girl made fun of him. He just clammed up, got all still."

"Did he ever express any desire to get back at anyone for that sort of a slight?"

"Naw, not Cory."

"Had he become more moody in the weeks leading up to his death?"

Bonebrake pursed his lips and shifted feet. "Hm. Come to think of it, yeah. Yeah, he did. I kind of put it off to the upcoming graduation. You know, school's out; a whole new chapter in a person's life kind of thing."

"Any chance he'd started using drugs?"

The answer was emphatic. "No way."

Abby looked at Bridger and shrugged. She had run out of questions a while back and now, it seemed, so had he. It was too bad, because Seth Bonebrake had proven to be the most forthcoming of the people they had interviewed so far. Nonetheless, they had no reason to waste his time or theirs.

There was little that this witness said that showed a dark side to their victim. The worst that he would say was that Cory Austin could tend toward moodiness and occasionally withdraw into himself, leaving the newspaper staff to find direction on their own. Nothing out of the ordinary for a teen-aged boy, aside from his IQ. Bonebrake did, however, suggest that something was eating Cory that last couple of weeks. No specifics, just an atypical distraction, which might have been laid off to the advent of graduation.

Seth Bonebrake had kept in touch with one other guy who had been on the newspaper staff and he willingly gave the detectives that contact information, but he assured them that they would hear a repeat of what he himself had just told them. Police types are accustomed to repetition, though, so they would find out for themselves. Just not that afternoon. Abby wanted a chance to review the file entries on Amanda Shaw, nee Ferguson, in order to be well prepared for their interview in Tumwater tomorrow. As for Bridger, he had other plans for the evening, plans he didn't share with his partner.

CHAPTER 18

"Never look down to test the ground before taking your next step;
only he who keeps his eye fixed on the far horizon
will find his right road."
- Dag Hammarskjold

The trip to Tumwater could be postponed no longer. The detectives had run thin on leads, and Amanda's name kept cropping up. In a couple of recent telephone interviews, two of Cory's high school buddies swore that Amanda had an abnormal crush on him, obsessively hanging around classrooms where she knew he would be, or lurking in the hallway near his locker. According to them, Cory didn't exactly reciprocate her feelings but he hadn't pushed her cruelly aside either. This was a kid who understood rejection. Therefore, his handling of her affections had required a special kind of finesse. But the detectives realized that Amanda's version may carry a different slant. According to the two students' stories, at one point, Amanda did a major ramping up of her efforts to gain Cory's attention, as in she'd do whatever it took. Had she gone so far as to stalk the boy? It was time to sort out the truth, for rebuffed affections ranked high on the list of murder motives.

Rather than suffer with battling CON in the deep ruts on the freeway due to delayed road maintenance, Bridger gassed up Big Blue, his old red pickup, and cleaned out the minor clutter on the passenger side, which consisted mostly of two hats and a grocery receipt. His '79 Dodge Ram had come to him in a factory blue, a color he ordered the pickup in because his then-wife Cyn loved it, but he preferred the nonstandard cherry red, so he'd had it repainted and never bothered to rename it. Abby hated riding in Blue, claiming that it made her bounce nonstop. There was little choice, though. It was either fight CON in the ruts or listen to

Abby complain about the bouncing. Bridger figured the decision for an easy one. After all, hearing aids had volume control.

Traffic on the short stretch of road between Portland and Vancouver tried a person's patience almost any time of day or season, but mornings saw more southbound commuters and, since the detectives were proceeding northbound, they moved along at a brisk rate. It frequently didn't work out so well and they thanked the traffic gods for the easy going. If only the entire trip had gone so well.

Shortly before the exit for Battle Ground, Washington – a few miles north of the city of Vancouver and the Columbia River – Bridger's phone rang. He answered, listened, and disconnected. When he turned to Abby, his face was grim.

She sensed his tension. "What?"

Bridger checked his mirrors for cars as he signaled to change lanes. "Vanessa Reilly was attacked about twenty minutes ago. The paramedics just finished working on her and she's being transported to OHSU. They're not sure if she'll make it."

Abby replied, "Shit."

- - -

Large, sprawling and perched on a promontory with one of the best views in the city of Portland, the Oregon Health Sciences University holds a nationwide reputation as a premier research hospital and is known as just about the top medical facility for any type of treatment in the area. Vanessa Reilly would be in good hands…if she lived. The caller hadn't told Bridger how serious her condition was, as he himself didn't have that information, but in case she was in more danger than Bridge guessed, they needed to get to her quickly. He had a strong hunch this attack was related to their case. It couldn't be coincidence. That kind of thing rarely happened, except in the movies.

It was almost four miles to the next exit. Four excruciatingly long miles. It seemed symptomatic of the entire case so far: Forever going in the wrong direction.

Once turned around, Bridger negotiated through the southbound traffic, which was heavy with commuters. While her partner drove, Abby made calls to whoever she could think of in an effort to find out more about Vanessa. Chris Reilly had been notified at work, where he dropped his tools, hopped in his pickup and peeled out. Capt. Shearer was still wrapped up in the abduction of the child from Tryon Creek Park and had little to add beyond what they themselves already knew. The hospital did nothing more than direct Abby to a particular ward.

Forty-five minutes later, Big Blue lumbered around the tight curves up the heavily-wooded Sam Jackson Parkway leading to the medical complex. The first parking garage was near capacity, causing them to lose precious time circling the floors for a free space. After that, another fifteen minutes elapsed as they wandered aimlessly through the convoluted hallways and breezeways that make up OHSU. Few would argue its qualifications as one of the best mazes in the world. Getting around efficiently just doesn't happen there. One can walk across a skyway from Level 2 of one building and end up on the third floor of the connecting building.

When they finally arrived at what they hoped was Vanessa Hoyt Reilly's floor, the nurse at the reception desk told them that Mrs. Reilly had not yet been assigned a room, as she was still in surgery. Abby asked what kind of injuries Vanessa had sustained, but the nurse wouldn't part with that information. They spent the next three hours waiting impatiently and asking questions, rarely getting anything close to a satisfactory answer. Chris Reilly milled around the waiting room, pacing and running his hands through his hair. He knew even less than Bridger and Abby did, and anything he attempted to say sounded barely coherent.

The officer who had responded to the 9-1-1 call – apparently made by the Reillys' oldest child, Dexter, who had walked partway to school with the twins before doubling back home – related to them everything he had seen, which fell short of specifics aside from a description of a massive quantity of blood in the family's living room. He had somehow located the children's grandmother, who whisked Dexter off to her place after picking up Sophie and Sonia from their classes, sparing them any additional trauma.

The neighbor directly across the street, a 71-year-old woman named Bertha Peck, had seen a man approach the Reillys' front door shortly after Chris had left for work at 7:40 a.m., but her recollection was of almost no help. She described the man as somewhere between five foot six and six foot one, with brownish or maybe black – no, wait, possibly ginger red – hair, kind of longish. He was on the plump side but not really overweight. And definitely white. Or a combination of white and something olive, like maybe an Italian guy. He might have had on a hat. Glasses? Let's see. Probably not, but he could have been wearing those little wireless round ones. Hard to remember. She didn't see any car. What brought her to even look across at her neighbors' house was a kind of shriek that she thought she heard, but the Reillys were a loud family, especially those twin girls. Always mouthing off. And that mom shrieking right back at them. It often sounded like a battlefield over there. Still, Mrs. Peck had peeked through her Belgian lace curtains to see what this particular shouting match might be all about. She had no idea, really, since she couldn't make out the words and she couldn't figure out what they were doing. Lord knows she tried.

Once the man went inside – which Bertha Peck thought he was rather pushy about – she continued to hear what she described as screaming but thought little more about it since she was used to their noise. Besides, there was nothing more to see, and Bertha was definitely a visual kind of a woman. In fact, once she thought about it, Mrs. Peck remembered seeing another man arrive shortly after the first one went inside. This second fellow she had a better description of, or at least more definite: thin, older. She hadn't watched what happened with him. Her failing bladder had called her away from the window. When next she looked, the scene across the street was deserted so she lost interest.

Fortunately, for Vanessa Reilly, Dexter had decided to ditch school that day. He said he thought his mother would be already headed off to the salon for her nail appointment or hair appointment or spa treatment of some kind. (Apparently, she had constant appointments, in the opinion of her son.) And she might have actually been gone had the attack not intervened. Dexter hadn't seen anyone lurking around their house as he trudged up the sidewalk, and he had been paying attention. He was, after all, playing hooky and didn't want anyone to catch him at it. His plan was to sneak inside the house unobserved and grab his skateboard from his room, then head off to the nearby park for a little personal rolling entertainment. His gruesome discovery likely ended any future truancy he might have attempted for the remainder of his entire life, as he had expressed the belief that his mother's injuries were the result of his bad behavior.

From what Abby and Bridger gathered, a forensics team was going over the Reilly house thoroughly while they cooled their heels at the hospital, hoping for news of Vanessa's medical condition. They tried talking to Chris but he was too consumed with worry to respond with anything close to a meaningful answer. Apparently, he cared more for his wife than Abby had given him credit for.

At almost 2:30 that Thursday afternoon, a doctor who looked like Leonardo DiCaprio with a buzz cut entered the waiting room and asked for Mr. Reilly. Abby's ears perked up and she made sure that she overheard every word the doctor was saying: that Vanessa came through surgery as well as could be expected, was hanging in there, alive but remained in a coma. Abby relayed this information to Bridger, who shook his head in frustration, or possibly dismay. Whichever, with Vanessa still unconscious, there was little more to be learned at the hospital.

While it felt too early to call it a day, neither detective had any idea of what their next move should be, considering this new turn of events. They had already phoned and rescheduled their appointment with Amanda Shaw. Maybe they both needed a break. But the problem, as they saw it, was that now it seemed they had the killer's attention and they couldn't afford to slack off.

With Capt. Shearer's permission, the two detectives decided to make a visit to the home of Bertha Peck in order to get her account of the morning's events first hand. By the time they got there, she had obviously been thinking hard and had refined her testimony. The passing hours, apparently, had sharpened her memory somewhat. Now she said solidly that the first man definitely had dark hair, no lighter than deep brown; on the slight side, not plump; and not tall, probably around five foot eight, but it's tough to gauge. Maybe as tall as six foot? Wearing khakis, gray, and one of those golf shirts, gray and white. As for age, hm, anywhere from forty to fifty-five, she guessed. And she meant "guessed".

Did she think she would recognize him if they showed her a photograph?

Yes, she was positive she would. Unfortunately, neither Bridger nor Abby had any photographs to present. They would need to revisit the people they had interviewed thus far and snap a quick shot of each of them. Would she mind if they came back later with some pictures?

Bertha Peck swelled with self importance and sighed as though put out at the idea, but Abby could tell she was secretly thrilled – or not so secretly, since Abby could tell even with her flawed vision.

By seven o'clock that evening, they had put together a file with photos of Randall Cross, the man taking his early morning walk who found Cory Austin dead on the trail; Seth Bonebrake, Cory's classmate and newspaper coworker; and Alan Garfield, the jogger who encountered Cory on an almost weekly basis shortcutting through Forest Park. Bertha Peck dismissed Cross and Bonebrake right away. Bonebrake was too tall and Cross was too fair skinned. Garfield? Something seemed familiar, but he definitely wasn't the first guy. Maybe the second? She shook her head. Her glimpse of him had been too brief.

They thanked her, promising to return with more photographs, probably the following morning. It was agreed that they should make it a priority to catch Lincoln Shin, Cory's math teacher, and the cross-dressing Toby Meyer for a picture, ASAP. Amanda Shaw would have to wait awhile longer, since clearly she wasn't Vanessa's attacker.

CHAPTER 19

*"Although the world is full of suffering,
it is full also of the overcoming of it."*

- Helen Keller

A persistent cloud cover had drifted in early Friday morning. Abby hated the flat gray of the landscape when the weather turned like this. Oswego Lake's usually vibrant surface shone glassy with the lack of wind, but its waters blended into the dark slate of rocks on the shore and the sky hung heavy. Abby hadn't slept well, nor had Malph, and she suspected that Bridger hadn't either. The sky wasn't the only thing weighing heavily on them. As usual, the dog took his mood from his mistress. He dragged himself from his bed to his breakfast bowl and back to his bed.

By 7:15, the detectives sat in the parking lot at Washington High School. Bridger held his digital camera in his left hand, at the ready whenever Lincoln Shin arrived. He'd parked CON close to where the teacher's ancient Gremlin had been the last time they were there, in hopes that Shin made a habit of parking in the same spot every day.

They heard him before they saw him. Even Bridger couldn't miss the rattle of the tailpipe, which had died long ago. In mere minutes of their arrival, the battered car pulled in, coming to a rest just three spaces away from where they sat. Lincoln Shin emerged a minute and a half later, dressed in loden chinos and a light tan jacket, gripping a valise as battered as the Gremlin and of about the same vintage.

Bridger shot a series of six or seven photos before Shin had moved far enough out of range for any more pictures to be of value. One down, one to go, he thought. However, getting a picture of Toby Meyer could prove to be a bigger challenge, considering the man's odd work hours. The detectives agreed to worry about that later. Maybe, if they were lucky, one of Darcelle's show flyers would feature a nice shot of Toby before transforming into Cher. His landlady, so happy to share with the detectives a few days ago, would hopefully prove to be a valuable resource once again. They had almost dismissed Toby as a suspect, considering he was far younger than Bertha Peck's description of Vanessa's attacker at forty to fifty-five years of age, but then they remembered his access to makeup and costumes. The guy could be any age he wanted with a few paints and powders. Best to cover all bases.

Bridger stowed the camera in the space behind the driver's seat, put CON into gear and merged into the throng of commuters converging on downtown. He and Abby rode along, neither speaking, for half a mile and then turned into a Starbucks. After a purchase of two grande bold coffees – Bridger adding cream to his – they were back on the road. Within five minutes, Bridger had a smile on his face and Abby had stopped cursing at the other drivers.

As they crossed over a snarled I-405, Bridger's phone played its tune. Capt. Shearer had gotten a call from a worried Cari Austin, rattling around in her mom's house and wondering about their progress. It had been five days, after all. Hell, Abby figured, it had been eleven years before they themselves had gotten involved, so maybe the woman could have a little patience.

"Look who's talking about patience, Abs."

"Shove it."

So far, nothing had come back on the cat's paw, but they knew it was unlikely to receive any sort of priority, especially considering the manpower currently dedicated to the Tryon Creek child abduction. Bridger had no report for Cari, but he had long ago learned how to satisfy people while saying pretty much nothing using many words and smiling a lot. Abby thought he would have made an excellent politician because of those skills.

She said, "Hell, let's just get it over with."

Bridger was often amazed at Abby's lack of compassion for the families of murder victims, having been part of one herself. He figured it must be her way of coping. Still, he wished she would soften her attitude sometimes, even if just a little bit. A quick stop by Cari Austin's house would only cost them an eight- or ten-block detour, so it really wasn't much of a time loss. The young woman deserved a personal update, at the least. Soon, maybe, they could bring her some real answers.

Cari came to the door as quickly as ever, wearing another boxy sweater and her signature baggy pants, looking anxious and expectant. Bridger worked his magic with empty sentences and a paternal countenance. The rich deep bass of his voice was soothing, his round vowels mesmerizing.

Tuning him out, Abby had no idea what he said, but Cari sounded satisfied. They declined her offer of coffee, having drunk enough on the short drive over to get both of them well on their way to jittery.

As the detectives started to step back outside, Abby caught sight of something she had nearly missed altogether. Few people knew she was a lover of jewelry. Squinting, she peered closer, saying, "What an unusual necklace, Ms. Austin."

"Oh! Um, thank you." Cari's hand jumped to the tiny gold chain and she fingered it self-consciously.

"A netsuke, isn't it?"

"Um, I don't know. It was my mom's. I found it yesterday as I was packing up some of her things. I'd never seen it before, but I wanted something of hers as a keepsake and I liked it."

Many years back, when Abby had first formed an interest in netsukes, she read that they originated in Japan. Of course, Rose Austin was Japanese so this one was likely genuine. Due to their high desirability, fakes flooded the market, Abby knew. She collected them and had been fooled once or twice, long ago, but most of the netsukes she had bought over the years had excellent provenance.

"Did your mom have a lot of these?"

Cari shook her head, a blank expression on her face. "No, I don't recall seeing any more. Mom didn't really keep knick knacks."

Abby wanted to say that netsukes were a bit more than knick knacks, but held her tongue. Instead, she said, "Well, this one is lovely. Is it some kind of animal?" She knew they often were carved horses, frogs, dragons, a pair of snakes, etc. Some even rarer ones depicted human forms engaged in various activities, like carrying masks or clasping something behind their backs. Her vision didn't allow her to make out what shape the netsuke that hung around Ms. Austin's neck took.

"Oh, no. It's a woman crouching under a hat. Mom loved hats."

"Would you mind if I took a picture of it so I can see it better once I find my magnifier? It's just so magnificent."

Cari appeared a little flustered, but that seemed to stem from delight at having something which someone else liked as much as she herself did. "Oh! Um, sure."

Abby snapped a couple of photos with her phone, thanked the young woman and then signaled to Bridger that she was done. They promised to keep her updated as often as they had anything.

Back in the car, Abby fished through her purse and brought out her magnifier.

Bridger chuckled and shook his head. "What was that all about back there? I thought you said you'd mislaid that thing."

"Hell, no. I knew where it was all along. Just wanted some pictures of that netsuke to study." She had already begun a thorough examination of the photos.

"So do you have something?"

"I'll let you know."

Bridger turned the key in the ignition and merged into the lane. It would be fruitless to push Abby until she was ready to share whatever idea had taken hold of her complicated Dalton mind.

- - -

A quick detour to Toby Meyer's Old Town apartment yielded better results than either detective had dared to hope. The landlady smiled at them when she opened her door, even going so far as to ask them in. She could put on a pot of tea and had a plate of freshly baked muffins on her counter. Apple bran, her personal favorite. Would they care for one? She would be happy to warm them up and bring out some butter. Abby thought the woman must be Bertha Peck's less-nosy but equally-lonely cousin. She left it to Bridger to decline the landlady's offer since he made a point of being polite where Abby just wanted to get right to business.

"Could we see that flyer again that you showed us a couple days ago?"

"Of course. Of course." The tiny woman bustled off down a short hallway, ducked into a room and darted back out, extending the flyer in her left hand as she hurried back, suddenly seeming infected by their rush.

Bridger took one quick look and said, "Yes!"

Without being asked, the landlady said, "You can have that."

"Thank you." The one photo of Toby Meyer featured as part of the cast showed the guy looking straight at the camera, only a head shot but a good likeness. They didn't want to dwell on Meyer's access to wigs and make-up. If Bertha Peck had gotten a good enough look at the men who approached the Reilly house, then she should be able to say yea or nay by viewing Meyer's picture on the flyer.

- - -

Forty-five minutes later, out in Gresham once again, the Reillys' neighbor, Bertha Peck, didn't answer her doorbell, leaving Bridger and Abby scratching their heads as they stood on her front stoop.

"I thought she was expecting us." Abby grumbled.

"Yes, me, too. Actually, I got the impression Mrs. Peck did little aside from watch the world from behind her curtains. It never occurred to me that she actually went out."

Abby laughed. He had said what she'd been thinking. It was usually the other way around. "I wonder where she's gotten off to."

Bridger shook his head, turning back toward the car. Abby picked her way carefully behind him, keeping a close watch for root heaves that the old oaks out in this budding suburb made into walking hazards. The local governments didn't like to take trees out, even when they'd begun a campaign of destruction. Abby sort of appreciated that, being a forest lover, but it was becoming more difficult for her to negotiate sidewalks in older neighborhoods because of the concrete-busting roots. Uneven surfaces could take her down nearly as fast as a Glock these days.

A brisk breeze rustled the leaves of a rhododendron that looked like it predated the entire city, standing close to fourteen feet tall. Bertha's yard had no fewer than five of the leafy granddaddies. Unless kept trimmed, the rhodies had a tendency to spread and become leggy. It appeared that Mrs. Peck had never taken a pair of shears to any of her plants, although someone kept the grass mowed and edged.

A yeasty aroma wafted over from a nearby bakery. Abby's stomach growled. Bridger didn't hear it, of course. Nonetheless, it had been over four and a half hours since breakfast and, with hopes of catching Bertha Peck before they took the seventeen-mile drive back into Portland, he suggested they stop into a little pub he knew about in the historic center of Gresham. They could pass some time waiting for Peck to return home.

Like many communities that had lost their identities with the overwhelming tide of urban sprawl, the majority of Gresham looked like an outdated strip mall on steroids. But its city council had concentrated a majority of its efforts on breathing life into the few blocks of older stone buildings that showed at least a hint of real character, and had given a facelift to some of the concrete boxes that had popped up. The result paid off. It wasn't a particularly large downtown, but the main street revitalized the town for a good two square miles. And with snow-capped Mt. Hood as a dramatic backdrop, the potential for more commerce to be attracted was definitely there.

The Pickaxe Pub resided on the ground floor of one three-story carriage house, with four tables lining the massive window looking onto the street. The detectives had their choice of seats, it being the slack time between the pub's breakfast menu – the full English one – and their Welsh lunch selection. With the Portland metropolitan area relatively close to the ocean – sixty miles as the crow flies – the Pickaxe featured a sizable number of fresh fish dishes. Abby zeroed in on the house-made crab cakes, a delicacy that was always irresistible to her. She had acquired a taste for even mediocre crab cakes during her growing-up days in Astoria. The Pickaxe Pub's were well beyond mediocre, according to a quote by a past Gresham mayor printed on the bottom of the menu. She and Bridger split a plate of three cakes and stuck with tap water for beverages.

Bridger checked in with Capt. Shearer and inquired about Vanessa Reilly's progress. There had been little change since yesterday, which they supposed meant that she was stable but still in a fair amount of danger.

"Not a lot we can do but keep our fingers crossed," Abby said absently, as she placed a $20 bill on the tab and they waved to the pub owner on their way out.

"Let's check on Bertha Peck again. If she's still not home, we can try to catch Toby Meyer and finish our interview."

CON pulled away from the curb in front of the pub, abundant sunshine streaming in through the windshield. The morning's oppressive clouds burned off east to west, Gresham benefitting earlier than central Portland because of that. Looking toward the city skyline and the hills, the detectives could see the receding shadows.

Fall, even late fall, in the Northwest is exceptionally pleasant. The temperatures hover below too warm and above too cool. Everyone who has any chance whatsoever takes each and every opportunity to spend time outdoors, for they know that, in just a few more weeks the days will turn dark, drippy and bone-chilling. The clouds will settle in for months, blocking even the most valiant efforts the sun makes to peek through. Abundant complaints about going to work in the dark and going home in the dark will be repeated to the point of overkill, and that's for a nine-to-five job. Cabin fever is a real, honest-to-God malady in Oregon by February. So September and October must be enjoyed to the fullest.

Abby rolled down her window to allow the mild breeze to ruffle her hair. Like a contented dog, she pushed her face further out. The short drive back to Bertha Peck's home provided a nice respite from the worries of the Austin case. Disappointingly, the house appeared to be just like they'd left it an hour and a half before, showing no apparent sign of life.

"Shit. Where the hell could she be?" Abby grumbled, as she followed Bridger up the path to the front door, her contentment of a few minutes earlier rapidly dissipating.

Her partner rang the doorbell and stood on the tips of his toes to peer into one of the three etched windows that decorated the beige metal door. While he moved his head from side to side, Abby listened closely for the sound of approaching footsteps. All she heard was silence. No, wait, was that a muffled voice? Bridger hit the bell again. Abby concentrated on the faint sounds inside. At the exact moment she identified a moan and yelled "Shit" again, Bridger leaned back and kicked the door. It flew open and bounced off the front wall of a small living room.

Bertha Peck lay mostly on her back with her legs twisted to one side, just to the right of her couch, a half-eaten bagel clutched in one hand. Bridger rushed to the woman and felt for a pulse. Abby could have told him that Bertha Peck was still alive, having heard the moaning, but she didn't waste the time. Her cell phone was out before Bridger had knelt beside the victim, and she dialed 9-1-1 without even looking at the keypad. Her eyes remained glued on Bridger and his efforts to assess their witness.

He knelt at Mrs. Peck's head and spoke in even, reassuring tones. It didn't seem to matter to the injured woman. Distress held her in its grip and she continued to groan. Bridger worried that her back might be broken, judging from the odd angle of her body. So far, she hadn't moved anything but her lips. Blood stained the shaggy carpet an overturned coffee table rested on, the majority of it congealed and tacky. How long had she been like this?

Sirens pulsed in the distance and Abby hurried outside to flag down the ambulance. The sun now seemed harsh in its brightness. A woman lay fighting for her life on this day of perfect weather, which cared not a whit about her desperate struggle. Three paramedics hopped from the truck as it came to a stop and ran toward her with their equipment, expressions of concern on their faces. Abby pointed at the Peck house and stepped aside before following them up the walkway.

While the EMTs ministered to Mrs. Peck's wounds and stabilized her for transport, Bridger said to Abby, "We've gotten somebody's attention."

"We sure as hell have." She bit the inside of her cheek. "You don't think the guy was inside when we came earlier, do you?" The idea made Abby angry, afraid that they might have missed an opportunity to prevent this attack.

Bridger shook his head. "I don't know. The blood..."

"Yeah, I saw."

"It might have been a couple hours, but probably no more. I hate to think we stood at the front door with a killer on the other side of it. So close!" He banged his fist against a nearby wall in a rare loss of composure.

Abby blanched. "Did we bring this on her? Would she still be okay if we had left her alone?"

"Don't, Abs. Don't go there. Mrs. Peck was a witness. She had to be interviewed."

"But Vanessa? Now Bertha Peck?"

"Abs —" He laid his hand gently on her shoulder.

"Don't call me Abs." She jerked away and looked toward the ceiling. "Damn it, damn it, damn it. We've got to catch this son of a bitch before he hurts anyone else." Abby's frustration threatened to explode beyond her control. She knew the attack on this woman wasn't something they owned. Still, the feeling of treading where they didn't belong tried to sneak in. Their failure to figure this out had led to Bertha Peck's present condition. She couldn't help believing that, despite knowing that they were doing their best. Or were they? What were they missing?

The Reillys' inquisitive neighbor now held onto life by a thread; that much was clear. Someone had tried to silence her, and it had to be related to their cold case. Abby and Bridger needed to sit down and retrace their steps, figure out where they had triggered a revenge response, who they had set off. She watched the ambulance drive away, praying to God that the woman inside it would live. A tear trickled down her face, one she wiped away with the back of her hand. In sadness or fury? Maybe both. As far as she was concerned, you could call it cotton candy for all she cared. It was an emotion to be dealt with when they had time for such things. But right now, she vowed to hunt down the man who had done this and see to it that he paid dearly.

CHAPTER 20

"When the Fox hears the Rabbit scream,
he comes a-runnin', but not to help."
           - Thomas Harris, The Silence of the Lambs

      Bridger and Abby spent the next couple of hours giving the responding officers their statements then headed over to the Gresham hospital to check on Bertha Peck's condition. The staff there explained that she had been flown up to OHSU, like Vanessa Reilly the day before. Over the phone, no one at Oregon Health Sciences could tell them anything other than that doctors were still working on Mrs. Peck. Status reports on Vanessa hadn't changed from the one Bridger had received earlier that morning. No surprise. A quick stop at PPB Headquarters gave them nothing aside from the satisfaction of having briefed Capt. Shearer on the events since they had last met with him. The two detectives took away little, if anything, new from the conversation.

      Exhausted and a bit dejected, Bridger suggested that they run down to the Leipzig Tavern for a drink. Abby gave the idea her enthusiastic approval. They rode the seven miles in Portland's end-of-the-week traffic without speaking, each absorbed in thoughts of the day's tragedy. And of the day before.

      Despite the relatively early hour of 4:45, the Sellwood bar was nearly packed. They had little choice but to make do with a couple of barstools, and thanked their lucky stars they were able to find two next to each other. On nearly all Fridays, most notably drippy ones, seats in the Leipzig came at a premium. Fortunately, the pleasant weather had lured a sizable number of people out of the bars and cafes, maybe for a last hurrah on the Willamette River. With the rainy season looming, most Portlanders wouldn't waste a beautiful afternoon.

A harried waitress with blonde hair making every effort to escape from a loose bun set Bridger's Knob Creek down in front of him with too much haste, spilling several drops onto the wooden bar. He used two fingers to wipe it up then licked them off before tucking into his glass. The bourbon went down fast, warming and calming him. Abby took slightly more time with her wine but they soon found themselves facing empty glasses and the danger of drowning their sorrows in too much alcohol. Abby reached into her purse, drew out a twenty and a ten, laid them on the bar and tapped Bridger's shoulder, motioning for him to follow.

Outdoors, she squinted in the bright sunlight as she faced him. "How about you take me home. You can come in. We'll order a pizza from Luigi's. I've got plenty of chardonnay and Knob Creek. If you get drunk, you can have the guest room." She looped her arm in his and started toward the car, adding, "Good thing you don't have that cat yet. Means there's nothing to compel you to drive your sorry butt home when you shouldn't."

Bridger just nodded as he dug the car keys out of his pocket.

- - -

At Abby's Lake Oswego townhome, Malph greeted his mistress with a long pink tongue lolling out the side of his mouth, two lower teeth protruding upward onto a portion of his lip. He skillfully dodged Bridger's attempts to pet him and trotted around the side of the cabana where both detectives knew he would sprawl on the deck in a heap and crank up the snoring within two minutes. Sure enough, by the time they came out, carrying their drinks, Malph had rolled onto one side and looked dead to the world. The sound issuing from his nose, though, made it clear he was very much alive.

While waiting for Luigi's Friday Special – this week it was fennel sausage, three types of mushrooms and caramelized onions smothered with shredded Gouda – Abby and Bridger settled into her deck chairs. Malph miraculously woke up long enough to transfer his round little albino body closer to Abby's legs.

Bridger sipped his bourbon, sighed loudly, and mused, "Two attacks in two days."

"Yeah," said Abby, too low for Bridger to hear, but nonetheless he knew she had said it.

"Abs, it's not our fault. Remember that. We aren't attacking these people."

"But it's because of us, because we haven't caught him – or her!"

This time, Bridger said, "Yeah."

Abby leaned her head against the seat back and sighed. "Shit. Okay, you're right. Laying blame won't help. We did set something in motion, though, and it's imperative that we stop whatever that something is."

"Abs, we're trying."

"But we're not doing enough!" She said fiercely.

"Blame game again?"

She shot him a look that said "Bite me" or maybe something less nice, then pressed her lips together in concentration. Bridger rubbed his hand down his face before taking another hit from his drink. He set his glass down on the tiny table between them and waited for Abby to work through her huff.

"What are we missing, Bridger? Come on, you're the eyes of this team."

He liked that she called them a team and wished he had the luxury of time to savor the feeling. But the fact was that they didn't have time to spare. They really did need to solve this case – or cases, now. People were getting hurt, maybe even dying. Where originally they had one dead person, they were dangerously close to two or three. Bridger had been almost ready to chock up Cory's death to a random attack, but that notion had been quashed since the two ladies – neighbors, no less – had landed in the hospital, lying comatose and holding onto life by a thread.

He counted off the witnesses they had spoken with so far, eliminating Bonebrake as being a tangential character only, along with the three old classmates they had interviewed over the phone. Two of them lived across the country and the other one had been interviewed merely in an effort to round out their victim. Sure, he had written in Cory Austin's yearbook, but only had contact with him in a series of math classes as far as the detectives could tell. Bridger was inclined to discount Toby Meyer as a serious suspect, but Abby wasn't so sure. For now, she would hold off judgment but put him toward the bottom of their list.

Neither of them felt that Randall Cross, the jogger who discovered Cory's body, had anything to do with his murder aside from being in the wrong place at the wrong time. As for Alan Garfield, well, maybe. He had professed to liking the kid he ran into on the trails occasionally, but who knew? People lie every day. It didn't seem all that far-fetched that Cory might have seen Garfield doing something he shouldn't have. They agreed that was a stretch, but they decided to keep Garfield on their short list anyway and have another chat with him soon.

That left Cory's dad, who had a pretty solid alibi, the Nerdlingers, Shin, Amanda, and maybe his co-workers at Burger World, none of whom had an obvious motive as far as they could see, although Amanda sounded like the most possible out of all of those. Problem was she had been in Tumwater at the time of the attacks on Vanessa and Bertha Peck. Or had she? Did they really know that as a fact? Even if she had been, there are always other people one can get to do one's dirty work.

As for Lincoln Shin, Abby didn't like Shin, but she couldn't find a way to pin this on him. At least, not yet. She would still keep digging. She wanted it to be him, if for no other reason than because of how he'd trained his dog. No dog should end up like Shin's had.

As for Cory's dad, nothing at all pointed to him except for statistics. Murders are usually committed by those closest to the victims, according to the odds. Gerry Austin, while close relationally, was distant emotionally not to mention physically. Abby discounted the usefulness of statistics, as did Bridger. But ex-wives can be troublesome, and children who require support payments are often more a thorn than a joy in the eyes of some parents. Could it have come down to simple economics? Dad got rid of one kid he was going to have to pay college tuition for? Did Cory have a scholarship? A fellow that brilliant, he must have. Something else to ask Cari.

They hadn't yet tracked down any of Cory Austin's co-workers at Burger World, clinging to the belief that the killer sprang from some sort of relationship at school. That still felt right. The Nerdlingers? Were they the ones who lured him onto that trail in the dark of night? That was possible but the detectives couldn't reconcile that scenario with the vicious attack. Unless...back to the scholarship idea. Maybe one of the Nerdlingers club members got beat out by Cory for it. Money was an age-old murder motive. Still, murder seemed like a hugely rash solution to the problem, but the world works in a far different manner now than back when the detectives were in school.

Abby repeated her question. "What are we missing?"

Bridger stood, tossed back the last of his bourbon, and said, "We're missing the identity of the killer."

Abby stuck her tongue out at him. She was about ready to punch him, but two short beeps of a horn from out front stopped her. Luigi's Special had arrived. About time something good happened.

CHAPTER 21

*"I think knowing what you cannot do is more important
than knowing what you can do."*

- Lucille Ball

Saturday morning, Abby slid onto the bench seat in Old Blue, working hard to suppress a yawn. Bridger knew her habits; she likely had stayed awake long into the night, plotting today's witness interview or ticking off known points of evidence in her mind. At the end of the day when they were on a case, Abby's brain opened up and went exploring. She might try to suppress the urge with a couple glasses of white wine – as she had last evening – but once she sank her teeth into a case, she couldn't let go. And it was undeniable that there was plenty gnawing at her the evening before that could keep sleep at bay.

The same went for him. His had been one of those rare nights when he saw more of his bedroom ceiling than the insides of his eyelids. At least, he had not added too much liquor into the equation, having limited himself to just two drinks.

Over Luigi's Friday Special, they had discussed where to go next. After only five days, the heat had ratcheted up to dangerously high, making it important that the detectives carefully weigh their next moves and choose their actions wisely. They had succeeded in pushing someone into a murderous rage, which had left two women fighting for their lives. Cory's killer was running scared and must be stopped – now – before they had more than one death to investigate. Why didn't he just come after the pair of them? They both wished he had. Things would have turned out much differently in that scenario.

Last night, when Luigi's pizza guy had showed up, Abby tipped him well with money from Bridger's wallet and served up a couple of slices apiece on paper plates. That Friday's Special came with extra garlic, since the man who took her order over the phone knew her preferences well, and a container of shredded Parmesan to push the flavor scales over the top. Still, she and Bridger chewed listlessly, their appetites all but gone. After they choked down just half of it, Abby had brewed a rare pot of coffee, and then Bridger had gone home. He wanted a clear head, and stopping short of having a third beaker of Knob Creek helped him keep it that way.

Amanda Ferguson Shaw had become their current focus. With Vanessa Reilly and her neighbor Bertha Peck each lying in a coma, a trip up I-5 to Tumwater sounded ideal. Actually, just getting out of Portland sounded ideal and they prayed that they could make it beyond Battle Ground this time. Amanda had not complained about their repeated cancellations. In fact, she said, Saturday would be better for her anyway since it was her day off. For their part, traffic would be lighter. Sounded like a win-win.

- - -

The day started out slightly overcast, nice for driving and not so nice for lounging on the lakeside deck, which neither had time for anyway. With a two-plus-hour trip ahead of them, they agreed to leave around 8:00. The clock read 7:53 as Abby buckled her seat belt.

Bridger turned to look at his partner on the passenger side of Old Blue. "Coffee?" he inquired. He already knew the answer. Abby wasn't fit company without at least one cup of coffee in the morning, optimally three or four. Her addiction to the stuff suited Bridger just fine.

"Sure."

"The Bean?"

Abby didn't care where they went, as long as she got a hefty shot of caffeine pumped into her system in the very near future. "Whatever."

A few blocks away, Bridger pulled to a stop at the window and, as expected, his young friend Marla smiled out at him and waved to Abby. "Hello, Ms. Dalton."

Abby acknowledged Marla with a nod, the most civility she could muster this morning, especially before her first cup. Despite her addiction to the stuff, she rarely brewed it at home. Maybe she would if Malph drank it but it was tough to pull together enough energy to grind the beans and fill the water reservoir, push the button and wait; even more so after a night like the one she'd just endured. And she hated to admit it, but restless nights had become an all too common occurrence these days. She feared she was entering a stage in her life where that would be the rule rather than the exception. Thank God for coffee.

The Human Bean served their coffee steaming hot, like Starbucks, to their everlasting credit. Because of that, the temperature stayed warm enough for as long as it took to drink it. Abby eagerly accepted the large cup Bridger handed to her and blew through the hole in the lid, impatient to cool it down to just under a lip-burning heat. Bridger set his in one of the two holders and pulled out onto the street.

Three minutes passed before Abby spoke. "Okay. As you could probably tell, I didn't get a lot of rest last night."

"Really?"

"Shove it." She glared in his direction.

"Sorry, Abs."

"Don't call –"

"— you Abs. Got it. So what kept you up?" He signaled to turn left onto Macadam Avenue.

"Aside from the obvious?"

He glanced her way. "Abs –"

"Don't –"

"Okay. Sorry. But, Abby, I know you. The obvious won't keep you up. It's the obscure that will."

She yawned as though to emphasize her weariness. "Yeah, you're right. Shit." About half a minute passed before she continued. Bridger laid it off to her wanting to organize her thoughts. "You won't believe this, but there are actually websites that sell murder memorabilia. It's called murderabilia. Is that fucking nuts or what?"

Bridger thought it was, as a matter of fact. "Really? Who buys this stuff?"

"Good question. My guess is sick assholes buy it. Not sure why anyone would want to pay good money for things once owned by creeps who prey on other people. I mean, how do you display something like that? And who do you show it to? What, you have a cocktail party and casually say, 'By the way, Joan, have you seen my Jack the Ripper jock strap?'" Abby shook her head in wonder at the crap humans collected.

"Anyway, I happened upon a couple of blogs while blind surfing, and couldn't let go, for God's sake. There's a hell of a market out there, looks like. The main sites I cruised had all these different topics, with links to murderabilia of famous serial killers: Ted Bundy, Charles Manson, John Wayne Gacy, you name it. They sell or auction off letters, envelopes, drawings, hair clippings, toenails."

"Toenails?"

"Toenails. Oh, and get this, they sell stuff under the heading of 'Bodily Fluids'. I don't even want to guess what that covers."

Bridger shuddered dramatically.

"There's layers and layers of that kind of depravity. Crime scene photos. Clothing. You can buy gift certificates. Honestly! Anyhow, I got hooked."

"Where are you going with this?" Abby didn't normally wander around strange websites without a reason and she certainly didn't have a prurient streak that would appeal to a hidden side, Bridger was sure. Police work had given her plenty of opportunity to indulge that but he had never seen her enjoy the dark side of human nature.

Abby sighed. "Shit, I don't know. I just couldn't sleep. But I couldn't do nothing so I started plugging in words and phrases."

"Murderabilia?"

"Don't ask. Not sure how I got there anyway. It probably doesn't matter. But it got me thinking about how murderers, especially serial murderers, like to take a memento."

"You don't think this guy is a serial killer."

"No, no, no. But maybe the cat's paw was some kind of memento. Ah, crap, I'm tired. None of that makes sense."

"Well, in an odd sort of way, maybe it does."

"Huh?"

Bridger drove without speaking for another mile or so. "Say the cat's paw wasn't sent to Rose Austin until later."

"But…"

"Hear me out." He paused in an apparent effort to think this line of reasoning through. "The cat went missing. We'll concede that."

"There seems to be no argument."

"Okay. Say Rose gets a letter with a photo of the dead cat. It tells her to do something, or to not do something. But whatever it was, Rose knew it was a serious threat. For some reason, she couldn't follow the letter's instructions."

"Why didn't she leave, run away, ask for help? Why not –"

"I don't have the answers. Just thinking out loud."

"So how did the paw get into the closet?"

"If she couldn't follow his instructions, he might have decided to send it to show her he was serious. Or maybe something happened later that caused Rose to become a bigger threat to the killer. He sent it as a reminder of what he could do. Rose still had Cari to worry about, remember."

Abby puffed out her cheeks in frustration. "Maybe, maybe, maybe. Hell, what we need is answers, not wild hare-brained ideas."

"You're right." Bridger smiled over at his partner, but she had laid her head against the seat back and closed her eyes. She could see almost as well like that anyway. And, for now, neither of them could see a conclusion to this case.

CHAPTER 22

"If you have anything to tell me of importance,
for God's sake begin at the end."

- Sara Jeannette Duncan

Bridger drove along deep in thought and allowed Abby to enjoy some much-needed rest. If she couldn't sleep at home in her bed, she did a fine job of dozing in the front seat of Old Blue. Bridger began to hum while she snored, the sounds blending into a funny sort of road music. They drove past the exits for Longview, Castle Rock and Chehalis, almost making it to Centralia before Bridger's phone sounded. Abby stirred, bolting upright as he answered.

When Bridger disconnected from the call, he glanced sideways at Abby. She had obviously been paying attention to his conversation, for she stared at him openly with a clear question in her expression. She didn't need perfect eyesight to make her point.

"What?"

At least this time it wasn't bad news. Or bad news of a criminal nature. Bridger didn't want to discuss the subject, but he knew Abby wouldn't tolerate that. Absently, he rubbed the gray-orange fuzz on the top of his bumpy brown head.

"That was Capt. Shearer."

"Yeah, I figured that out when you said, 'Hi, Captain.'"

Bridger licked his lips and gripped Blue's steering wheel hard.

"Spill it, Flynn."

"Okay." He drew a deep breath, stalling a few seconds more.

"Bridger, honest to God, if you don't –"

"Okay. Okay, Abs. Sorry, don't call you Abs, I know." The woman had the ability to turn Bridger to mush where usually he had the upper hand with folks. Abby Dalton was a formidable force and a person you wanted to keep on the good side of. "Okay, here's the deal. Somehow someone leaked a story to the media." He cringed, knowing how Abby hated dealing with the press.

"And?"

"Well, they got wind of a new angle in the Austin case."

"Shit! How?"

"I don't know. Capt. Shearer doesn't know. He's no happier about this than we are." Bridger emphasized "we" to try to defuse his partner's anger, which she currently appeared to be directing toward him.

"Damn. So what do they want?"

Bridger would have been relieved by her apparently calm answer had he not worked with her for so long. There was more vitriol coming, no question. Probably well deserved vitriol even. Abby didn't just hate the press, she despised them. And with good reason. Too many of her interviews had been twisted to portray a slant that hadn't existed in the real world, too many held-back clues had been discovered somehow and splashed across headlines, and too many cases had been compromised or complicated by a reporter's irresponsible quest for a journalistic scoop.

He swallowed hard. He hated this part as much as his partner did. "There's a press conference scheduled for tomorrow morning. The local TV stations want to see the new cold case squad. The Oregonian will be there, too. Maybe others," he added loudly, as though Abby were the person with poor hearing.

"What? There is no cold case squad."

"Technically, there is."

"Damn and double damn. Shit and hellfire."

They rode along for the next half hour with Abby staring at nothing out the side window. The sky grew flatter the further north they traveled. The freeway, Interstate 5, which cuts through a western Washington valley, has only rolling hills, long straight stretches, and little scenery in that area. The nondescript towns break up the monotony, but do nothing to pique motorists' interest. It becomes difficult to stick to the speed limit. Once out of the Portland-Vancouver metro area, they had made good time, partly because Bridger never worried about being stopped. He didn't

143

have anything like professional immunity, especially in Washington, but he did have a sixth sense – and years of experience – about where the State troopers would set up their radar.

Just over two hours after crossing over the Columbia River, and following the instructions on his GPS, Bridger took the exit that would lead them west of the freeway to Lakeside Street in a community of moderately upscale homes with views of Black Lake. The address read Olympia, but Amanda Ferguson Shaw's house was closer to the town center of Tumwater.

It can be tough to tell where Tumwater leaves off and Olympia, the state capital of Washington, begins. The area, though, situated at the southern end of Puget Sound, has a reputation as an exceptionally beautiful setting, especially for a couple of water lovers like Bridger Flynn and Abby Dalton. In fact, the name Tumwater itself stems from the Chinook word for a waterfall. And, while Tumwater Falls doesn't have the utter magnificence of, say, Multnomah Falls in the Columbia River Gorge, it is a pretty little cataract. The detectives wished that they could make a short detour to appreciate Tumwater's beauty, but they had a killer to catch, which meant that side trips were too big a luxury for them to take.

At the Ferguson Shaw house, a dark cedarwood contemporary structure obviously designed to take advantage of the view, they were pleasantly surprised by the woman who answered the door. In the yearbook, Amanda's senior picture had depicted a chubby-faced girl with a serious acne problem, thin brown hair worn short with nothing one might define as style. It had looked as though her parents disallowed make-up in high school, so her complexion had come across as wan and her eyes had seemed to sink deep into her skull.

But now, at twenty-eight, she had shed the baby fat, learned how to apply eyeliner and mascara without looking like she was wearing any, and sported an end-of-summer tan which showed off her dark brown eyes nicely. Her hair, though, was still fine and thin, but she had made the best of it with vibrant highlights and an airy cut that complimented her heart-shaped face. An easy smile led all the way up to her eyes as she welcomed them inside.

Abby hadn't known what to expect, but the Amanda who stood before them momentarily knocked her off her game. Eleven years had changed the previously awkward girl into a woman overflowing with confidence and poise. On the foyer wall, a picture of two children, a girl and a boy, on either side of a tall man one-arm hugging each of them hung in the middle of a collage of what could only be family photos.

The detectives made themselves comfortable in a pair of matching barrel chairs off the spacious kitchen in a room they assumed functioned as the family room. Bookshelves filled with leather-bound classics and a few RK Travel books flanked both sides of a marble-fronted fireplace. Abby could picture herself nestled in this plush chair with a volume of Jane Austen's "Pride and Prejudice", losing herself to another time and another country. The rattling of a tea cup brought her back to the present day in Tumwater, Washington.

Amanda steered them to the point with a direct, "You came about Cory Austin?"

"Yes," Bridger replied. He summarized the pertinent highlights of the last week for her, beginning with the discovery of a new clue and ending with the attacks on Vanessa Hoyt Reilly and her neighbor Bertha Peck. Amanda's tanned face drained of color at the mention of the brutal attacks the two women had suffered.

"They're not out of the woods yet," said Abby, confident that Bridger was paying close attention to Mrs. Shaw's demeanor.

Remembering their omission with Toby Meyer in his interview, they next asked Amanda about her whereabouts the night Cory was killed. Her alibi seemed airtight. Police reports the detectives had reviewed said that she was staying at the beach with cousins, getting an early start on what was forecasted to be a beautiful weekend. If they thought it strange, considering it was a school night, they quickly dismissed their doubts, recalling that the last couple weeks of the school year is all wind-down to summer vacation. Even more so in a student's senior year, like Cory's. He should have enjoyed two weeks mostly taken up with commencement practice, senior trips, cleaning out lockers and skipping class. Lots of skipping class. If you hadn't learned it by then, you probably weren't going to. Unfortunately, he had been denied all of that.

Amanda told the same story to Bridger and Abby that she had told to the cops eleven years before. Her cousins still lived in the Portland metropolitan area. She would be happy to supply their latest contact information for verification of her story. That weekend at the Oregon coast had ended up even better than expected. No one in the family would forget it, partially due to the announcement of a long-anticipated pregnancy and partially due to the welcome news that her aunt's cancer had gone into remission.

As for her crush on Cory Austin, she freely admitted it. "I was a geeky, shy teenager. I had a brain, but not a lot going on in the looks and personality departments. That can be tough at that age. Cory was exceptionally smart, and nice to me. He seemed to 'get' me." She used air quotes. "But he didn't seem to like me in the same way I liked him." She shrugged. "High school was painful for me. I didn't really fit in anywhere." Her face clouded. "Cory's death was devastating. Not because I thought I stood a chance with him, but because he was so nice."

They asked her about reports of her stalking Cory, and she laughed it off as absurd. "What girl doesn't try to show up where their 'love interest' will probably be? But stalking? Seriously? Geez, I'm embarrassed it came across like that to some of the other kids. I had a simple schoolgirl crush on him."

Was she jealous of Cory's infatuation with Vanessa Hoyt?

"No, not really. All of the guys lusted after Vanessa Hoyt. Probably half of the girls did, too!" She laughed easily.

Amanda hadn't known about Frizz disappearing, nor about his severed paw. She paled again when she heard. "Oh, God, that's just awful. Poor Cari, having to find it."

"Did you know Cari well?" Abby asked.

"Fairly well. She worked on the newspaper with her brother, as did I. We did some projects at the Austin house, just because it was convenient. But interact at school? Not so much. She was a sophomore; me, a junior. You know how that goes. I didn't avoid her, just didn't really cross paths."

If the detectives wanted to put Amanda in a starring role for Cory's killer, their visit was fast casting doubt on that hope. She seemed about as likely as the current pope to have stabbed her classmate. After a few more questions aimed at cementing her alibi with her family at the beach, they turned their focus to Toby Meyer. Amanda's face darkened at the mention of his name, her shoulders drooping perceptibly. She had little of a specific nature to say about the guy but nothing of a positive one. Abby wanted to know why.

Amanda furrowed her brows and pursed her lips. "I can't really put my finger on what it was about Toby. He just – hm. He just wasn't right. There was something – something secretive about him."

He likes to dress in women's clothing, Abby thought, but figured that wasn't what Amanda meant. What other secrets did Toby have, or how else was he deceptive?

Amanda painted them a picture of a young man who sort of walked in the shadows but never missed a beat, wasn't quick to volunteer for projects unless it was a real plum but spent a lot of time on minutiae, a guy who carefully watched everything going on around him, almost like he was waiting for something to go wrong so he could pounce. An opportunist? Yeah, that's exactly what Toby Meyer reminded Amanda of, an opportunist.

"How did that manifest itself, Amanda?" Abby asked.

"Hm. Well, he just seemed to be where he thought he might be needed. Like the last issue of the *Post*. He was right there, ready to slide into Cory's place when Cory didn't show up and deadline was looming."

"Do you think he engineered that?"

She thought for a few seconds before shaking her head. "No. It just happened. Again, that opportunity thing."

"Any other times?"

"Yes, but I'm not remembering what they were. He was so much a part of the sidelines, like a presence you can't put your finger on. Slick. He was slick."

"Did Toby use drugs?"

Amanda shook her head again. "I don't know." She smiled. "Actually, I was so naïve, I didn't realize anyone used drugs. I mean, I heard that kids did, but I couldn't point to anyone specific."

"Did Toby do anything you'd consider mean? Ever see him punch another student, kick a dog, say, or throw rocks at cats?" Abby was floundering, unsure what direction she wanted the interview to take now.

"No."

Bridger sensed his partner's break in concentration and posed his own question. "Amanda, did you ever walk on the trail where Cory was found?"

She looked out the windows toward the quiet waters of the lake. "Yes. Yes, I did." She bit her lip. "Never after he was – never after. But a few times before. God, could that have been me?" She shivered.

They didn't think so. By now, they were convinced that Cory wasn't a random victim, but that was a thought they decided to keep to themselves. Amanda had only walked the Forest Park trails twice, according to her, and those two times had been with a friend from another school during the month of March, before that friend moved to California.

They wrapped up the interview and Amanda disappeared from the room for a few moments. When she returned, she carried with her the most recent addresses and phone numbers of her cousins. The detectives had little doubt by now that Amanda's family would back up her story of a beach weekend that fateful day eleven years ago. But they were troubled by her familiarity with the trail Cory died on. The timing was too close for comfort, and there are miles and miles of trails in Forest Park. Why had she been on that particular one? Coincidence? Neither liked dealing with coincidences. In fact, neither believed in them.

CHAPTER 23

"As we acquire more knowledge, things do not become more comprehensible, but more mysterious."
— *Albert Schweitzer*

The drive back from Tumwater Saturday afternoon left Abby and Bridger tired and deflated. Amanda Ferguson Shaw was not the smoking gun they hoped she would be, despite their lingering suspicions. With Vanessa Hoyt Reilly and her neighbor Bertha Peck still in critical condition, uncovering the identity of Cory's killer and the women's attacker seemed more important than ever. And more elusive.

Discouraged, they had not spoken much during the two hours and twenty-five minutes it took to get home. What little information Amanda had given them of any value had been about Toby Meyer, and it was more in the way of her gut feeling than tangible, useful facts. They already knew something was off with the guy. His livelihood dressing like Cher told them that much. But impersonating a celebrity wasn't criminal. Weirdness wasn't against the law. Murder was. They needed to find the person who had viciously killed a young man. Granted, it could still be Toby Meyer, but Abby wasn't convinced. Bridger always reserved judgment until he had hard evidence so, for now, he didn't have an opinion.

Late Saturday afternoon, Old Blue pulled to a stop at Abby's gate under a sky that looked as though it hadn't brightened all day. Bridger might have liked to share a meal and some conversation with Abby but she did not appear interested. With the promise that he would return at 7:30 the next morning, Bridger waved goodbye and drove off. In fact, he had a lot on his mind anyway. In a fortuitous turn of events, he had managed to unearth a phone number linked to the Children of Allah. Whoever controlled the group would probably not allow any of its members to take

149

outside calls, but Bridger had special persuasive powers he intended to put to the test. And tonight was as good a night as any to give it his best shot.

- - -

At the Dalton cottage, Abby dragged herself through her gate and down the short path to her front door before Malph found the energy to trot over and greet his mistress. Inside, she first fed her dog – priorities well ordered, if you were to ask Malph – and poured a short glass of pinot gris while massaging her neck. The hours in Blue had taken their toll on her back. Whenever she tried to explain to Bridger about the bouncing and its effects, he became even more deaf than usual.

Once she'd worked the kinks out and allowed the wine to help relax her tensions, she fished a couple pieces of pizza out of the refrigerator and sat down at her computer to go surfing. She set her phone on the desk beside her keyboard and brought up the picture she'd taken of the netsuke that dangled from Cari's necklace. As Cari had described, it appeared to be a figure of a woman crouching beneath a wok-shaped hat. Interesting, but not particularly intricate. Abby owned much nicer netsukes herself.

She typed in various keywords and explored Google images.

"Look at this one," she said to Malph. He glanced up from his place at her feet, most likely hoping she was showing him something along the lines of a Milkbone or offering a bite of her cold pizza. Indeed, what she had on the screen was a foo dog netsuke. A bit far afield of the mark. She varied her word searches, but gave up after a half hour. She was impatient to find useful information, and no crouching woman had appeared. So she abandoned the subject of netsukes and went exploring more sinister avenues.

First, she wandered into "Asian hate crimes" and "Japanese discrimination" and "Pearl Harbor survivors Northwest". Maybe the results would be better with "Japanese cat mutilations" or "Asian blood rituals" or…hell, she didn't know. Her fingers took over for her. And led her to Asian secret societies. While something of a broad subject, maybe it could be narrowed down a little. She had to start somewhere.

Abby waded through a couple dozen sites that appeared to be more social than serious, tending toward dinner parties and costume balls, for lack of a better description. A few seemed to have organized for spontaneous political purposes, much like the "Occupy" movements of the early 2010s in America. But a couple of the groups, with sites as secretive as they themselves seemed to be, piqued Abby's curiosity. She focused on one called the Devil & Dragon Society. Particulars were sketchy, but she gleaned from her sources that the Devil & Dragon Society was an underground group of intellectuals and rebels who originally joined together for the purpose of shaping Japan's political future.

According to something called Floor13.gov, a site which a privileged few, like Abby, had access to, the Society dated back to the Sino-Japanese War in the mid-1890s. Much of what was attributed to their actions appeared to be for the greater good. But they also had a more ominous side. Numbering among their members were a few officers with, according to a couple reports, "the special function of persuader". Some of those officers seemed to have interpreted their job descriptions to be more along the lines of assassins. Their targets looked random, but Abby had scant knowledge of Japan's history. What she could tell was that, once in their gunsights, you were pretty much toast. Further information showed that, in order to set the officers, including these special persuaders, apart from the other members, they wore a distinctive netsuke which identified them as holding that rank.

Abby sat back in wonder. Just when she had given up on her netsuke research, it had come looking for her, it seemed. Originally attracted to netsukes for their unique and beautiful carvings, she had no idea they had ever possessed an evil function. What one article said was that these miniature sculptures had a dual use, suggesting that they were more than decorative. At the time they were invented, in the 17th century, the robes worn by men had no pockets, so the netsukes hung from their belts and had tiny secret compartments. The most intriguing ones were minuscule boxes that allowed their owners to store personal items they wished to carry with them, much like a lady's tiny purse. Or, for a special persuader, possibly some curare.

The Devil & Dragon netsukes given to the persuaders were carved with the member's unique personal identifying symbol, like a sitting pig or a sleeping dog or two squirrels intertwined. In

151

addition, it also had the triple shield that served as the Society's unifying sign. Regular members merely had the triple shield netsuke, which served as their membership token, without the extra ornamentation.

From further online sites that took special permission to gain access, Abby learned that the formation of the D&D had been seen as necessary in order to keep the country's representatives who were serving in the Diet – the Japanese form of parliament, somewhat similar to our Congress – walking a straight line, or at least walking the line the Society wanted them to walk. These intellectual ideologists had a vision for Japan that they wished to not be confounded by their government. But ideology worked only up to a point. Beyond that, it had been found that physical pain or threat of death worked even better. And sometimes it worked better yet if the threat was occasionally carried out. Over the years, the D&D Society had repurposed itself so that, in modern times, it leaned more toward greed and violence and had shed much of its former altruistic bent.

Abby had no idea what this might have to do with Rose Austin and, right now, she didn't care. Her eyelids had grown heavy and her mind was spinning. The clock read 12:58. It promised to be another night lying awake for hours before sleep would come, but she could no longer stay at the computer. She had a damned press conference to attend in the morning. How in the hell had that happened? Damn this cold case commitment. How long had it been since she'd curled up with a good book and snuggled with her dog? *Far too long,* she muttered in answer to her unspoken question.

"Come on, Malph. Time for bed."

The bulldog hoisted himself up and followed her to their room, unaware that his mistress's mind was working overtime.

CHAPTER 24

"New roads, new ruts."

– G.K. Chesterton

Sunday morning, Abby called Bridger before 6:00 a.m. "Pick me up in half an hour." She didn't wait for an answer, just severed the connection.

The press conference was scheduled for 10:00 o'clock and they didn't have anything concrete to tell reporters, not that she really cared, but maybe they could at least eliminate one of their possible suspects and narrow down their search. It would help to be able to announce that much and then get the hell out of there quickly. Press conferences were a waste of time, if you asked Abigail Dalton. They had work to do. Urgent work. She had an idea that had taken root late last night, the seed of which had germinated and grown as she slept – or, rather, drifted in and out of sleep – and now she felt that she might be onto something of substance. The solution was still a long way off and the killer's motive still far beyond fuzzy but it was the best direction they had open to them yet. She allowed a little ray of hope to sneak into what had been days of roadblocks. Malph nudged her leg.

"Oh, yeah, guy. Sorry. Daydreaming here." Malph never waited more than five minutes past his idea of meal time before stepping forward with a reminder. And meal time, for him, was defined as ten minutes after Abby's feet hit the floor in the morning and 7:00 o'clock sharp in the evening, or ten minutes after she returned home from wherever she'd gotten off to, whichever came first. He wasn't one to let the rules slide either.

With Malph's stomach satisfied, Abby splashed a couple handfuls of cold water on her face, brushed her teeth, put on a minimum amount of make-up and pulled her hair into a smooth ponytail. Outside, the sun had already begun burning through yesterday's persistent clouds, steering Abby toward the choice of a crisp white blouse with French cuffs, black jeans – as close as she came to formal attire, begrudgingly donned for the television cameras – and a lightweight blue-gray blazer. That was the most effort she would make. It wasn't as though she planned to come home and watch herself on TV.

At 6:32, she heard CON idling out at the gate. Leaving Malph lounging in the sun, she locked up and went to meet Bridger.

"You're late," she said, as she clicked the seatbelt home. "I need coffee."

They drove away toward the Human Bean. As Abby finished adjusting her position in the seat, she glanced over at Bridger. What she could see was a blurry profile staring straight ahead. Even her sunglasses weren't helping to define him clearly – something which never really happened anymore – but he seemed unnaturally quiet and stiff.

"Hey, everything okay?"

"Tell you in a minute."

"What?" She hoped it had nothing to do with Zach again. Bridger's full attention would be required today.

"Hold on." They had already reached the Bean, it being only a couple of short blocks from Abby's cottage. Marla leaned out of the kiosk window and greeted them with her heartiest smile.

"Hi, Miss Dalton! Hi, Mr. Flynn! What can I getcha?"

Abby wanted an extra bold brew – it sounded like she was going to need it – and Bridger surprised them both by ordering the same, no cream. Bridger paid, including a nice tip for his favorite barista as Abby observed, sensing his false cheer toward Marla.

"What gives?"

Marla handed their drinks out to them.

"Bridger?"

He drove ahead and pulled into an empty spot, leaned his head back and closed his eyes. "Got a call just before I left the houseboat. Bertha Peck died this morning."

Abby groaned and then clasped her hands in front of her face. "Oh, damn," she said, quietly. "Damn, damn, damn."

"Yeah. She never regained consciousness."

The two detectives sat like that for another five minutes, each dealing with the news in their own way and trying to figure out how they should proceed, or even whether they should proceed. Abby went back to doubting their investigation had any value at all. In fact, she wondered, were they doing more harm than good? Intuitively, they both were aware of all the rhetoric about the person who wielded the knife was the bad guy. Like the saying: Guns don't kill people; people kill people. It still didn't make them feel any less guilty. If only they had gotten to Bertha earlier. If only they had caught Cory's killer already. If only, if only, if only.

It was Bridger who broke the silence. "So what's up?" His voice sounded weary to Abby.

"Huh?"

"You called early, said come in half an hour. Why the rush? What's up?"

"Oh, just this shitty little thing called a press conference."

Bridger chuckled despite his desolate mood. "Yeah. Fun."

"No, it's not fun. It's crap. I'd say we skip it –"

Abby felt Bridger's head whip around.

"I'd say we skip it except that Capt. Shearer's got enough on his hands with the child snatching from Tryon Park. And now this."

Bridger nodded. "He sure does." It had been six days and almost no progress had been made on finding the toddler kidnapped from her mother in the heavily-wooded Lake Oswego park. Until last evening, Abby would have said the same thing about their cold case, a years-old murder that took place in Portland's beautiful Forest Park. But now maybe, just maybe, she was onto a lead that could bring justice to their victim.

"Seriously, Abs, why the early call?"

She sighed. "Well, we have this damnable press conference at 10:00. We need to come up with something to tell the reporters."

"Capt. Shearer –"

Abby put up a hand. "Yeah, yeah, the captain has some idea of what to say, I know. But we haven't exactly cleared things up much since we started working the case. In fact, now we have two dead and one fighting for her life." She wiped her eyes and sat up with a start as something occurred to her. "Oh, hell. Do you think the press has connected Vanessa Reilly and Cory Austin? And have they caught wind of Bertha Peck's death?"

Even as she asked these questions, she winced, knowing the answers. Of course the press knew the connection between Vanessa and Cory. The two were classmates. That would be a cakewalk to find out. And Bertha Peck was Vanessa's neighbor, attacked the day after Vanessa had been attacked and in the same way. Stabbed. Just like Cory Austin was stabbed eleven years ago. Stabbed just a few short days after the new "cold case squad" was formed. These were investigative reporters they were dealing with. And, while Abby detested reporters of any kind, she would begrudgingly admit that most of them were highly proficient at their jobs. No doubt they had been keeping a watchful eye on both of the women's conditions. They may have even known about Bertha's death before Capt. Shearer did. This turn of events complicated their case beyond the obvious. And now more than ever they needed something positive to report at the press conference or, as Abby would say, they were in deep shit.

She turned to face Bridger. "Okay, here's what's happening. We're going to Toby Meyer's apartment, right now, ask those questions we didn't get answers to the last time. Like what was his alibi the night Cory Austin was killed. I think we're going to find out that Mr. Meyer has been hiding something, but it's not murder."

Bridger looked at his partner in admiration. It was actually a good idea and he was delighted she had taken charge this morning. He felt another guilt pang over allowing himself to be sidetracked by Zach's entanglement with the Children of Allah. His son's new life with them could be sorted out in a couple of weeks, likely without any serious consequences between now and then. The people involved in the Austin case, well, they were another matter. Nothing about their current case had come without consequences so far.

CHAPTER 25

"Every man is a borrower and a mimic;
life is theatrical and literature a quotation."
- Ralph Waldo Emerson

The detectives didn't bother stopping at Toby Meyer's landlady's door. They decided to let her sleep in this morning. It was Toby they wanted to talk to. Why bother with a middleman – or middlewoman in this case? Eventually, though, they feared their fist pounding might awaken her anyway, for Toby proved to be a heavy sleeper. It took nearly two minutes of nonstop knocking for the Cher impersonator to come to his door, and then he only opened it the length of the security chain.

Peering out through bloodshot eyes, he sounded grouchy. "What?"

"We need some answers, Toby." Abby stood directly in front of the apartment's resident, who did not look at all rested this morning. He had neglected to remove his false eyelashes after the previous night's show and much of Cher's heavy makeup remained on his gaunt face. Even through the crack in the door, Abby was almost envious of the negligee he wore, or at least the garish color of it. Some might say it was flashy but, on the right woman, it could be called sexy. Next to her, Abby felt Bridger struggling to stifle a snicker.

"Come on, open up."

"Jesus, it's not even 7:30! And it's a Sunday, for Christ's sake!"

"Watch your mouth around the lady."

It was Abby's turn to stifle a snicker. Bridger never swore, but Abby did not have similar qualms about the use of colorful words.

Toby reluctantly opened the door and stepped back to allow the detectives entry. He struck a defiant pose, though, arms crossed over his coral and lime lace-covered chest. This was another one of those times that Abby sorely missed her vision. She would have to rely on Bridger to take in every detail about the apartment, do a thorough scan of the place and its resident and describe it all to her later. He rarely overlooked anything pertinent, but sometimes a woman's perspective made a significant difference.

They didn't expect Toby to offer them coffee or tea, or indeed any social amenity, so Abby cut to the chase. "We didn't get a chance to ask you about your alibi last time we spoke."

Toby smirked. "My alibi?"

"The night that Cory Austin was killed," she prompted.

"Oh."

"What did you think I was referring to?"

"Oh, nothing. Yeah, Cory Austin. Yeah." He rubbed his face. Cher's wig would have greatly improved his appearance, considering that the false black lashes looked out of place with just his short blonde hair. It didn't help that some of the adhesive had let go at the corners of his eyelids, allowing the falsies to flap with each blink. "Um, yeah, that night I was at a senior party up on Mt. Hood."

Abby frowned. "A senior party?"

"Uh-huh, yeah. I *was* a senior, you know, dear one."

"Wasn't that a school night?"

"Ha! Yeah, a school night. Like that mattered." He glanced at her, then did a double take. "Oh, hell, you're serious. Um, yeah, it was a school night." Toby watched closely as Bridger made a circuit of his living room.

Bridger had been wandering around slowly, letting Abby ask the questions. She seemed to have come with her own agenda so, as usual, he would make the most of his best sense, vision, while his partner gathered the audio portion of the information they had come for. Toby's apartment was small and mostly tidy, not given over to much in the way of personal items like family photos or meaningless baubles. As Bridger reached the doorway to a tiny hall with two doors – a bedroom and a bath, probably – he thought he heard a bump. Abby glanced his way, which confirmed his suspicion.

Toby's ears reddened, although Abby missed it. "That'll be Gaga, darling. She gets impatient."

"Girlfriend?"

He laughed. "Sure, dear one. Let's say that."

"O-kay. Where were we?"

Bridger continued his tour of the room, Toby keeping a wary eye on him. "Um, school night."

"Yes. Didn't your parents care that you were out at a party on a school night?"

He laughed again, this time without even a hint of humor. "My parents. Let's see, did they care? Um, no. Not ever."

Abby wished she could see the fellow's face, for she believed he would look as lost as the child his voice made him sound like. She was certain they were getting close to the reason Toby Meyer had chosen the path that he had. Generally, Abby didn't believe in blaming parents for everything that a child did wrong, but sometimes they needed to shoulder about 99 percent of the responsibility. And this was looking like one of those times.

Gaga started making noise again, now with more animation.

"We'll wrap this up, Toby. Can you give us a list of who was at this party on Mt. Hood, exactly where it was, and what time? And then we'll check it out. That should eliminate you as a suspect." Or not, she didn't add.

"Sure." The bluster had gone out of Toby Meyer. Abby almost felt sorry for him. And she hoped that maybe he might someday find a way out of this lifestyle of confusion to a better happiness. He probably wouldn't, but one never knew. Miracles do happen.

- - -

Back in the car, Bridger tweaked the adjustment on his hearing aid in anticipation of the upcoming press conference, plus he wanted to hear whatever Abby had learned from their encounter with Toby Meyer. He had seen little in the apartment to set off alarms. If the fellow wanted to have a relationship with Lady Gaga, who Bridger guessed was another man from the show, well, that was his choice. It might reinforce their idea that Toby had a possible crush on Cory Austin but Bridger hadn't found any evidence so far to support that either. And, anyway, even if they did, would it really mean anything?

"So can we eliminate him?"

"Almost. We need that list of kids at the party to confirm it, but I think it will absolve him of further suspicion."

Abby spent the next fifteen minutes filling Bridger in on what she had learned from her Internet surfing Saturday night. She wanted for him to commend her with a "Good job" or play devil's advocate so she would have a chance to pick out the weak spots in the theory. Instead, he stayed silent for a long while and she wondered whether the idea of a secret society hit too close to home for Bridger, considering Zach's recent defection to the Children of Allah.

When he finally spoke, his words surprised Abby. "I think you may have just breathed new hope into the case, and into solving Bertha Peck's murder."

She smiled despite the gloomy news the morning had begun with. How could the sun shine so brightly when a woman had died such a senseless death? It was reminiscent of the day Cory Austin had died. Beautiful, clear, blue sky, one of Portland's finest by all appearances. But the ugliness of a young man's death put a shadow over the sun and sucked the light right out of the world.

Bridger started CON's engine. "Well, we're already late. Nate – sorry, Capt. Shearer wanted us there by 8:30 to prep for the news conference."

"Shit."

CHAPTER 26

"In politics a week is a very long time."

- Harold Wilson

Capt. Shearer did not notice that the two detectives were almost forty minutes late. As expected, the Tryon Creek abduction still occupied much of his attention. What little attention it didn't occupy was taken up by Bertha Peck's death early that morning.

Abby asked, in her usual pointed manner, "Did Peck have help leaving this world, Captain?"

The question almost seemed to take him by surprise. Knowing Shearer for one of the top professionals in the Bureau, Abby chocked it up to fatigue. Had the man been home even once during the past week or so? The bags under his eyes carried the look of limited and restless sleep.

"My detective is investigating now. I haven't had a report from him yet. We do know that Mrs. Peck was pronounced at 5:51 by one of the nurses doing her rounds before shift change."

"Which is when?"

"Seven o'clock."

"She could have been dead for a while."

Capt. Shearer shook his head. "There were monitors."

"Hmpf." Abby had forever been skeptical of monitors and other types of gauges. In fact, she believed there were ways around every machine made by man. "What about Vanessa Reilly?"

"No change in her condition. And, before you ask, yes, she is being watched."

"What do we say to the press?"

"You don't have to say anything to the press about Bertha Peck or Vanessa Reilly. It's not your problem." He smiled in a conspiratorial fashion. "I will handle it. Considering my detectives are hard at work on the cases, the answers will necessarily be of a somewhat generic nature."

"Thanks, Captain." Abby added, "We would greatly appreciate any updates, though, whenever they become available."

"Certainly." Shearer nodded.

Bridger and Abby moved on to their reason for being there, spending just shy of twenty minutes with the captain going over what the "cold case squad" should say to the reporters about the Cory Austin case. Since they had little evidence of a concrete nature, they would play the game of vague comments and obfuscation, a term and concept Abby had come to know and love, especially when applied to press conferences.

The bright spot of the morning came when a uniformed officer poked his head in the door and asked if he could borrow the captain for a quick word in the hallway. Shearer returned smiling. There had been a minor breakthrough in the child snatching case, enough of one to maybe take the heat off of the lack of progress in their cold case. Maybe. Hell, progress in any case was welcome as far as Abby was concerned. And, while she felt they had made some headway, she wasn't about to share their newest theory yet. It was too soon and too uncertain. She fingered her watch, growing impatient to get done with this nuisance the media called the public's right to know and get on with their investigation. Jesus, she hated reporters and their incessant meddling.

To make matters worse, it looked like the press conference would be getting started at least ten minutes behind schedule. Abby could not understand what held things up. Everyone had been present and in place long in advance of 10:00 o'clock. It seemed to be an unwritten rule that you never begin on time.

When they finally got the room under control and Capt. Shearer was introduced by his public information officer, he opened by sharing the good news about their development in the Tryon Park kidnapping, which got reporters all excited for about a minute and a half. Their attention span, as Abby well knew, lasted only as long as it took to write the latest breakthrough on their notepads, or iPads, or whatever the hell it was that they used these days. Then they thirsted for more. Nature of the beast, she guessed.

Once the thrill brought on by the announcement of the break in the abduction case died down, Shearer explained to the press there had been an appointment of two outside contractors – Abby and Bridger – to work on old unsolveds for Portland Police Bureau, carefully avoiding the words "cold case squad".

"As you know, the first case these detectives are looking into involves a teenager named Cory Austin who was murdered in Forest Park shortly before his graduation back in 2002. Some possible new evidence came to light within the past few days, causing Ms. Dalton and Mr. Flynn to re-examine the files and re-interview some witnesses. They have been gracious enough to come in this morning to share some of their methods and speak about how they are conducting their investigation. I believe Ms. Dalton has agreed to be the spokesperson, but please remember their time is limited."

Capt. Shearer ceded the microphone to Abby, who walked forward wearing a businesslike expression, which was about a thousand times friendlier than she felt toward the people in the room. Bridger stepped up beside his partner, intending to be her eyes in as covert a manner as possible. For the next three minutes, Abby gave the reporters a quick rundown of their approach to the handling of an old unsolved, and the Cory Austin case specifically. Then she took a deep breath and opened the floor to general questions. Eleven or twelve hands shot up immediately. Bridger knew that Abby would want to avoid the most eager and the most familiar among them, so he pointed to a nondescript woman in the third row.

The young reporter asked the obvious. What was the new evidence? Abby answered with what everyone expected, "We can't divulge that information at this time." She loved saying that line. It was like sticking her tongue out at the media while waving her hands with her thumbs in her ears.

She looked around as though deciding who to choose next and pointed vaguely toward the back of the room. Someone would shout out a question; she didn't have to be precise. Most reporters didn't care about making eye contact; they just wanted to gain control of the floor. She heard a voice she knew, a voice that had been on Portland television for over two decades. It was a voice that Abby despised. She gritted her teeth. Beside her, Bridger stiffened in response to her tension.

"Where did the new evidence come from? Can you tell us that?"

In fact, Abby could, but the history she had with this fellow struck a stubbornness chord within her and she answered his question without giving him anything of intrinsic value. "Yes, Kerry, a family member came forward with it. Next?"

While Kerry tried to ask a follow-up, as Abby knew he would, someone in the front row wanted to know how she and Mr. Flynn had gotten together to form this cold case squad. Mr. Flynn heard enough of that question to jump in. Besides, he figured that, if he took the opportunity to speak, no one would grow curious about his silence. And it would allow space and time to deflect the anger emanating from his partner beside him.

"First of all, we are contractors working on old unsolveds, as Capt. Shearer said." He intentionally avoided using the words "cold case squad", figuring the fewer times they heard that phrase the less likely they were to repeat it. "Ms. Dalton and I worked together over the years on several task forces, beginning with the one formed to capture Snowy Forbes." Bridger was in comfortable territory now. He rambled on about old times until someone hollered another question, this one about who they had been talking to since they reopened the case. Abby trotted out her version of "no comment" again.

Next, a round-cheeked man with a bored, self important expression slowly stood up and asked, in a grating whine, if they had made any real progress in the past week. Not what progress they had made, but if they had made any. Abby wanted to ask him if he'd had a bowel movement in the past week but, instead, she answered, "Yes, we have. Quite a lot, actually. As a matter of fact, we are at this moment closing in on the killer."

Bridger heard that, too. If he'd been a cursing man, he would have come forth with some rich words himself right about then. As it was, he rapped his partner's shin with the side of his shoe behind the dais, just to get her attention and discourage her from volunteering any more off-the-script comments.

Pencils flew across tablets, giving Abby an enormous amount of satisfaction and giving Capt. Shearer a sudden bout of heartburn. He might have been thinking that Bridger would have been a better spokesperson whether he could hear the questions or not. Abigail Dalton simply had too unpredictable a temper. The woman needed to be muzzled.

A few questions were asked about Vanessa Hoyt Reilly and her neighbor Bertha Peck, which received pat answers. Fortunately for Bridger and Abby, as Shearer had assured them, those cases were not theirs. They might have appeared to be connected, but they belonged to the detectives assigned to them, not the "cold case squad," which the press persisted in calling them, nudging Abby dangerous close to the point of eruption.

After the allotted time allowance, Capt. Shearer cut the questions off, to Abby's vast relief. She exited abruptly. Bridger followed her out of the room, steaming. When she stopped long enough for him to catch up, he glared at her, red faced. She knew he was angry, but couldn't see how upset he had become. For once, she thanked the macular degeneration.

Abby didn't want to be there, she didn't want to be part of a "cold case squad," and she didn't want to play nice with reporters. Her partner was livid and she didn't want that either, but she couldn't seem to do anything about it. So she said exactly what she knew would get to Bridger most. "I think that went well, don't you?"

Without waiting for a reply, she turned on her heel and walked off to the ladies' room. He would stew outside for a while, maybe with Shearer, maybe alone. She didn't care. What would Shearer do because of her mouth? Fire them? Well, that would suit her just fine. She hadn't wanted any of this to begin with. Besides, she really did think they were closing in on the killer. And thinking back over the week, they had come quite a long way from Cari's discovery of the cat's paw. The cat's paw. The damned cat's paw…

"Oh, hell!"

CHAPTER 27

"Just as courage imperils life, fear protects it."
- Leonardo da Vinci

Abby crashed through the bathroom door, nearly knocking down a female sergeant heading in.

"Sorry, officer. Excuse me. Bridger! Bridger!" Rarely had anyone heard Abigail Dalton yelling in fear and few in the police bureau had ever seen a blind woman running and screaming in the hallways of Central Precinct. Bridger momentarily forgot his anger when he caught sight of Abby rushing gracelessly toward him, her face a mask of raw terror.

"Shit, Bridger. Take me home! I've got to get home right now!"

He didn't waste time asking her why. Once again, he took it on faith that she had a good reason. Her word was enough. He grabbed her arm and held onto it as they ran toward the parking garage to retrieve CON. Thankfully, the media trucks had already left the area. Add to that traffic on Sunday was light, especially in the heart of the city, which wouldn't begin to come to life until after noon. Nonetheless, the trip to Abby's townhouse took thirteen minutes. Even though that was a near record time for the distance, to Abby it was an eternity. A woman with an unusually stoic mien, today she couldn't sit still. Her heart palpitated and she was short of breath. Even Bridger could hear what sounded like panting. Her hands shook and she chewed the inside of her lip. Hot tears leaked from the corners of her eyes.

Bridger pushed his little car hard, ignoring traffic signals as they turned to yellow, once or twice blowing through red lights when he could see no approaching vehicles. Beside him, his partner agonized. She twisted the material of her blazer into crumpled wads of blue-grey silk. Now and then she laid her head against the side window, but sat back up as though an electric current had shot through her. And she rocked. Lord, did she rock. And she sighed – huge, heavy sighs, which turned into heart-wrenching moans.

Bridger didn't speak. If Abby wanted to tell him something, she would. Right now, she seemed incapable of forming words. Moaning and sighing were the only sounds escaping her.

At last, the smart car slid into Abby's parking lot. She had the passenger door open and was out before Bridger had brought CON to a full stop. He noticed that Abby's gate hung open several inches. That was odd, considering how meticulous she was about keeping her place locked up tight. She disappeared inside the yard and was barely out of his sight when he heard her anguished scream. "Oh, no!" He didn't realize she was capable of such volume. "No! Malph! Malph!"

Bridger ran after his friend and partner. He found her standing in the middle of her herb garden, looking confused and dazed, turning first in one direction, then in another, yelling her dog's name. Finally, she doubled over and crumpled to the ground on her knees, head in her hands, shoulders sagging.

"He's got Malph. Oh, dear God, he's got Malph."

Bridger sat down beside her. All he could think to do was hold her. Weak with emotion, she leaned into him, as a small child might after a bad dream.

"Bridger, he's got my Malph." Tears flooded her eyes and cramped fingers dug into the flesh of his arm. They squeezed with an intensity born of white hot anguish. He winced.

For once, Bridger didn't know what to say. He stroked her hair gently and hugged her close, hoping to help her find solace in his arms. They sat there for a minute or two like that, her shoulders shaking, both feeling lost. Bridger pushed back at the guilt that kept trying to leach its way in. If he hadn't insisted on working this cold case, Abby's beloved Malph wouldn't be in danger. Bridger wouldn't blame Abby if she hated him right now. He was the one who had gotten them into this and now the one thing that mattered most to his partner was gone. Malph was far more than a dog to Abby; he was the child she could never have. At least Bridger had Zach and JJ. All Abby had was that silly albino bulldog. And now he had been taken from her.

Slowly, a sound other than Abby's sobs crept into Bridger's consciousness and he felt Abby's body stiffen and twist. He looked in the direction she had turned. An elderly woman stood in the adjacent yard, waving toward them and calling out.

"Ms. Dalton! Ms. Dalton!"

Abby pushed herself up off the ground and struggled to her feet, with Bridger trying to assist. Awkwardly, they made their way over to the fence separating the two properties. "Mrs. Fitzhenry?" Abby said, wiping her face with the back of her hand and attempting to compose herself. She knew her neighbor by name, but only because the older woman had brought over some kind of baked goods, brownies maybe – Abby hadn't really cared – the day Abby moved in, and introduced herself. Abby had been polite but made a point of keeping to herself afterwards. She believed privacy made the best neighbors. Whatever could this woman want now? It wasn't really the time for chit chat.

"That's right, Ms. Dalton." She smiled as though pleased that Abby would remember her name, but then her expression grew somber. "Ms. Dalton, are you okay?"

Abby took a deep breath, as yet uncertain whether she could trust her voice. "Yes, thank you." Bridger stood beside her, watching and listening carefully. He sensed this could be important.

"You're sure?"

Abby caught something curious in her neighbor's tone. "Yes, Mrs. Fitzhenry, I am sure. Why do you ask?"

"Well, there was a man in your yard earlier. He seemed to be sneaking around. It didn't look right."

"Well, no, of course it wouldn't."

"No. And Malph didn't like him."

Abby gasped at the mention of her dog. "Malph? You know Malph?"

Mrs. Fitzhenry winked, a subtlety lost on Abby. "Oh, sure. Malph and I are good buddies. He often visits me when you're gone."

"How in the –"

Mrs. Fitzhenry crooked her finger in a beckoning fashion, "Come this way." Abby followed her over to a corner hedge. "See here, the fence stops before this hedge, and this bush is quite loose, so Malph just waddles his way right on through." She smiled, displaying more gums than teeth. "He doesn't like to be alone, you know."

As if on cue, Malph came trotting up behind Mrs. Fitzhenry. A tiny whine escaped him when he saw Abby. He plunged into the bush, quickly came out into his own yard and raked a paw down his mistress's leg, at just about the spot Bridger had kicked with his shoe earlier. It took every ounce of strength for Abby to maintain even a scintilla of self-control, and not the least of it due to the renewed pain in her leg.

- - -

Later, inside her own cottage, Abby discussed with Bridger what they had learned from their unlikely witness. As he left Abby to love up her dog, clearly worlds beyond relieved that Malph was okay, Bridger had gone out to the car to retrieve the pictures they had taken of their possible suspects in the Austin case.

As he showed them one by one to Mrs. Fitzhenry, she proved to have excellent eyes and wholly reliable description skills. So now they knew who had been in Abby's yard, likely in an effort to grab Malph. But why?

Of course, Abby believed that she had brought this on herself. She'd swear up and down that the bold assertion she had foolishly blurted out before the television cameras – the one about them closing in on the killer – had driven Cory's killer to repeat his "warning" of eleven years ago by coming after her pet, just as he had done with the Austins' cat Frizz. Given the chance, he would have stolen Malph and cut off his paw in an effort to silence Abby, just as he had done with Frizz.

The man didn't understand who he was dealing with. Harming one hair on her dog's body would have been tantamount to attacking a member of her family, which would only have served to enrage Abigail Grace Dalton. They both knew that she would have stopped at nothing thereafter to utterly and completely destroy the man. The result, naturally, wouldn't have been pleasant. As things stood, just having made the attempt set in motion events he wasn't going to like.

CHAPTER 28

"Hope, deceitful as it is, serves to lead us to the end of life along an agreeable road."
                                                    - La Rochefoucauld

For once, noon came and went and Abby didn't think of food. The events of the morning had reduced her appetite to nothing more than a vague concept. Her mind whirled, busily putting in order the facts they already knew and searching for slots to plug in the suppositions they had come up with. There were still too many loose ends dangling about to suit Abby, but it was just a matter of time before they all fell into place. That's the way it always worked with Bridger and her.

Their next logical move should be another visit to Cari Austin. A few days back, Abby had taken a cursory look at a tiny figurine known as a netsuke that Ms. Austin wore around her neck, but Abby had only paid attention to the shape it represented, the crouching woman. She had felt an instant connection to it, along with the sensation that it held immense importance somehow. The nature of that importance had been murky, too ill-defined to lead Abby in any discernible direction. Because of that murkiness, it hadn't occurred to her to study any detail carved into it on the reverse side but now that little omission might hold the key to a murder motive.

Absently, Abby reached down and rubbed Malph's stubby ears while she telephoned Cari Austin to inquire about how soon they might come by to look at the netsuke again. As she murmured into her cell phone, Bridger answered a call on his. Capt. Shearer wanted to know just what had happened that morning to make them flee the building in a hair-on-fire panic. Fortunately, the press hadn't caught wind of their sudden flight from headquarters or it might have put an entirely new spin on the freshly formed cold case squad, an unwanted label that had attached to them despite their best efforts to discourage the media from their fond use of the term.

Bridger assured the captain that everything was fine, false alarm, although he left out the part about them having indeed identified who the killer was. He wanted to have further confirmation or, in reality, absolute certainty beyond that of Abby's neighbor's account. While Mrs. Fitzhenry seemed on top of things, one couldn't be too careful when it came to making accusations of murder. Bridger believed in being utterly positive. Abby was setting up the appointment that would place them on the road to doing just that.

- - -

Less than an hour later, after dropping off Malph at a safe house – otherwise known as his chosen doggie day care, run by a retired Oregon State Police lieutenant – Abby and Bridger sat at Cari Austin's dining room table, the young woman seated with them wearing an anxious expression and a shapeless puce sweater over an off-white blouse. Fall had fully entrenched itself now. The days were staying cooler, but so far remained dry. The forecasters said that was all about to change though. Light cardigans were on their way out in favor of coats and rain jackets. Umbrellas would not be far behind.

As Cari and Bridger looked on, Abby held her magnifier in one hand and the netsuke in the other. After two minutes, she surfaced from her intense scrutiny with excitement shining on her face. "Look here, Bridger. Just look!" She shoved the little figurine across the broad expanse of mahogany to her partner, along with her magnifier. The mark of the triple shield was unmistakable, even to Abby. Bridger examined the netsuke for a long time before he said, "Huh!"

"Yeah!"

Abby had already explained the significance of the triple shield to her partner: that it served to identify the netsuke's owner as a member of the Devil & Dragon Society. The presence of the shield mark on the crouching woman netsuke held huge meaning if what they believed turned out to be true. Meanwhile, though, they had no intention of sharing any of their suspicions with Cari. While it was quite possibly a breakthrough development, the younger woman didn't need to know all of the specifics yet. For a bit longer, she could continue to think of her mother as just another shy Japanese immigrant. At Cari's look of puzzled expectation, Bridger once again issued forth a ration of empty words said with high enthusiasm that seemed to mollify her, at least for the time being.

Next, Abby asked if Cari had found any more of her mother's belongings from the years that she lived in Japan: old books, papers, journals, keepsakes, trinkets, souvenirs, anything that looked personal from that era. Good fortune continued to rain on them, for it turned out that she had recently run across some boxes she thought might have come over with her mom way back then. They had what appeared to be Japanese characters printed on their sides. She had not yet gone through them. In fact, they had not been opened in what looked like a very long time, judging from the brittle, discolored packing tape, maybe not at all since arriving in Portland. Cari had never seen them before. The detectives were welcome to take a look inside for themselves.

Abby smiled at Bridger, and her partner smiled back. Neither especially relished the idea of an afternoon spent pawing through piles of forgotten old stuff but both knew that was often where they found their most valuable clues and sometimes even the solutions to their cases. So they accepted Ms. Austin's offer of tea and settled in for a long session of old-fashioned searching.

- - -

While the detectives busied themselves rifling around in her mother's possessions, Cari channeled her nervous energy into baking, a direction Abby could fully appreciate. As the dining room table transformed itself into a sort of time machine, spinning tales of Rose Austin's escapades from the 1970s and 1980s, the new lady of the house took over the adjacent kitchen, scurrying about, measuring cups of flour into a bowl, adding in teaspoons of baking soda and salt, tossing in a few pinches of herbs and beating in eggs and cream. Somewhere close to twenty minutes later, the scent of rosemary emanated from the oven and Abby's stomach growled without shame, loudly reminding her that she had skipped lunch.

Their tea was refreshed and a dish of butter slid in alongside one of the boxes, with a knife perched atop the pale

172

yellow slab, which was soon accompanied by fresh, hot scones and a stack of napkins.

They were on their second box and their third scone when Cari exclaimed, "Oh! I almost forgot!" She took off upstairs, leaving Bridger looking at his partner and wondering aloud whether they were expected to follow. Abby responded by buttering the remaining bite of her rosemary scone and sliding it onto her tongue. "Mmmm."

She heard footsteps pounding down the flight of stairs and then Cari burst into the room again. "I found Cory's cell phone." She tossed it onto the table with a triumphant flourish, then skipped back into the kitchen to work on a second round of baking.

CHAPTER 29

*"When Fortune empties her chamberpot on your head,
smile and say, 'We are going to have a summer shower.'"*
                                                    - John A. Macdonald

Abby and Bridger looked at each other in stunned disbelief. They simultaneously grabbed for Cory's phone but Bridger came out the victor, holding it high in the air like a champion boxer who just won the latest round. Abby called him an asshole but in a barely audible voice. Bridger looked the phone over, marveling at how far technology had come in the past decade. His natural response was to power it up but, after eleven years, its natural response was to lie dormant in his hand.

"Did you happen to find the charger, too?" Abby called over to Cari, saying a silent prayer with her fingers crossed.

"Huh?"

"The charger?"

"Oh. Uh, no, no charger." Cari stopped measuring flour and wiped her hands on a towel. "I guess that's a problem, isn't it?"

"Sort of," said Abby, massaging the back of her neck. *Shit. Of course it couldn't be that easy.*

"Mind if I ask where you found it?" Bridger asked. The original investigating officers must have done a thorough search. So how had they missed it? Those detectives all had excellent reputations, aside from the egotistical Derek Moss. None of them would have overlooked a victim's cell phone, even back in 2002, when teens weren't attached to the devices by umbilical cords.

Cari blushed again. "Uh, in my mom's dresser. I went to sort the drawers out so I could donate some of her clothes and there it was under a stack of her camisoles." She went on to explain, "Sometimes she used to take Cory's phone away as a kind of punishment. I'd forgotten about that. I guess she hid it in her underwear drawer."

"Cory got in trouble?" Abby asked.

Cari made a noise that almost sounded like a scoff. "Well, sure. He was a nerd, but he wasn't perfect."

"I meant right around the time of his death."

"Oh. Um, hm. Yeah, I guess he did." Cari put a finger to her lower lip and tapped a couple of times. "Yeah. That's right. Mom had taken away his cell phone. I remember, because he got a call at the house. I mean, on the landline."

"That night?"

Bridger looked over at Abby, having noticed the sharpness in her words. He moved nearer in an effort not to miss anything. The chances were good he would miss plenty anyway but he could watch closely for signs of agitation and further work on his lip reading.

Cari replied, scratching her head. "Uh-huh."

Abby hadn't read anything in the reports about a phone call the night before Cory was found dead. She assumed it hadn't been mentioned back in 2003, as any investigator worth his salt would have found that significant. There was a little tingle of excitement at the prospect of a lead this worthy of following. "Do you remember what time?"

"Um, after dinner. Maybe eight?"

"Was it already dark out, Cari?"

The young woman thought for a minute. "Almost."

Abby glanced around, but couldn't see anything that resembled a phone. However, she knew one could be lurking in a corner somewhere and she would never see it. Bridger realized what Abby's visual search meant, having caught onto the conversation about a call. His eyes swept the room casually before he asked Cari, "Where was the phone?"

"We had one in the kitchen and one by my mom's bed. I think that was all."

"Which one did Cory use that night?" Hope upon hope that he had no choice but to talk where Cari could have listened in, although the young woman was so afraid to bother anyone, she probably would have covered her ears and hummed la-la-la-la-la until her brother was finished with his conversation.

"The upstairs one."

Abby's heart sank. "So the one in your mom's room?"

"Uh-huh."

"Damn," Abby mumbled, although no one heard.

Bridger asked, "Who answered the phone? Was it you or your mother?"

"Um, mom."

"So you don't know whether it was a girl or a boy?"

Cari shook her head and grimaced, apparently upset at being the cause of further frustration just when she had hoped that finding Cory's cell phone might be a cause for celebration. In fact, it was, but the detectives wanted more. She hugged herself and backed out of the room, almost as though she didn't want to be asked any additional questions that she might have a disappointing answer for.

Abby said to Bridger, "Well, that tells us why he didn't have his cell phone on him that night. But what happened to the charger?"

Bridger shrugged. "Who knows? In Rose's addled state of mind of late, she might have planted it in the yard, hoping to grow some little ones."

Abby chuckled. Inch by inch, they were making progress. If only it weren't so painstakingly slow.

Bridger picked up Cory's cell phone and studied it. What a coup to have found it. Unfortunately, it was useless as it sat. The phone, a Sanyo, dating from back in 2002, had probably been state of the art at the time. That was the first year that cameras became an added feature so the detectives desperately wanted to see what Cory had deemed photo worthy. But where to find a power cord? Electronics stores only carried the newest inventory. Ditto department stores. Pawn shops maybe?

Bridger nodded his head and waggled his finger in the air to attract Abby's attention. "Allow me." He put in a call to someone known as Little Casper, a man he claimed could get you anything your heart desired. Casper wasn't a detective; far from it. In fact, he might be about as opposite a detective as one could get, but he had a wicked knack for locating odd, rare or hard-to-find items. Abby knew something about this contact of Bridger's and had always figured the man for a five-finger liberator, but she would be the first to admit that people like Little Casper came in handy at times. This could be one of those times.

While Bridger hooked up with his guy, Abby pulled another handful of papers from the second box. More receipts and mundane scraps of household records. Cari stuck her head into the room before timidly stepping in. Then, looking more like she had pulled herself together, she went to the counter and brought over the plate of scones, like a peace offering, but Abby waved her away and stood to stretch.

Tucking his phone in his pocket, Bridger walked back to the table as Abby was rotating her neck. "I'm going to run Cory's cell phone over to Casper's place. He thinks he's got a charger that will work." He looked at Cari and spread his hands in a conciliatory gesture, "I assume there's no problem with that."

Cory's sister blushed, as though no one had ever asked her permission for anything. "Oh! Sure. Of course, no problem."

Bridger left the two women in the Austin kitchen with a table top full of boxes. Abby sighed, wishing her eyesight was good enough to allow her to drive the cell phone over to some questionable character in some questionable part of town. Instead, here she was, stuck wading through a dead woman's forgotten and probably worthless old papers. And with her core vision next to nonexistent, it was some very heavy wading, heavy wading through deep mud that had bits of marsh grass twining through it. A couple hours of this took its toll. After another forty-five minutes, a dull headache had begun to form.

She leaned back in her chair and rubbed her eyes. "Shit."

"What?"

Abby had momentarily forgotten that she was not alone. "What?"

"Oh! I thought you said something."

"No." Abby's phone jangled. She snatched it up, relieved to have the interruption. "Yes?" She listened, smiled and pressed "End".

While Abby had been talking, Cari put her last batch of cookies in the oven and was now wiping up and doing her best to appear as though she couldn't hear Abby's phone conversation.

Abby cleared her throat and said, "That was Bridger."

Cari glanced sideways, then noticed Abby looking over her way. "Oh! What?"

"That was Bridger just now on the phone."

"Oh. Good. Any luck?"

"As a matter of fact, yes. He's on his way back. Seems his buddy Casper did have a charger that works with Cory's old phone. Of course, it will be a while before the phone is charged up, probably even before it will fire up at all, but at least we've taken the first step and found the equipment."

"Woo hoo!"

"Woo hoo indeed!" Where had that come from? This diffident young woman could barely make eye contact with a stuffed toy and here she was saying "Woo hoo" and pumping her fist in the air like the Oregon Ducks' No. 1 fan. Maybe there was hope for her yet.

The timer dinged. Cari jumped and yelped, "Oh!" Grabbing a pair of hot pads, she flung open the oven door, releasing a cinnamony breeze. In a few seconds, a dozen snickerdoodles rested on the counter. Cari turned off the heat and resumed her culinary tidying as though she couldn't bear a moment of idleness.

Abby, distracted by the aroma, said, "Shit," but more quietly this time, and got up to sneak over for a cookie before settling back into the task at hand. The salty sweetness definitely helped her get through a few more pieces of old Austin family history. She picked up her magnifier and tried to focus. Soon, it all began to look alike and the words on the pages began to lump together in a blur. Receipts, bills, correspondence, notes, pictures, etc. ad nauseum. Why did people keep this crap? She opened the third box and pulled out a folder, upending it and spilling the contents onto the table. She puffed out her cheeks in anticipation of more of the same boring dross she'd been shoving around the table for what seemed like an eternity.

Wait a second, what was that? She thought she had seen a familiar insignia stamped on a letter. She pawed through a couple more notes. Yes, there it was again! The triple shield. The Devil & Dragon triple shield. It was emblazoned on what appeared to be a small handbook, but the writing was probably in Japanese. Something Asian, at any rate.

"Well, I'll be damned." She released a breath and nodded to herself. "Finally." Now, if only she could read the characters. Abby wondered whether Little Casper also had an interpreter among his questionable bag of tricks who could help them out with that. She leafed through the book's thirty or so pages, catching an occasional glimpse of numbers and what might have been names. Frustrated by another roadblock, this one being of the language sort and not of the technology sort, Abby cursed again, three times, but in a whisper. Then she grabbed another snickerdoodle. She may not be able to read Japanese, but she could sure as hell eat German.

CHAPTER 30

"You always pass failure on the way to success."
- Mickey Rooney

Abby finished licking the last of the cinnamon sugar off of her lips in lusty pleasure as she heard Bridger closing CON's door curbside in front of the Austin house. A few seconds later, the doorbell rang and Cari trotted down the hall to let him in. When he entered the kitchen area, his teeth shone white with a wide smile cutting a crescent in his brown face. Cari made a little squeak of delight at seeing his expression and Abby felt Bridger's enthusiasm rubbing off on her. Maybe working cold cases wouldn't be so bad after all. At least it might keep him from seriously considering that cat he'd been threatening to get for more than a week now.

Bridger immediately located an electrical outlet on the kitchen island and plugged in the charger he had bought off of Little Casper, then cradled Cory's cell phone in it. An hour or two might pass before it ingested enough juice to power it up, but there was plenty else for the detectives to do in the meantime.

Abby covertly showed Bridger her discovery of the Japanese handbook with the triple shield insignia. She then suggested they take a break and go get some coffee. Cari overheard her comment and immediately offered to brew up some for them but Abby gently refused, saying they had already put her to far too much trouble. She deserved a rest. Could they bring something back for her? Of course, they knew she would never allow anyone to go to any bother over her so neither was surprised when she declined.

Bridger drove them to the Starbucks a mere seven blocks away where they could talk with little fear of eavesdropping ears.

To be doubly sure, they grabbed the table furthest away from the bulk of the others and sat huddled with their grande iced Americanos. The detectives were, as the saying goes, cautiously optimistic. The case seemed to be coming together now, although in bits and pieces. They believed they knew who, they obviously knew how and when, and were now well on their way to finding out why. Abby was almost positive the answer to that lie in the handbook she held in her hands, which a translator would hopefully confirm. And Bridger once again came through with a resource. And, in fact, that resource came, secondhand, through Little Casper. Abby marveled at the man's infinite usefulness.

It worked out that they could meet the translator at a Chinese restaurant in the westside Portland suburb of Beaverton, in an eatery situated across from the pricey private Jesuit High School where the man cooked American breakfasts every weekday morning. They should drop by, say, around 10:30, after the main onrush of diners had come and gone. Sure, he was Chinese, but the guy spoke fluent Japanese. Korean and Vietnamese too, in case they had a need for help with anything in those languages. Abby knew the place well, for she often patronized it for its eggs Benedict, which she proclaimed the best in the entire metropolitan area, and had discovered that its Bloody Marys weren't too shabby either. It made little sense in a Chinese restaurant, but that's just the way it was.

Naturally, the detectives would have preferred to take care of business sooner, but mid-morning Monday was the earliest time the man said he would be available. Having made that appointment, Bridger and Abby gathered up their things and departed Starbucks for Cari Austin's house once again.

At the door, the young woman could barely wait to share some news, as evidenced by her flushed cheeks and tightly clasped hands. Cory's cell phone had come to life. "The light's glowing!" It looked like she wanted to applaud its performance.

"Wonderful," Abby said with mock enthusiasm, although she had to admit that it was a sign the phone might eventually reveal its secrets, which they hoped would confirm their budding suspicions.

But now, Bridger explained to their victim's sister, he and Abby had decided over their coffees that a quick interview of all the former Nerdlingers club members as they could locate was in order, ASAP, as in right now, today. He was sorry to have to interrupt the phone's progress but they really had to take it with them. Leaving with a promise to let Cari know the minute they found out anything of interest, Bridger escorted his partner out to the smart car where they continued their discussion of how to handle the interviews.

"I'll ask each Nerdlinger whether he or she called Cory that evening and you observe their physical response in that nonchalant, casual way you have, Mr. Flynn. I'm pretty sure they'll all deny it but we need to eliminate them as suspects."

"Yep. Let's go."

Sunday afternoons can be good times to find people at home, and so it proved that particular Sunday. The detectives had carried with them copies of interview sheets from the original files. In fact, CON's "trunk" area had the appearance of a file cabinet that had been involved in a tiny tornado. But the documents did provide them with names and addresses. The addresses, of course, being over ten years old, were for the parents of the Nerdlingers members, or at least those that still lived where they had when their kids attended Washington High. Only four of the eleven did. It helped, nonetheless. They managed to locate three Nerdlingers from the parents – all local – and another four from Abby's phone-calling charm and manipulation. All in all, they spoke with five former club members in the space of three and a half hours, which took longer than they had anticipated due to the neighborhoods being cast over all parts of the Portland metropolitan area. Despite the time and distance, they counted themselves lucky that so many Nerdlingers had put down roots so close to home.

Just shy of eight o'clock that evening, the pair slid into a booth once again at the Leipzig, ordered their usual drinks and asked for menus. Abby couldn't speak for Bridger, but she was famished. Three scones and two snickerdoodles didn't constitute an adequate day's nutrition, although it most definitely qualified as a week's ration of sugar and empty calories.

As Abby sipped a chilled chardonnay, she sighed and said, "Well, if my ears didn't deceive me, the Nerdlingers were all honest when they said they weren't the ones who called that fateful night, right?"

"Right." Bridger swirled his bourbon. "None of them appeared to be deceptive in the least, judging from their body language. We can try to locate the other half dozen, but I think we know who made the call."

Abby's eyebrows shot up before she realized that Bridger probably was right. She opened her mouth to say so when her phone rang. She answered, "Hello?" Shoulders visibly relaxing, she smiled and said a few words Bridger couldn't hear before disengaging.

"That was Malph's day care. I asked him to keep Malph until we catch our guy, just for peace of mind."

"Good idea. And I should stay at your place tonight. Just for safety."

Abby gasped in simulated horror. "Oh, lord, we'll scandalize Mrs. Fitzhenry!"

"Seriously, Abs."

"Yeah, seriously." They each took a sip of their drinks when the waitress came over for their dinner orders. Once she had left, Abby rubbed her temples. "Shit. I'll be glad when we have enough to arrest this son of a bitch."

Bridger knew she looked forward to that even without hearing it. And to getting her dog back. And to reading a book on her deck again. Frankly, he couldn't blame her. It all sounded good to him too, as did hammering out a little jazz on the piano at The Woodstocker. Although he really was enjoying the thrill of the hunt again. Probably always would. Abby interrupted his thoughts.

"By the way, did PPB ever find Cory's computer?"

"Not that I heard."

"We should stop by Evidence, light a fire under them."

"Sure. Right after we discover what's on Cory's cell phone, decode Rose's Japanese handbook and inventory the rest of the items in her unpacked boxes."

Bridger might have meant for that to sound light-hearted and a touch facetious, but it mostly came across as tired and worn out. He almost apologized, but instead ordered another bourbon. Maybe it wouldn't help, but it sure would taste good, along with that Delmonico steak that was coming up. Then, later, maybe a nightcap at Abby's. Tonight, he felt like drowning his sorrows, something he almost never did.

In a rare reversal of roles, Abby was the one to exhibit a newfound level-headedness. She could tell that Bridger's mood had folded in on itself, and this was no time for that. She needed him here, now.

"We have to inform Capt. Shearer of our suspicions. I'm sure he realizes Vanessa Reilly is in grave danger, but his officers need to understand that the list of visitors should be restricted to pretty much law enforcement personnel. Until the killer is caught."

Bridger looked up and across the table at his partner with something close to bewilderment. Maybe he'd been too preoccupied with his son's latest lifestyle changes to think straight but he realized that Abby had hit the nail squarely on the head. He decided to shake off his self pity and pulled out his cell phone. The call to Shearer went straight to voice mail so Bridger left a message.

"Sorry, Abs. I should have thought of that. Got sidetracked."

"Zach still?"

Bridger nodded, then realized she probably couldn't see that, especially in the dimness of the tavern. "Yes. I've been trying to get in touch with him, but the Children of Allah either don't answer their phone or tell me 'Moshe' is meditating, or something else equally full of hooey." He stared into his glass. Abby felt a stab of pain for him, knowing how much he cared for his son, whether the kid realized it or not. Zach had always been a difficult child, his acting out not altogether unwarranted, but heartbreaking nonetheless.

"Let's wrap this case up first, then we can go kick some Allah ass."

That elicited a grin from Bridger, despite his obvious worry. "Yeah, you're right." Before he could say more, his phone played the tune Abby had come to recognize as the one that identified Capt. Shearer. She listened to one side of the conversation with growing dread.

Bridger clicked off. "Nate said —"

"Yeah, I got the gist. Our guy's flown the coop."

"Uh-huh."

"That's not good."

"Nope."

"But the captain has posted more guards at the hospital?"

"Doubled the manpower. Cut off visitors."

Abby pinched the bridge of her nose. "Shit."

Their food came and they attacked their meals, eating heartily despite the bad news.

After close to 15 minutes of cutting and chewing and thinking, Abby twirled the last bite of spaghetti Bolognese around her fork and tipped her head back to swallow it with a dramatic finale. She believed carbs helped her strengthen logic, so her diet that Sunday focused heavily on pasta and sugar. Bridger zeroed in on protein, which she hoped would clear his mind and set him on the right track. They needed to be at the top of their game, so once Bridger had spoken with Shearer, the wine and bourbon had been replaced with strong, black coffee. Neither really thought their quarry would come after them, but it wouldn't do to get lax now. After all, Abby didn't want to leave Malph an orphan.

CHAPTER 31

*"Truth is something you stumble into when
you think you're going someplace else."*

- Jerry Garcia

CON's digital clock read 10:41 when Bridger pulled up to Abby's cottage later that night. She slipped on her tinted glasses, hitched her purse up onto her shoulder and stepped out onto the narrow sidewalk. The parking lot on a Sunday evening always filled up early, making it difficult to find a spot, even for a car as petite as a little Smart For Two. Maybe Bridger could find room in the far row, over by the weedy field. While her partner went in search of a space, Abby felt her way into her yard, instantly missing Malph's familiar snorts and harrumphs but happy in the knowledge that he was safely snoozing away at doggie camp.

She left the gate open for Bridger. As always, it had been locked, a habit from way back. Somehow, when Cory's killer had come looking to harm her Malph, he had bypassed that piece of security. Abby was puzzled by that, but Mrs. Fitzhenry had been adamant that she had seen someone *inside* Abby's yard. Probably climbed over. The fence was high enough to discourage scaling, but not so high as to make it impossible.

Her neighbor must have already retired for the night, for Abby could see no lights on over at Mrs. Fitzhenry's house. She herself had left none on either. Of course, she had departed early in the day, when the sun was high. Now, the lone solar yard lamp did little to illuminate the short path leading to her front door, although light was not much help to Abby at this point in her life. Nothing was vivid or sharp for her anymore when it came to her vision. Those days were long gone. Granted, lighting did improve what she could see, but it was probably more important to a person who had fully functioning eyesight.

With macular degeneration, you learned to rely on peripheral vision. It often is the sole visual perception available to you. And it sometimes works best if you turn your head slightly away from the object you want to focus on. Illogically, this actually provides the most optimal view, awkward as it may seem. In other words, to see toward the right, tilt the head several degrees left. Of course, with macular degeneration, really focusing doesn't ever happen. You may get a sense of shapes, even enough of a sense to identify what you're looking at, depending upon the stage of the progression of the disease. MD mostly ate away at your core vision, but with tools you could limp through.

Abby's glasses had some central magnification, but the periphery was merely tinted glass. So when she turned her head a certain way, she was looking not in the direction her gaze would suggest, but where she had trained her limited vision to concentrate. That's how she entered her house, and that's how she spotted her would-be attacker. And Abby didn't leave a night light on either, so the man hiding inside her kitchen didn't notice the doorstop on the floor next to the counter.

He lunged to grab her as she came in and his left hand caught a fistful of her blouse. Instinctively pulling away, she heard it tear.

"Shit! Asshole!"

Abby feinted right while reaching into her bag, guessing he would have a weapon and wanting to level the playing field. A hand closed over her arm and gripped hard. She yanked away, but he held firm. Panic took hold and she kicked blindly at his legs.

"Ow!" She'd connected well.

"Hah!"

His grip faltered slightly.

Abby pulled and twisted, feeling his nails dig deeper into her flesh. She kicked again. He stumbled, but regained his hold. She heard something whiz by her ear, brought her knee up, bumping him hard, and slipped out of his grasp.

"Bitch!" The man took another swipe at her and she jumped sideways, praying he would have trouble keeping his balance for at least the few seconds she needed. He had obviously been well trained at some point and it showed, especially in his speed, although his skills were more than a touch rusty. But so were Abby's. Plus, she had gone blind in the meantime.

Her assailant tripped on the little iron quail she used to hold her door open on warm days. "Ooof!" She heard him crash against the wall.

She threw a heavy vase from the counter in the direction of the sound and it collided with some body part.

He cursed again.

Abby rushed sideways. Where the hell was Bridger? How damned far had he gone for a stupid parking spot?

The man righted himself quickly and lunged again.

Abby felt the prick of a knife graze the muscular part of her left arm.

"Shit! You bastard! Son of a bitch!" A roiling anger carried her backward as she continued rifling through her purse, her hands growing slick with blood. Finally, she located her snub-nosed Beretta, a silly gun she never thought she would need but one that fit tidily in small bags and worked well in close quarters. She squeezed the trigger and heard a surprised scream.

"Never bring a knife to a gunfight, you stupid shit."

At the same moment, the kitchen burst into light and Bridger stood framed in the doorway. In an instant, he assessed the scene before him: Abby aiming her weapon at the intruder's midsection as he teetered, maybe on the brink of falling to the floor or maybe on the brink of hurtling toward her again; it wasn't clear.

At the sudden glare, the man glanced over his shoulder and, apparently realizing he didn't have any good options, dropped his knife. Bridger kicked it away, grabbed the intruder's arms and pinned them behind him while Abby found something to tie his hands with.

Adrenaline spent, the guy crumpled, instantly favoring one leg.

Bridger looked down and saw that the fellow's left foot had been shattered by a bullet. "Well done, Abs!"

"Meant to hit him somewhere else," she muttered.

From the angle of the gun, her intended target appeared obvious. "You want to put that down, Abs?"

Abby looked at the gun in her hand, almost as though startled to note that it was still there. Then she lowered it and laid it on the counter behind her. "Damn it, he's bleeding all over my floor." She found some kitchen jute to wrap around his wrists and then shoved him roughly toward the door. "Let's take him outside."

The man screamed as his weight came down on his ruined foot. Abby pulled him along. He howled with every step. "God, stop! Stop!"

She wanted to march him the entire six miles to Central Precinct, but settled for tethering him to the lamppost in the middle of her yard. At least, there, he would merely bleed into the bark dust which surrounded her lavender bushes. Bridger removed his hearing aid so that their captive's protests wouldn't reach his ears. Abby saw him do that and said, "Coward," but wished she had the ability to tune him out, too. While Bridger watched the enraged fellow rant, Abby placed a call to Capt. Shearer.

- - -

It was after 2:30 a.m. Monday morning by the time Abby and Bridger laid their heads on their respective pillows. With the danger past, Bridger could have gone home, but exhaustion overtook him and he fell asleep on Abby's couch even before she could get a blanket for him. She managed to round up a pillow and coverlet and pile them atop his chest, figuring that he would at least have them close if he got cold. Then she double-checked the locks and fell into bed without undressing.

Earlier, Lincoln Shin had refused to talk, immediately invoking his right to speak to a lawyer. The police detectives who accompanied Capt. Shearer to Abby's cottage acknowledged Shin's request, but took their time getting him to a phone. He sat in the back of a squad car for over an hour while Abby and Bridger answered questions. The police lights and general melee surrounding the events of that Sunday night, including uniformed officers and detectives milling around, all had caused quite a stir in the parking lot of the Lake Oswego townhomes.

Mrs. Fitzhenry stood with a few of the other neighbors, watching, when they led Shin out. Abby, Bridger and Capt. Shearer accompanied the officers as far as the gate so Abby could explain the earlier sequence of what had gone down.

"Ah, I see they caught him, Ms. Dalton." The tall, bony Irishwoman smiled smugly at the man in cuffs. "Serves him right for sneaking around where he doesn't belong. Malph's okay then, Ms. Dalton? I haven't seen him for a day or so."

"Yes, Mrs. Fitzhenry, Malph is fine. He's off at a slumber party. Coming home tomorrow. I suspect he'll be paying you a visit then."

Abby received a smile and a nod for her comment.

The five or six people gawking at Shin continued to speculate among themselves about crime rate in Portland spreading out to Lake Oswego, and Mrs. Fitzhenry observed how she would sleep better that night with this man behind bars.

Abby and Bridger followed Capt. Shearer back inside to wrap up the night's interview. Shearer looked happier and more rested since the break in the Tryon Creek abduction a few days before. Abby and Bridger had the harrowed, weary appearance the captain had worn when they began the Austin case. At least, now they could see some light at the end of the tunnel. But with Shin remaining tight lipped, they still needed answers. Maybe Rose's handbook held some. Or Cory's cell phone. Their meeting with the translator had seemed so far in the future but now they feared 10:00 o'clock would come all too quickly.

After another forty-five minutes, they shook hands with Shearer, closed the door behind him with promises to get in touch later on in the day. Then Bridger collapsed on the couch while Abby fetched a blanket for him before falling into bed herself. Her arm throbbed where Shin had sliced it open, but that didn't keep her awake. Nothing could.

CHAPTER 32

"Crime, like virtue, has its degrees."

- Racine

Barely six hours later, Bridger awoke to the delicious smell of strong coffee. Abigail Dalton was brewing a pot without being badgered and/or cajoled? Bridger slowly pushed himself up, a whisper soft blanket tumbling off to one side, stretched his neck and yawned loudly. His back creaked as he stood. He followed his nose toward the aroma, rubbing the side of his face to help shake off a lingering drowsiness.

"Good morning, sunshine." Abby greeted him, looking fresh, clad in comfortable jeans and a loose lightweight V-neck sweater. He eyed her there, standing in the kitchen, slurping from an oversized mug. She held a steaming one out to him. "Bet you could use this."

"Thanks."

"You're welcome."

After several deep, appreciative swigs, he asked, "How's the arm?"

She shrugged. "It'll survive."

"Think it can still handle the weight of a book?"

"Pretty sure."

"How about walking Malph?"

"Absolutely."

"Paddling a kayak?"

"Yep."

"Nothing to worry about then."

In the aftermath of the melee of the night before, Bridger and Shearer had tried to call an ambulance for Abby, but she refused, saying the stab wound was just a scratch. Eventually, they had given up and Bridger bandaged it with supplies from her home first aid kit.

Another yawn escaped him. "Oh, by the way, we need to get Cory's cell phone plugged in again."

"Took care of it already."

"Well, aren't you the efficient little lady?"

"You'd better believe it."

"Okay then." Bridger took a deep drink of his coffee before checking the time on his watch. "Ready to go?"

"Damned right I'm ready."

The two detectives put their mugs in the sink, Bridger scooped up his keys and Abby grabbed the few things she needed. It took nearly five minutes to walk over to where Bridger had found enough space to park CON the night before.

"Shit. No wonder it took you so long. Good thing I had a gun."

Bridger either didn't hear that or pretended not to. Abby knew he frowned on her carrying a firearm, but it had saved her more than once so she intended to continue to keep it in her purse. Which, by the way, she would need to replace after blowing a hole in it last night. There had been no time to actually extract the gun before pulling the trigger. Lucky for Lincoln Shin because, if Abby had taken the care to aim better, the man might have sustained far more serious injuries than a mere shattered foot. Although Bridger harbored a secret inkling that Abby may have meted out some poetic justice, what with the case already involving a severed cat's paw and a football star's crushed foot. However, he probably would never know the truth on that score. She almost certainly would not own up to it either way. The woman liked to maintain a certain amount of mystery.

Once they reached the car, it didn't take them all that long to get out to Beaverton. Their route took them cross-country, skirting downtown and avoiding the usual heavy traffic altogether. Their arrival at the old Chinese joint was perfectly timed, if maybe a few minutes early.

Inside the restaurant, they were greeted by a blonde hostess whom Abby recognized from virtually every previous visit. She seemed to be the only hostess ever on shift. Bridger explained that they were there to see Mr. Jiang, and the woman ducked into the kitchen. When she returned, she led them to a booth in a remote but well-lit corner of the bar.

"Can I get you anything while you wait?"

"Just water," answered Abby. Bridger nodded.

Abby fished around in her makeshift purse for Rose's handbook. She didn't know where anything was in this bag, which frustrated her to no end. Everything should be in its place, a rule particularly important for a blind person. Finally, her fingers closed around it. She pulled it out and laid it on the table, just as a waitress brought their glasses of water, followed by the man they had come to see.

Bridger stood. "Mr. Jiang?"

The man bowed his head slightly. Bridger introduced himself and gestured for Mr. Jiang to sit.

Abby offered her hand. "Mr. Jiang, a pleasure to meet you. I am Abigail Dalton."

The man bowed his head again before taking her hand. After he had arranged himself comfortably on his seat, Abby slid the book across in front of him, then placed a small cassette recorder on the table and asked, "Would you mind if we taped our conversation? Just so we don't forget anything. It is very important."

"No, of course not." Mr. Jiang motioned to the waitress and, within a minute, a drink appeared in front of him. It had a lime garnishing the rim but, other than that, was unidentifiable. Abby wished she had ordered a Bloody Mary instead of water, but thought it might have appeared impolite. Now she wondered.

Jiang took a sizable gulp, set his glass down and began reading aloud from the handbook. The revelations were damning. Rose had kept impeccable records. As they suspected, this wasn't a handbook at all. The title was as much a cover as Rose Austin's entire persona had been.

In these pages she had written names, dates and locations of murders, who had done the killing, and whatever evidence she had to back up her claims. There must have been a dozen different assassins identified, including Shin and a man named Hiroki. Most of the killers, but especially those two, had been involved in several brutal attacks on entire families, not just a specific member who had strayed and needed to be used as an example. Their bloodlust was frequent and legendary. By the time Jiang had finished reading and looked up, his eyes had grown to the size of saucers and his face had gone as pale as bone china.

Bridger saw the look and groped around for some words to reassure Jiang, but none came.

Abby sensed the man's discomfort and said, "Thank you, Mr. Jiang. The young lady who wrote this has quite an imagination, don't you think?" She beamed at him in that disarming way of hers as she hit "Stop" on the recorder and gathered up their papers and the little book. They had been vague about their purpose when setting up the appointment, so now Abby felt justified in whatever fiction she could come up with on short notice. "She's done a great job on this script, I'd say. It's going to be a thrilling mystery. Your reading was perfect."

Jiang looked from Abby to Bridger before grinning and nodding. He turned a bit red, as though embarrassed that anyone would think he could have possibly believed the preposterous claims in the "handbook" were true. "Yes, very good imagination. Very good. Thrilling mystery." He stood and nodded his way back into the kitchen, saying several times, "Very good imagination."

Bridger winked at Abby, an old and abiding habit, one he would have to break now, considering she would not be able to see that – probably not ever again. He cleared his throat. "Quick thinking, Abs."

"Don't call me Abs." Her voice sounded weak.

He took a closer look at her face, which had gone as pale as Jiang's. He understood. Her supply of bravado might be running low. The little book wasn't fiction like she had tried to convince their translator, but full of some very ugly truths. Something like a hundred thirty men, women and children had been slain by the Devil & Dragon henchmen, according to Rose's records, and they had not died easily. Shin and the others had seen to it that they suffered as much as possible. Torture had been a form of entertainment for them.

"Fucking monsters." She closed her eyes, as though she might block the images evoked by Rose's little book.

"Yes, Abs, monsters indeed. But we got one of them."

"Yeah." She sighed. "Let's get this damned thing down to Shearer. He needs some good news." In fact, this would start his week out very well. And they both knew that Capt. Shearer didn't need another one like the last week had been.

Bridger didn't want to bring Abby down any further by pointing out that a break in their case would likely mean they'd have to endure another press conference, so he kept silent on that subject. Let the captain be the one to tell her. It might even be possible to put it off for a few days, although considering the tenacity of the media it didn't seem very likely.

CHAPTER 33

"A hunch is creativity trying to tell you something."
– Frank Capra

Down at Central Precinct, Monday morning was in full swing. The weekend had been an active one, with a shooting other than Abby's to contend with, not to mention the usual assortment of burglaries, assaults and drunken brawls. Capt. Shearer's good mood was short lived. The news that Bridger and Abby brought him, though, did kick it up a notch. It gave them all hope that they had found another nail to pound into Lincoln Shin's coffin. However, Shin's defense lawyer was the best in the state, and a tricky bastard, if you asked pretty much anyone in law enforcement. Still, Rose's methodical recording of murders and her backup details went a long way toward making the detectives optimistic about sealing a conviction. Plus, they had Vanessa Reilly's case as a bonus, which would likely compound the years Shin would spend behind bars. And if Forensics had found some good stuff at the Bertha Peck crime scene, that could add to the prison sentence, too. Hopefully, about six lifetimes.

The detectives weren't done yet, though. Bridger asked Shearer, "Any sign of Cory Austin's computer?"

The captain cringed, looking sheepish. "Yeah. Here's the deal on that. It got shipped over to the Evidence archives, of course, and Rory, who runs the desk there, has been on vacation. The relief officer is pretty much useless. That's why he's assigned there – and other places like that. It's archives; almost no one needs evidence that old. Anyway, according to our records, the computer is there somewhere. Digging it out is the tricky part. I'll put another call in." He made a note on a pad beside his phone, which rang the instant he laid the pencil down. He had a triumphant smile on his face when he hung up.

"Vanessa Reilly is ready to talk."

Bridger cupped his ear, as though he hadn't heard. Abby thought he probably just wanted to have the words repeated, they were such sweet ones.

"Yes, Vanessa Reilly is awake and apparently anxious to talk. Shall we go?"

Bridger and Abby followed Shearer's official car in CON, winding up Sam Jackson Parkway once again, only this time with a far less grim reason. Half an hour after the call, the captain and the detectives stood beside the ex-cheerleader's bed. She still sported a prize-winning bruise that spread across her broken nose and her split lip looked painful, but there was fire in her eyes, which had cuts and contusions around them as well.

Abby acted as scrivener while Shearer conducted the interview and Bridger watched with an alertness honed to perfection by years of observation. Occasionally, one of the Eyes & Ears detectives had a question or two to clarify something. Mrs. Reilly told them a story that further tightened the noose around Mr. Lincoln Shin's neck. Clearly, vengeance was on her mind. It might have come eleven years late, but at least it came.

She wept when they broke the news of Bertha Peck's death. Abby began to think there might be some actual substance to the woman after all. Sometimes it took a heartbreaking tragedy for a person to realize the value of life. The past week had seen Vanessa Reilly mature at a remarkable pace. Apparently, eye shadow and nail polish had dropped several slots on the list of things she cared about.

One piece of information, though, absolutely stunned them: the identity of the man who had rushed in to save her. Neither of them would have ever guessed. Fortunately, Bridger had made sure they came prepared by bringing the photographs he took to show Bertha Peck the day she was assaulted. Now, Vanessa gasped and pointed excitedly when she recognized her white knight. Her eyes grew bright with tears. Bridger, almost speechless, finally managed to tell Abby the man's name.

"Well, I'll be damned."

Shearer was the only one in the room left in the dark.

Once back outside, as the captain and two detectives stood in front of the medical center, Abby pulled her sweater tighter around her. The sun was midway into its annual journey south and had already lost much of its strength. The time for heavier layers was firmly upon them. Soon, they would need to switch to waterproof layers.

Capt. Shearer shook each of the detectives' hands. "Thanks for working this case."

Bridger smiled and said, "Happy to, Nate."

Abby stood by, the men looking at her as though they expected an echo of their cheery sentiments. She figured anything she said would be taken as encouragement, unless she voiced exactly what was on her mind, so she opted to remain quiet. When the silence stretched out so long that it made Bridger uncomfortable, he said, "Well."

Shearer scratched the back of his neck. "So what's next?"

Bridger replied, "Uh, I guess we'd like to observe the interview with Shin."

"Of course. It's planned for a little later this afternoon. I think his attorney will be showing up around 2:00. Let's hope he'll let his client do some talking."

"Yeah. Could be a short interview with Jerome Moore as his lawyer. Meanwhile, I think Abby and I will go check on Cory's cell phone. See if it's ready to share its secrets."

"Good. Good." The captain said, as he turned to leave, "Keep me in the loop on that."

"Will do."

Abby slipped on her glasses before they started off toward CON. She could almost see Bridger glancing at her sideways as they walked. Well, he knew she wasn't crazy about working cold cases. What did he expect? That she would turn cartwheels at Shearer's praise? He'd better get over that idea real quick. What she most fervently wanted was to pick up Malph and spend a little time sitting lakeside before fall gave way to winter. This case had already eaten up too much of the best weather the Northwest had to offer.

In the car, Abby put in a couple of calls, one to Cari, telling her they would like to drop by the next day with all of the newest news, then to Malph's day care to ensure that she could get her dog back ASAP. In fact, they decided to pick him up on their way to Abby's townhouse. It would only cost them five minutes, if that. She cleared a spot behind the seats for the dog to ride. It would be tight, considering the space taken up by files, but the distance was short and Malph wouldn't mind as long as he was on his way home.

Back at the cottage, while Malph scampered around and reacquainted himself with his yard, Bridger and Abby powered up Cory's eleven-year-old cellular phone. Having done some earlier research on the model, they knew that it was the first year to feature a camera. This was what they'd been waiting for. It took a little maneuvering to figure out how to go backward in technology but they finally accessed the dead teenager's photos.

"Bingo!"

Abby nearly applauded when she heard that. "What?"

"Get your magnifier. You're going to want to see this."

Impatiently, she rummaged around in her purse until she found it, grabbed the phone from her partner and scrutinized the screen. "Yes! The netsuke!"

"Uh-huh." Bridger drew out the two syllables into what sounded like four.

They did a high five and said, "Yes!" in unison.

Abby put the magnifier to her eye again. "Fantastic. Just fantastic." She leaned in closer. "Wait a minute."

"What?" It was Bridger's turn to ask.

Abby looked up at her partner. "This isn't Rose's netsuke."

"What?"

"Huh-uh. It's not a crouching woman under a hat. This one's different. I think what we've got here is Hiroki's netsuke, Bridger. I'd stake my life on it!"

"What?" He said again.

"Hiroki's netsuke," Abby mouthed as well as upped the volume.

The pair stood frozen for a moment, both wondering whether it was true and, if so, what it meant.

A bark from outdoors brought them back to the moment. Abby shook off her shock and went to open the door for Malph. Bridger felt the bulldog brush his leg as he squeezed by him on his way through the room to his bed. They pondered the import of the netsuke photo as they watched the dog complete a couple of circles before settling deep into its cushion. From all appearances, there would be no visiting Mrs. Fitzhenry in the near future.

Abby shifted her attention back from Malph to Bridger. "If this is Hiroki's netsuke, and I definitely think it is, then that means Cory found it. Do you think he understood the significance of it?"

Bridger gazed out the picture window at the lake, mulling the question over. "Well, he was a smart kid."

"But he was a kid."

"Yes, he was a kid. However, I do believe he grasped the importance of this netsuke. Or at least that it had importance. Otherwise, why take a picture of it?"

"Good point," Abby conceded. "So now the question is where did it go?"

They both spent some time thinking about that. Cari had not found a little figurine other than the crouching woman, that much was clear, and she had been pretty thorough in packing up her mother's belongings, by all appearances. Was there a safe deposit box? Surely, she would have mentioned finding a key to one. Besides, the Devil & Dragon men sent by Hiroki to locate the netsuke would have made their own inquiries in that area, and they had come up empty. No, something else happened to it. But what?

Struck by a new idea, Bridger said, "If it's not here and not in a safe deposit box, then Cory must have sent it off somewhere."

"But where would he send it?" Abby tried to think like a teenager and found it almost impossible.

"I don't believe he'd have put any of his friends in danger."

"Nor do I."

"Beyond school friends, he didn't know a lot of people other than his mom, his sister, and –" Bridger snapped his long, brown fingers. "His dad."

"You think?" Abby frowned. She herself had come up with no better answer. Still, the world is a huge place and it sounded like a long shot. Bridger seemed quite sure though.

"Where else could he send it? This makes sense, Abs."

Unwilling to concede, Abby argued, "But wouldn't Rose have had a shit fit about that?" She couldn't imagine Rose letting go of her only leverage, especially giving it up to the man who had deserted her.

"Well, yes, she would have. If she knew."

"What?" Abby started to argue again, but Bridger cut her off.

"Hear me out on this." He stroked his chin a couple of times as he organized his thoughts. "Cory's dad has run off to the middle of nowhere." Bridger knew about absent dads, his own often on the road for musical gigs; then he himself not so present for his two kids due to work shift issues and overtime. "So seventeen-year-old Cory is now the alpha male, at least in his mind. He's trying to step up and be the man of the house. Then Frizz the cat turns up missing. I think he saw the severed paw. And he finds this object, this netsuke, then comes across the handbook. A lot is happening at once. He puts two and two together."

"That's more like one and one and one."

Bridger gave her a dirty look, but realized she had the advantage of blindness on that. He went on, "He knows something's up."

"How does he make that leap?"

"Not sure. Just thinking out loud. Maybe he finds a translator like we did, gets a reading of the handbook. As for the netsuke, it could be researched on the Internet, and I'd bet that Cory knew his way around the Web. The netsuke has unique markings. You yourself found quite a lot on the Web about the use of them in a secret Japanese society. He could have, too. And the cat – too much for coincidence. Plus, he's scared and angry. So he comes up with a loose theory, or possibly several theories, but none of them bode well for his family."

Bridger stopped to catch his breath and try to read Abby's reaction. Her expression remained skeptical. He forged on, "We've heard from his classmates that he wasn't himself those last few weeks. He's troubled. I think he's terrified for his mom. He could have learned more than we even know. Anyway, he's found the netsuke and has realized that it's dangerous. Maybe not how dangerous or quite in what way, but he instinctively knows it can hurt his mom. So he sends it off to his dad, who lives far enough away no one will think of looking there, with a cryptic letter pleading for him to keep it, hide it, don't tell anyone about it, don't lose it, but keep it safe." Bridger finished with a flourish that, had he been vocal about it, would have said, "Ta da!"

Abby chewed on that for a couple of minutes, then admitted, "That does make a certain amount of sense." Standing abruptly, she said, "And, well, that's something we can easily confirm." She strode over to the file and grabbed it, then handed the folder to Bridger. "Find Gerry Austin's number and I'll give him a call and ask."

"Now?"

"No time like the present, as my mom always said."

Bridger recited a number and she punched it into her phone as she ambled out onto her deck. It was time for them to get some answers. And, by God, they would. If Cory's dad picked up.

CHAPTER 34

*"It is a mistake to look too far ahead. Only one link
in the chain of destiny can be handled at a time."*
        – Winston Churchill

Gerry Austin was home and he did answer, although he sounded thoroughly perplexed. Beyond simple introductions, Abby had to explain their purpose for phoning. Twice. She and Bridger had not deemed it important to speak with Mr. Austin since reopening the investigation into Cory's murder. Not so far, at least. Apparently, Cari hadn't either, for her father professed to be totally unaware of any recent activity.

"Wow. I thought all of that was over and done with a long time ago."

Abby rolled her eyes. It was a case gone cold, not dead. She bit her tongue. "No, sir. It's just been waiting for new evidence, which came in last week."

"Uh-huh. Well, good."

He still sounded perplexed but didn't ask what the new evidence was, so Abby didn't tell him. Instead, she got right to her point: the netsuke. Did he remember a package from Cory arriving shortly before his death? She asked and held her breath. It had to be what happened; it made the most sense. Bridger had her convinced at this point.

"A package? Let's see. Wow, that's a long time ago. Hm. Um, no, I don't think so."

Abby released her breath, deflated. "Are you certain? Please think hard, Mr. Austin."

The ensuing silence stretched on for so long that Abby wondered whether the connection had been severed, but then he said, like a game show contestant suddenly realizing the answer, "Oh, oh, yeah. That's right. I remember now. He did. He sent a funny little thing. It looked like an ogre, sort of. Odd doodad.

Foreign. Maybe Japanese, like my Rosie." He chuckled. "Anyway, I figured it was for Lacey's birthday."

"Lacey?"

"Yeah, my fiancé back then. She's my wife now."

Abby's patience was quickly running out. She didn't have much to begin with and they needed to wrap this up. Mr. Austin didn't seem to share their sense of urgency. "Wasn't there some kind of note with it? Why would you think it was for Lacey's birthday?"

"Well, the timing, of course. It arrived just a couple of days before." He paused again. "Hm, a note? Yeah, probably. Cory always wrote notes."

"Sir, did you know anything about Rose's background?"

If he thought that an off-the-wall question, he didn't let on. "Oh, not much, especially about her time in Japan. She was a pretty secretive little lady. But it didn't matter."

Abby sucked in a lungful of air. If he only knew how wrong he was and how her background did indeed matter. "Okay. About the note, do you happen to remember what it said?"

Bridger had come outside by now and stood at Abby's elbow, trying to hear at least her side of the conversation. Malph sat on the deck between them, looking up at his mistress, his stub of a tail wagging ferociously.

Mr. Austin couldn't remember anything Cory had written in the note accompanying the ugly little object. Abby still contended that any letter would have cautioned his father to keep the item safe and hidden, but maybe the kid was more casual about it. After all, Gerry Austin lived in a tiny town in the middle of Colorado. Who was going to notice a funky little ivory figurine called a netsuke? At least, that was the kind of logic a seventeen-year-old would adhere to, even a highly intelligent one with a whole lot to fear.

"Okay. So this little, um, thing came in the mail and you thought it was for Lacey. Does she still have it, by any chance?"

Bridger leaned in, hoping to hear the answer to this most crucial of questions.

"Oh, Lord, no. It's been gone for several years now. She wore it on a chain now and then." Gerry Austin chuckled again. "I don't think she liked it very much. Couldn't blame her; it was pretty hideous. But it was from Cory. She didn't really know him, but she knew how much I loved him, so she wore it for me. Somehow it went missing one night when we were out to dinner. We got home and it just wasn't around her neck." Abby could almost hear him shrug. "No big loss."

She slumped. If Bridger hadn't caught the answer through the phone, he'd understand by Abby's body language that it wasn't what they wanted to hear. He stood back while she asked Mr. Austin a few other questions before thanking him for his time.

Just as she was about to hang up, Gerry Austin asked about Cari. "How is my daughter? She never calls. Blames me for running off. She's right, but I sure miss talking to her."

"She's doing well, sir. Just fine."

"And my Rosie?"

Abby closed her eyes tight. Of course Cari hadn't called him about Rose's death. Otherwise, he wouldn't have needed to ask about his daughter. She kicked herself for not being prepared for this. His voice held an eagerness that made Abby believe he cared deeply about his former family. She said, in as gentle a manner as she could muster, "I think maybe you should call Cari. She can better explain her mother's, um, condition." Abby confirmed that Gerry Austin had Cari's current contact number and clicked off as hastily as she could.

The two detectives dropped into the chairs on the lakeside deck. Abby said, "Damn!"

Bridger said, "Ditto."

Ten minutes passed with each deeply involved in their own thoughts before Bridger sat up straight with a start. "Actually, Abs, this might not be so bad." Before she could protest, he went on. "In fact, it might even be better this way."

"Yeah, right. How the hell do you figure that?"

"Hear me out." Bridger stood and began pacing as he explained. "See, we now know for a fact that Hiroki's netsuke existed. We have Rose's handbook evidence, Cory's cell phone picture, and now dad's corroboration. And we don't have the burden of its physical presence. No one has to worry about the D&D continuing to try to get their hands on it. No one has to worry about the chain of custody, not to mention protecting it any longer. Its loss, well," he spread his hands wide, "is pretty okay."

"That's not how a real cop would think."

"I'm a retired cop. I think like one who wants to find a solution the easy way."

"No, you don't. But I like your optimism. You've convinced me that it might indeed be all right after all."

One of Abby's neighbors – probably Mrs. Fitzhenry – must have been microwaving some popcorn, because the scent wafted across Abby's yard and made her mouth water. "Shearer's not expecting us for another hour and a half. What do you say we go get some lunch?"

They debated their options, finally deciding on a nondescript Thai café a couple miles up the road along Macadam Avenue. Abby could feed her taste for their pungent drunken noodles while Bridger could stick to his diet of veggies prepared however suited him, if he wanted. For once, they had little to discuss aside from what they hoped to hear from Shin's interview and who would tell Cari what part of the story.

After a much-needed break over a meal with no problems to solve, plates were cleared, roles were meted out for the next day's progress report, and the two detectives left, satisfied all was in control, except that Abby knew Zach's predicament still lingered in the back of his father's mind.

CHAPTER 35

*"Half the world is composed of people who have
something to say and can't and the other half who have
nothing to say and keep on saying it."*

— *Robert Frost*

Jerome Moore, Lincoln Shin's lawyer, was late. However, no one thought a thing of it. The man had a long-standing reputation for indulging in self importance. When he finally arrived, he brought with him no apologies, only a fat briefcase and an air of superiority. Abby could smell it on him like a bad body odor. She had no fondness for attorneys in the best of times, and this wasn't one of the best of times. Bridger tolerated lawyers far better than his partner, but then that could be said about a great many things.

Once Moore had arranged himself with the coffee and stapler he'd demanded, another forty-five minutes passed while Shin and his mouthpiece consulted, at which point the lawyer stormed out of the room in a huff. Apparently, since being confronted with the evidence of Rose's handbook and the hint of what Vanessa Reilly might say, the schoolteacher wished to make a statement, against Jerome Moore, Esquire's advice. Abby nearly rubbed her hands together with palm-chafing glee. She loved it when a suspect decided to blow off his attorney and spill his guts. This was turning out to be a really good day after all. And it couldn't happen to a better guy than Lincoln Shin.

The partners of Eyes & Ears took their places alongside Capt. Shearer and a few others in the secluded viewing room to observe the lead detective conduct the interrogation, which turned out to be more of a monologue on Shin's part, despite frequent admonitions from Jerome Moore, who had returned to his client's side with a great show of theatrics and more vociferous advice.

Nonetheless, Shin cleared up a lot of questions that Abby and Bridger had been pondering, along with some gaps that Vanessa Reilly was unable to fill in, and created some more that they hoped other witnesses would be able to answer. Witnesses like Alan Garfield, the mystery guardian angel who swooped in and saved Vanessa from Shin's lethal clutches. Abby and Bridger didn't know how he fit in, just that he did. Shearer surprised them with the welcome news that Garfield had volunteered to come by Central Precinct at 4:30 that afternoon. Those interview rooms were going to be buzzing for several hours! Double feature.

A department secretary with a flirtatious manner offered to bring Bridger a latte from the lobby Starbucks. Abby piggybacked an order onto her partner's, to the obvious chagrin of the young woman. Meanwhile, Shin sang for a couple of hours before his attorney convinced him to cool his jets for a while. The detectives weren't sure that he hadn't simply run out of steam. They had what they needed for now anyway. Further details could be pulled from him later. Besides, Alan Garfield had arrived twenty minutes earlier and they were anxious to hear what he had to say. No one wanted to risk the chance that he might get cold feet.

Another interview room was set up, this one with more comfortable chairs and a pitcher of iced water. Abby and Bridger would be permitted to ask questions after the lead investigator had completed his official interview.

Watching Alan Garfield from behind the one-way glass, the detectives were struck by the man's easygoing, nonchalant demeanor. He came off as almost humble, answered questions with an economy of words and did not embellish in any manner. He recounted what happened at Vanessa Reilly's house swiftly and confidently, then went mute. Nothing more needed to be said, in his view. They had their facts. His past and his personal life were private. If there was anything pertinent about either of those, he had no intention of sharing it. After just thirty-five minutes, the officer left the room and told Abby and Bridger, "He's all yours."

They smiled and went in. An hour and twenty minutes later, their smiles had doubled in size. They shook hands with Alan Garfield and thanked him for his help and a lifetime of service. They had a lot to tell Cari Austin in the morning. Most of it very good news.

Capt. Shearer ran into them at the elevator. Jerome Moore, Esquire had left nearly two hours before, declaring Shin hands-off for the rest of the day. The captain had his coat on, ready for a rare night out with his wife. Sometimes, dates with Mrs. Shearer had to be impromptu, like this one. Bridger and Abby had other plans, at least one of them delighted to be cutting the day short, relatively speaking.

That evening, the atmosphere at the Leipzig Tavern was decidedly more celebratory than it had been in well over a week. Abby and Bridger clinked glasses to congratulate each other on a fine conclusion to their first case.

Bridger beamed at his partner. "Nice job, Ears."

She almost said, "Don't call me Abs," but then realized that he hadn't. Instead, she said, "Don't get used to it. I'm still not onboard for cold cases."

"Aw, come on, Abs. You can't tell me you didn't get a lot of satisfaction out of this."

"That's beside the point."

"No, it's not. That's exactly the point."

"I don't want to argue, Bridger. Let's just say it's too much like work."

He sighed. He didn't want to argue either. Best to let it be for now. They were celebrating; that should be enough for tonight. At least, they had Eyes & Ears, the agency. What they built it into remained to be seen. Bridger signaled the waitress for another bourbon. When she brought it, they ordered Leipzig's legendary meatballs two ways: in a garlicky marinara sauce and in a creamy béchamel. He knew for a fact they could agree on that, paired with a Caesar salad and cheese bread. Bridger would step off his diet for one more night. Maybe that sort of attitude would spur Abby to rethink some of her own ideas.

An hour and a half passed with neither bringing up the topic of cold cases again. They still had this one to finish up, although much had fallen into place today. And tomorrow would see more filling-in of the holes. Alan Garfield's somewhat abbreviated story only went so far. If they had the time, it would be nice to see if they could pry a few more secrets from the former D&D guardian. Or was "former" an accurate description of his status with the Society? Maybe his commitment was truly a lifetime one.

Their appointment with Cari Austin had been scheduled for fairly early in the morning. By nine o'clock, Abby felt like she'd hit a brick wall. The tensions of the past week and a half finally took their toll. Bridger couldn't hear the weariness in her voice, but he could see the change in her face.

"Time to call it a day, Abs."

She gave him no argument, not even an eye roll or a "Don't call me Abs."

CHAPTER 36

"A politician divides mankind into two classes:
tools and enemies."

- Friedrich Nietzsche

"Lincoln Shin killed my brother?" Cari Austin had refused to let the detectives across her threshold until they disclosed the identity of her brother's killer. She absorbed the news slowly, visibly astonished. "But why?"

Abby was happy to answer her question, almost as happy as she was that Shin turned out to be their killer. The man had rankled her from the first time she met him. Even before, in fact, from the instant he careened out of his overgrown driveway in that heap of a Gremlin, causing her to bump violently against CON's door. And that dog of his. How could anyone train an animal to be so nasty? What he must have done to that creature to turn him into such a mean-tempered dog she shuddered to think. Abby could hate Shin simply for that.

"Sit down, Cari. It's kind of a long story."

"Oh! Can I get you some coffee? Tea?" The young woman looked from Abby to Bridger and back to Abby.

A mere week ago, Abby would have been tempted to scream at Cari's unremitting eagerness to please, but she had grown used to it, so now she bit her tongue and swallowed her annoyance. "No, thank you, dear." She added "dear" as a further aid in keeping her temper in check. Out of the corner of her eye, she thought she might have seen Bridger grin.

The trio arranged themselves in the Austin living room. Abby breathed deeply and launched into an explanation of the history of the Devil & Dragon Society. Since it was the first time either detective had mentioned a secret Japanese society to the young woman, Cari looked understandably puzzled.

At seeing this, Bridger assured her, "It will all become clear."

Abby went on. "You see, your mother was one of the honored few in the Society's special ranks."

Cari sucked in a surprised breath.

"Yes. We did some research, and have confirmation from a witness. That's one reason I was so interested in your necklace, or rather the little figurine that dangles from the chain. As I told you, it's called a netsuke. They are quite ancient. Originally, netsukes had several uses, most notable among them being a belt weight for men, or a tiny compartment to hold small items. But those were the everyday uses. The D&D used them as membership badges, and the one your mother carried proves she had an elite status. Regular members only had a small bit of ivory or bone with the Society's identifying triple shield carved into it. In addition to the shield, each 'officer', for lack of a better term, chose his or her own design and had the netsuke custom made in that shape. Rose's was the crouching woman under the wok-shaped hat, which must have held some special meaning for her."

Bridger took up the story from there, explaining that the Devil & Dragon Society had been formed sometime in the late 1940s, when a group of politically minded intellectuals wished to exert a sort of covert control over the Japanese Parliament, or the Diet. As it happened, the Society changed purpose with nearly every change of its upper echelon. Cari's mother Rose joined the D&D in 1977, at seventeen, after lying about her age. Her brains took her very far very fast, and she became an officer within two years. Rose Nakamura was an impressive young woman. But youth and ideology can be a lethal mixture.

Soon, Rose discovered that many of the other officers did not share her purity of motives. Instead, they possessed highly selfish plans, ranging from plots to influence results of elections to fashioning bills favorable to their personal fiscal futures. Rose seemed to have come in at one of the Society's less beneficent times.

Abby wanted to tell the next part. "Somehow, your mother uncovered some very damaging information about an up-and-coming Japanese statesman named Hiroki, a man being groomed for great advancement in the country's government, quite likely the top spot. I don't know, was it still emperor at that point? Sorry, I'm not real good with Japanese government stuff.

"Anyway, the best we can reconstruct from what one witness has told us – and he's not real forthcoming – your mom absconded with Hiroki's netsuke, which was linked to a hell of a lot of crimes. Hiroki had once been among the most feared assassins in the Devil & Dragon Society, one of those special agents who went over to the dark side, if you will. When he entered public office, most of his D&D friends – which, of course, were the worst of the lot – thought the netsuke had been destroyed. But Hiroki's colossal ego wouldn't allow him to part with it. To him, it signified the many lives he had taken, the power he gained from the souls he'd stolen. But the power-hungry fool didn't think through the consequences of keeping this gruesome souvenir, for its existence had the ability to also be the pivot point of his downfall.

"Rose, of course, knew all about Hiroki. As Bridger said, she was one smart cookie. She'd been watching Hiroki. Somehow, she got her hands on the netsuke and a fistful of damning papers proving its true owner, and a little book that contained names of the dead, disabled, cheated, blackmailed – whatever Hiroki was into. And, believe me, he was into a lot. Anyway, she hightailed it out of Japan damned fast. Left everything. Never looked back. She didn't dare. She knew Hiroki would squash her like a bug if he found her.

"Well, the news of the theft spread quickly and prevented Hiroki from even thinking of chasing his goals. Just the fear of exposure, which would have meant a certain death sentence for him, kept him from pursuing his dream of ruling his country. It also made him a deadly bitter man. He changed his life's goal to simply finding your mother."

"That's absolutely right," Bridger added. "And Hiroki had a vengeful streak the size of the Pacific Ocean. When it was discovered that his netsuke had gone missing at the same time as Rose, naturally he jumped to the correct conclusion. Immediately, he sent an army of his best men to look for her. The rogue agents in the D&D had their spies, and the rumblings in the underground there mentioned the Pacific Northwest as a place Rose had likely gone to hide. Hiroki assumed Rose would try to disappear among the Asian community in a large city, so he dispatched men to the more major metropolitan centers. Shin – whose real name was actually Aito Himura, by the way – happened to land in Portland, where he assumed the identity of Lincoln Shin, with some forged teaching credentials. He spent years, ultimately, combing the city, first asking around about the recent arrival of a young Japanese woman named Rose Nakamura, then just watching for her."

"She didn't change her name?" Cari asked, apparently catching onto the spy mindset and finding this idea unbelievable.

Abby shook her head. "No. She probably didn't think anyone would try looking in a town like Portland, Oregon. In the grand scheme of things, Portland's not really very large."

"But it is part of the Pacific Rim!"

"Yes. In hindsight, I'm sure Rose realized her naiveté, only by then it was too late. But thirty years ago, it was hard for a person of Asian descent to blend into a smaller community, so her choices were somewhat limited. And fairly soon, she fell in love with your dad and got married, so it became a moot point – at least in her mind. She was now Rose Austin. No one had found her, it seemed, and she settled into a happy, normal life. She actually got by several years before anyone did discover her. And that's why Statesman Hiroki never ascended to the greatness he coveted."

"But once so much time had passed that he couldn't run for office anyway, why not drop the search for mom?"

"Oh, the D&D had already found your mom. They found her pretty early on. But the netsuke, that was another matter. They watched Rose like she was a poisonous snake, but she never went near the netsuke. At least not while they were looking. And believe me, they were looking. Besides, remember, Hiroki hated your mother with a burning passion for ruining his chances to become the grand ruler he envisioned himself to be. He devoted the remainder of his life to making her pay. Only he wasn't about to let himself be connected to her demise when it came. That's where he had to finesse his revenge."

Deep in his pocket, Bridger's phone vibrated and rang. He excused himself. Even from the next room, Abby could hear his frustrated tone, and guessed that things with Zach were nearing the boiling point. She wished that problem could be solved as easily as the Austin case, and as quickly.

CHAPTER 37

*"Conscience is a cur that will let you get past it
but that you cannot keep from barking."*

— *Anonymous*

Cari sat quietly, soaking up the surfeit of information they had just thrown at her. Abby heard Bridger mumbling in the hallway, raise his voice, and then abruptly end the call. He marched back into the room and sat beside her, rigid. A minute passed, then two.

Finally, a question they would have liked to avoid occurred to Cari. "Who's the witness?"

Abby nodded at Bridger, allowing him to handle this subject in the hope that he would get his mind back on this case. His voice was strong, betraying none of the frustration Abby had heard in the telephone call. "A man named Alan Garfield. Or, that's his name now. We don't know what he was called when he was born. Mr. Garfield often jogged the trails in the West Hills, where he saw your brother quite a lot. That was sort of by design more than by accident."

Cari was watching Bridger closely as he answered, and she didn't miss his ending comment. He had left it dangling, ambiguous, so that, if she wanted clarification, she could ask. It gave her control of the amount of information the detectives fed her. Apparently, she wanted to know everything, for she urged, "Explain Garfield's role again, please."

Abby took another deep breath. This was the part that had them scratching their heads. "I'll try. First of all, let me say that Alan Garfield is, beyond doubt, a guardian angel, a hero like your mom. He originally came from Japan, like your mom. And, like your mom, he was part of the Society. You see, the Devil & Dragon Society assigned each of their officers, again for lack of a better term, a sort of secret guardian angel, someone to watch their back. Garfield was Rose's. The top guys knew they had some bad eggs in their ranks and this was their way of providing at least some protection for their people. Garfield stuck with Rose from her earliest assignment through the time she fled the country. She, of course, had no inkling of his existence. But he knew everything about Rose. However, when she disappeared, his obligation ended. That didn't stop Garfield. Oh, no. He took his life's work to heart. Where she went, he went, obligation be damned. No one could get near your mom without going through Alan Garfield. He was her invisible shield, although she never knew."

By this point, Cari had started to cry. "Why didn't he save Cory? How could he let that happen to my brother?"

Bridger reached over and placed his hand lightly on the young woman's shoulder. "That was Garfield's one failing. He had fought them off before. Many times, in fact. He thought he still had it all under control. Unfortunately, he was wrong."

Abby plucked a tissue from her purse and Bridger handed it to the young woman. "Cari, he's been suffering almost as much as you have since Cory's death. That's why he made sure he was there for Vanessa. True, Shin hurt Vanessa, and pretty badly, but at least Garfield got there before he could finish the job."

"That was Garfield, too? Huh." She took some time to process this. "He didn't call the cops though. Why not?"

This had puzzled the detectives, too. They had come to the conclusion, since Garfield had been vague about the reason, that he felt the need to maintain his anonymity in case Cari still needed his protection. His allegiance to Rose descended to her children, too. It was also possible that he remained suspicious of police type people, not having trusted the ones in his native country. Or the timing of Dexter's arrival might have played into Garfield's failure to call 9-1-1. Whatever the reason, they figured it would remain a bit of a mystery, Alan Garfield being disinclined to answer fully all of their questions. Sometimes loose ends dangled and nothing could be done about them. Garfield had no obligation to explain himself beyond what he had done, and apparently felt no compunction to do so. However, that wouldn't diminish anyone's gratitude for his heroism.

Cari asked, "So did Shin kill our cat Frizz, too?"

Abby answered, "Oh, yeah. He sure did. That was his warning shot. Cory didn't quite understand, didn't know what was up, just that something was. He started acting – shall we say – off, not like himself at all. Apparently, he dropped hints that he knew what was going on. He said all this at school, pretty vocally, too. We're surprised you didn't hear any of it."

Cari blushed. "Cory protected me from *everything*."

Bridger shifted in his seat and said, "Yeah, my son protected his little sister from stuff, too."

Abby thought she heard a wistfulness in his voice. They might be able to address the issue of Zach's newfound lifestyle soon, now that they had solved the mystery of who murdered Cory Austin. However, there remained a bit of mopping up yet.

"But Cory thought the football star had killed his cat?"

"Yeah. That's the sad part. He really did. At least, at first. He thought Chris Reilly had cut off Frizz's paw and then let him bleed to death, so he booby trapped Chris's locker. Did a pretty ingenious job of it, too. Just went after the wrong guy." Bridger had assumed a comforting voice, meant to walk Cari through a difficult subject. He was talking about her brother, after all, a guy she idolized.

"So who called Cory that night?"

"Vanessa Reilly, of course."

"Really?

"Yep."

"Why?"

"Well, see, Shin convinced her it was just a harmless prank. And while she normally loved attention, Cory had been pretty blatant about his crush on her and she was growing bored with it, so this was a way to get him to leave her alone and have a little fun, too."

"Some fun."

"Yeah." Bridger shook his brown bald head in sympathy. Clearly, Cari had a lot to digest. At least, though, she now knew what had happened.

"Why did Cory buy her story when she called? I mean, it was eight o'clock at night and starting to get dark."

"Because he *wanted* to believe it. Remember, he's an eighteen-year-old boy with raging hormones. Those pesky things always get in the way of logic and reason. As for time of day, who cares how late it is when you're that age? Also, darkness brings with it a shroud of secrecy, so he's thinking maybe, just maybe…Things can happen that wouldn't otherwise happen when it's light out."

"Okay." Cari still didn't sound convinced. Maybe her hormones hadn't caused the nightmarish sort of insanity that they normally did in teenagers. "So did he ever realize it was Shin?" It appeared that she had yet to untangle all the twists.

"Not until the bitter end. He found your mom's handbook but he didn't know how to read Japanese. The kid had resources, though, and a hell of a brain."

"You said 'hell'."

"Bite me, Abs. Anyway, he finally did figure it out, or at least most of it, and threatened to tell. That was his fatal mistake. Typical, though, especially for a guy his age. Naïve, yes, but fatal nonetheless. He wanted to protect his family. Those hormones again. With your dad not around, I suspect that Cory tried to step into the role of man of the house." Bridger spread his hands wide. "Besides, he was really, really upset about Frizz. He wanted the guy to pay for that. It's possible that the cat's death was the catalyst that ultimately set Cory gunning for Shin. He just didn't know what kind of person he was dealing with. After all, Shin was a trained assassin once upon a time. He may have lost his edge, but he still had a deadly lethal side. Your brother's threats didn't put much of a scare into him. Shin just needed a way to lure Cory to a secluded spot. And, voila, along comes Vanessa."

Cari bit her lip. "Vanessa. And to think we idolized her." She shook her head and smiled with a look of disgust. "Why didn't she tell? She must have known it was Shin after he asked her to call Cory and then he turns up dead."

Abby answered. "Oh, she knew all right. She may not be real bright but that didn't get by her. Vanessa says Shin tricked her into calling and then told her that she'd better be quiet about it or she would be the one arrested for murder. He used a knife from her kitchen, said her fingerprints were all over it, so he had her convinced that the cops would think she'd done it. She was terrified."

"Didn't she have an alibi?"

"Remember, Cari, this is Vanessa. Shin didn't have to cover all his bases, because he knew she wouldn't think things through. Just mentioning the knife and the fact she had made the phone call convinced her that Shin was right; the cops would put her away forever. Besides, any man that will do what he did and then frame his student for it, well, I sort of understand her inability to come forward. She just froze with fear."

"She's a coward! At least he hurt her, too!"

Bridger and Abby recoiled at Cari's outburst. Indeed, Vanessa could have told the truth eleven years ago, taken her chances and hoped the police would believe her over Shin. Of course, they knew she didn't have that kind of virtue inside her, nor that kind of courage. Nonetheless, Cari had a right to be angry. Vanessa had paid, though, and would continue to pay for years, possibly for a lifetime. Sadly, Bertha Peck had become an unnecessary casualty of Vanessa's shameful secret.

Cari abruptly changed the topic. "Why didn't mom just give Shin what he wanted?"

"We won't ever know that. But I'd suspect that she couldn't, in good conscience. The ramifications of relinquishing Statesman Hiroki's netsuke, coupled with that damning documentation that she possessed, would have been too devastating for her native country. It would have given the man a dangerous amount of power and, with nothing to stop him politically, might possibly have allowed him to attempt a coup. She had to risk losing everything over that, even her children. I'm so sorry."

"Oh, no, no, no. I mean, she was a hero, wasn't she?"

"Yes, Cari, she was. What she did took a lot of courage. And exacted a steep price, one she had to live with for so many years, not to mention living with the fear of losing you, too."

"I was wondering about that. Why did Shin let me live?"

"I think Rose and Shin were at an impasse. She had something he badly wanted, and he had only one piece of leverage left. He probably didn't want to use it unless he absolutely had to, because without it he would have no control at all. But that one piece of leverage was a biggie, so he bargained that she would maintain the status quo, and that was at least a fairly acceptable second best."

"Um, okay, I sort of get that." She sat across from the detectives, deep in thought. "If this guy was such a good assassin, though, how come Vanessa and her neighbor weren't killed right off?"

Good question. Abby held up her hand to indicate that she had an idea about that so Bridger let her take over. "Well, Cari, for one thing, it had been decades since Shin's initial training. According to your mom's handbook, he did some maintenance of his skills, but his life here was as a schoolteacher so he didn't really need to be super proficient at killing people anymore. Time passed; everything seemed to be humming along smoothly. And then there was that hidden gem, Alan Garfield. Garfield's sole purpose was to watch over Rose and, as we know, he never forgot that. So when we stirred things up again, he was on high alert. And Shin's rustiness allowed Garfield just enough time to knock him off his game, saving Vanessa's life."

Abby bit her lip before continuing. "As for the neighbor, Bertha Peck, that's a tough one. I think Bridger's and my arrival at her house interrupted Shin. I truly believe he was on the other side of the door when we got there, and he panicked. What once were nerves of steel had weakened over the years and he simply panicked and ran off before finishing the job."

This was a conclusion Abby had come to after many hours of contemplation. The time table worked out so that this could only be how it had happened. She had beaten herself up a little bit about not sensing Lincoln Shin's presence at the Peck house as she and Bridger were just a few feet away, knocking on Bertha's door. The poor woman lay dying on her floor and they walked off, grumbling about the fact that she hadn't answered. What the hell good was a heightened awareness as a counterbalance for the loss of one's vision if it didn't kick in at a life-or-death moment like that? Forgiving herself would take some time.

Bridger tried to dispel Abby's feelings of guilt with the argument that she couldn't possibly have known. After all, they had just driven from Washington High where they had watched Shin park his car, get out and walk inside the school building. How were they supposed to guess that it wasn't like any other day at work? He wondered, had the teacher noticed them sitting there in little CON? If so, Shin had given no sign, but then he had been trained in his previous life to remain cool under such circumstances. He might have just ducked inside the lobby, waited until he saw the detectives drive away, and sprinted back out to his dull gray Gremlin.

As for knowing where to go once inside his wreck of a car, had he followed them the evening before? Or, an even more unnerving thought occurred to Bridger, had he been following them for days? Bridger figured he must have been. And he would have laid bets that Shin saw him taking pictures that morning, guessed at the reason for them being there, and raced like a madman out to Gresham in order to silence Bertha Peck before they could get to her. It was a risky move, but what did the man really have to lose? If they got there first and Ms. Peck identified Shin from the photos, his goose was cooked anyway. But, of course, they had not driven there directly. Instead, they had stopped for coffee, made a detour by the Austin house, and dropped over to Toby Meyer's apartment to pick up the flyer featuring a picture of him in the currently-playing Darcelle's revue. No reason to think that time was of the essence. Bridger would take some time forgiving himself for that slip-up.

CHAPTER 38

"Belief is harder to shake than knowledge."
                                                    – Adolf Hitler

"Wow." Cari sat back, head hanging, looking thoroughly dumbfounded.

Abby could understand how she felt. Bridger sympathized, too. They had dumped a lot of information on the young woman. Eleven years in the dark about what happened to her brother, now they had given her the answer. A conclusion wonderful and awful at the same time.

After what felt like an eternity, she found her voice again. "Um, I'd really like to thank this Mr. Garfield personally."

Bridger looked at Abby, who opened her mouth, then snapped it shut. Neither had anticipated this and neither had a ready answer. Bridger was the one who finally made a decision. "That's real nice, Cari. We will convey your desire to him."

Cari recognized the stall for what it was, judging by the prickle in her voice. "But why wouldn't he be all right with that?"

"Some people don't like being in the spotlight. Alan Garfield comes across as an intensely private person. We just need to pass it by him first." Bridger continued to study her reaction, wanting to ensure that they left her as satisfied as possible. Granted, it would of necessity be a bittersweet satisfaction, but still it might provide a solid foundation upon which Cari could begin to rebuild. Every inch of her being must be aching with a renewed sense of loss by this point, so whatever comfort they could give her would best be given now.

"Mr. Garfield and my brother were friends, right?"

Abby answered, "Of a sort, yes."

"Well, that – I mean, it would be really cool to talk to him about Cory. He *knew* him. And he protected Mom." Cari's face had turned a scarlet shade, as though she might be on the verge of tears. Abby looked away, uncomfortable. She hated to see a person cry. And, while she believed, were she in Cari's shoes, she would want to meet Garfield, too, she knew better than to make promises they couldn't keep. She could, however, vow to use her not-inconsiderable persuasion skills to see that the meeting happened.

"We'll do our best, Cari." Abby nodded at her partner, who correctly interpreted her signal. The detectives stood.

"We should be going now. Let you digest all this. Get some rest. It has been our pleasure helping you." Bridger offered her another business card. She pushed herself up off of the sofa and reached for it.

"We know this has been very difficult for you. Please, call either of us for any reason. Any reason at all." Bridger's voice was soft and friendly.

Cari threw her arms around his neck and squeezed tight, then kissed his deep brown cheek before stepping back and saying, "Thank you. Thank you." When she released him, her eyes were brimming.

Abby had turned away, but she didn't even feel the young woman's intention or she would have tried to deflect Cari's enthusiastic hug aimed her way. Instead, she patted the girl's back and said, "You're welcome," hastily in an attempt to shorten the duration of their bonding. They said their goodbyes, adding in promises to stop by again soon and further assurances that she should indeed call them anytime she felt like it. Then Abby took hold of Bridger's arm, her recent concession that she needed guidance to safely maneuver outside and down the steps to the curb.

Once inside CON, Abby heaved a sigh of relief and shortly followed that with a suggestion that they celebrate their victory. Bridger raised an eyebrow, forgetting again that she couldn't see that. He cleared his throat as he glanced at his watch. 10:22. "Rather early for a drink, don't you think?"

"Hell, yes, which is why I say let's toast with some Salt & Straw ice cream cones."

Bridger groaned. His diet had already taken several lethal hits over the course of the Austin case. Voodoo doughnuts, a burger oozing fat, carb-laden pasta and meatballs in a cheese sauce. Now ice cream? But he knew it was fruitless to try to deny

Abigail Dalton anything once it appeared on her radar. He put the little smart car in Drive and sped off toward Northwest Portland.

Less than half an hour later, the detectives of Eyes & Ears sat on a wrought iron bench in Portland's picturesque Rose Garden, a vast park covering several acres in the West Hills that overlook the city toward the east. Abby polished off the last of her mint and caramel and cookie dough triple cone, then made a show of cleaning off her fingers. Bridger's simple pistachio one scoop had long since disappeared.

Against a backdrop of cerulean blue, puffy cumulus clouds floated lazily north, a few of them parting for Mt. Hood's jagged summit in the distance. The vibrant oranges and yellows of the oaks and birches lining the East Portland streets lent the scene the character of an autumn watercolor.

The old friends sat companionably, each entertained by their own thoughts for ten or fifteen more minutes as a class of what appeared to be sixth grade students walked solemnly through the rows of Mr. Lincolns and Gold Blushes with a thirty-something teacher leading them in a nature lesson. They watched her smile and nod and point and murmur, and mercifully keep the children under control.

Eventually, Bridger shifted in his seat and cast his arm over the back of the bench. He rubbed the fuzz on his chin as he stared out over the skyline. "So, Abs, tell me what you see."

She laughed, surprised. "What?"

"Yeah, just look out there. What do you see? Describe it for me."

Abby sat up, straightened her back and folded her arms. She opened her eyes wide, donned her sunglasses and peered down from their place on the hill as though concentrating.

"Okay. I see soft shapes, Bridger, as you know. Everything is fuzzy lines and colors. In front here," she gestured, "the trees, they're deep green and almost like an abstract painter would put them on a canvas. The city itself is nothing more than boxy clumps in varying shades of mostly gray and brown. There's a streak of slate blue, which must be the river, and then a riot of different colors. The center is kind of a black hole. But then Mt. Hood towers over it all, standing there big, bold and magnificent."

Abby took off her glasses and wiped her eyes. "Well, no, I

can't see that clearly, actually not well at all. But I know. I *know* what it looks like. My mind fills in the blanks that this damned disease has created. It's a handsome city, and that mountain is so beautiful." She turned to face him, realizing that her voice had dropped dramatically. "Sorry. You probably didn't hear any of that last bit."

He beamed at her. "Oh, but I did. For once, I had my hearing aids turned up. Put fresh batteries in this morning. And I was watching you. You felt a lot of that, probably even more than seeing it." He hesitated, still looking at her, his smile fading slowly, "It's easier for me, isn't it, Abs?"

Abby kept her eyes on his face, wondering whether he was referring to their disabilities or their newfound partnership, or something else entirely. Where once she might have been able to tell, now she could not. Her vision was faltering, day by day. The changes were subtle, but relentless. She dreaded losing what little she had left. It would be awhile yet, but what then? Already, she couldn't read Bridger's expression. His features had become indistinct, like someone had smeared Vaseline on her glasses.

Suddenly, aware that she could too easily find herself on the brink of a pity party of her own making, she answered, "Yes, I think it is easier for you. But probably not in the way you mean. I think it must be easier because you know what you want." She realized then that she did envy Bridger his convictions. She'd thought she wanted nothing more from life now than a good book and her dog Malph at her feet, but did she really? In fact, the past week and a half had been quite the adrenaline rush, and wasn't that a gas? Hadn't she felt more alive faced with the mystery, the puzzle, the research? Yes, even the danger. Maybe it wouldn't hurt to work on a cold case now and then…

Abby shook her head. Foolishness. They'd set up the agency to work simple domestic cases, nothing more. Bridger, in his sneaky fashion, was using his charisma to nudge her beyond her comfort zone and she had almost fallen for it. That damned Flynn Effect at work again. No, the Austin case was a one-off. In reality, she was bone tired and, therefore, prone to becoming vulnerable. That's all. With her jaw set, she said, "So tell me what you see out there."

Bridger had watched Abby's emotions warring with each other. Now he leaned forward, elbows on knees, and watched the grade schoolers disappear around an evergreen hedge before answering.

"What do I see? I see a bustling city full of diverse people, individuals wanting to connect, get a job, fall in love, build a family, enjoy life. It's a city proud of itself, with a river in the middle which cuts the place apart, but bridges which pull it together. It's a huge expanse of land, a community full of dreams and hopes, some fulfilled, some dashed. And, yes, all of that with the incredible backdrop of Mt. Hood. What a wondrous, looming peak, like Portland's own guardian angel. Today it stands there, looking fantastic and majestic." He sighed. "Some days, though, it has a shadow falling over it."

"Are you sure you were a cop?" Abby snickered. "You sound more like a poet."

"Oh, sorry. I hate poetry."

"Me, too. At least, we agree on something." Abby reached out and touched Bridger's hand. "Seriously, Bridger, that was lovely."

"Thanks."

A jaunty labradoodle trotted up to Abby with a ball in its mouth and laid it at her feet. She picked it up and tossed it, the dog running off, panting, to fetch it.

"And that shadow over Mt. Hood? It's there now, isn't it? The Children of Allah? Zach?"

"Yeah."

"Want to talk about it?"

Bridger looked over toward the dog, who had reversed course and was running back toward its owner. "Not really."

"Have you been able to reach him?"

"No." Bridger hung his head and shook it. "I call over there every day. They won't summon him to the phone. I don't think he even gets the message that I've called." He slapped his knee.

"Bastards."

"Yeah."

Abby would have expounded further, but Bridger's phone rang. She stewed over how to best lure Zach away from the clutches of the cult that had its hold firmly over him while her partner listened and interjected an occasional, "Okay."

After three minutes or so, Bridger disconnected. "Uh, that was Capt. Shearer."

"*Capt.* Shearer? Not Nate?"

Bridger blushed. "Capt. Shearer. He needs us to come to the precinct this afternoon."

"And why would that be?"

"Uh, to prep for a news conference at 4:00."

"Tell me you're joking."

"Sorry, Abs."

"Shit."

CHAPTER 39

"You can never plan the future by the past."

– Edmund Burke

Capt. Shearer's call had ruined the magical moments enjoyed by Bridger and Abby as they sat on a park bench, taking turns describing the city view from the Rose Garden. With a press conference hanging over their heads in a few hours, they decided it would be best to each snatch some rest and meet up again around 3:00.

Back at her Lake Oswego townhouse, Abby waved after Bridger as he drove off in CON, then sauntered slowly toward her gate. Her legs felt like cement. The comedown after the high, she supposed. Like always, the welcome sound of Malph's deep-throated bark thrilled her. What a lovely way to be greeted. The albino bulldog did his best to wag the stub that served as a tail, and his mistress rewarded him by showering hearty good boys and vigorous back rubs on him. He trotted after her, bumping his snub nose into the backs of her legs, as she made her way inside the house to rid herself of her purse.

Less than five more minutes passed before Abby had sunk deep into one of the Adirondack chairs on her deck, a small fleece blanket wrapped around her shoulders. Two weeks ago, she had begun "The Charm School" by Nelson DeMille and now was more than eager to return to the book. She knew how the story went, and the ending, because she had read it more than once, but sometimes she liked to revisit a favorite author and spend a few weeks going over old ground. Nelson DeMille was at the top of her list of writers worthy of re-reading, so now it felt especially right to curl up with him for even a short time. It would be a pleasure to escape into the novel and emerge in a couple of hours, invigorated by the cleverness of the characters, delighted by their smart dialogue and awed by the twists DeMille inevitably conjured up. It might even take away some of the pique she was feeling because of their appointment with the media.

A few miles away, on Bridger's houseboat, he sat covering a little familiar territory as well, having queued up *Gran Torino*, starring his favorite Hollywood cop Clint Eastwood. Clint always had a drop-dead fabulous line or two worth quoting. Bridger absolutely loved hearing the husky voice say something grouchy, like, "Get off my lawn," especially when the man who owned the voice stood there holding a rifle. Not that Bridger was a big fan of firearms, but he would admit that they did have a place in this world.

Now, a couple hours of watching a macho old white guy saying and doing whatever he wanted, well, that would do Bridger a vast sea of good. He slouched deep into his chair, remote in one hand, a power tea drink in the other. He considered making a batch of popcorn, but that would entail getting out of the chair and his energy level felt nearly depleted. Pressing the "Play" button and lifting the tea to his mouth seemed about all he could handle.

With the movie still in its start-up mode, not yet advanced as far as the title, Bridger's thoughts drifted to his partner. Since the onset of the macular degeneration, Abby's sight had been seriously compromised and continually deteriorating. But the universe demands balance, so something positive had to be countered by something negative. Abby's positive was a heightened sense of intuition. She had asked about Zach more than once lately. He probably should have opened up to her, picked her brain for ideas. In fact, he was at a loss what to do next. Maybe he'd try calling the Children of Allah again after the movie ended. He would probably get the same response they always gave him, but something had to be done. Zach should at least be given the chance to hear him out.

While he was allowing himself to agonize over his son's situation, Bridger almost missed his favorite scene, so he brought his focus back to Clint. Better to keep his mind on today and the Austin case wrap-up.

Shortly before 3:00, as Bridger pulled CON up to Abby's gate, he halfway expected to find her house dark and empty. It didn't seem beyond the realm of possibility that she would – well, not exactly run off, but skip out on the upcoming press conference.

She hated them that much. Instead, though, he watched her slide through the townhouse gate with grace and poise, looking as though she anticipated a pleasant afternoon in the company of old pals. Bridger braced himself. This had to be some kind of trick.

The ride to Central Precinct went without incident, Abby rambling on about some book she was reading and acting like the two of them were heading out on a date. Bridger would almost have preferred grumbling curses and invectives, for that is what he expected. His partner this serene, calm and collected didn't jibe with her earlier reaction to the news of the scheduled media frenzy. Well, he decided with more than a small amount of resignation, let's see what happens.

As they turned onto the final block leading to Central, TV news vans lined the street. Abby shifted in her seat and said, "Damned vultures."

Bridger caught her tone if not her precise words, and chuckled. "That's more like my Abs."

"Don't call me Abs."

Ah, yes, his Abby Dalton was back. Whatever had briefly gained hold of her had released its grip. Now Bridger and Capt. Shearer could worry about nothing more than her usual remarks rather than what she might have up her sleeve. Nonetheless, Shearer deemed it wise to have Bridger take the lead this time. It was decided that he would give a summary of how they closed the Austin case and keep Abby's participation to a minimum.

At the appointed time, the captain introduced them, touting their success with great fervor, but noting there would be a very limited period for questions at the end. Overseeing the Austin case, he'd come to the obvious conclusion that Abby possessed a lack of tolerance so he promised to keep the session short. With the recovery of the child abducted in Tryon Creek Park and now the capture of a murderer eleven years after the crime, the media's attitude had mellowed, viewing them more as champions, unlike the earlier press conference when they had little progress to report. At that time, there were more accusations than accolades being thrown around.

Bridger gave a brief recap of their actions leading up to catching Shin, then fielded some questions, with a bit of help from the captain and even from Abby, although he wanted her role to be a silent one, smiling and nodding, rather than a speaking one. It was safer that way.

The press conference was winding down when Abby heard the voice belonging to the same man that had goaded her into making a rash claim the previous week during the Q&A.

"So does the cold case squad have another case lined up?"

Abby didn't give Bridger a chance to even open his mouth. "No, sir, because we're not a cold case squad. We're a couple of retired detectives. We have a modest little agency called Eyes & Ears over in Sellwood, where we do simple domestic sorts of tracking: helping mom find pop, or mom find daughter, or boss find the money someone got away with. We aren't a cold case squad," she emphasized. "We handled the Austin case as a favor to our old friend Captain Shearer." She smiled sweetly and stood aside. Bridger and Shearer both swallowed hard, as if fearing she might continue and dreading what she might add. Then the captain took the dais and concluded with a few diplomatic remarks, essentially cutting off any more questions. Reluctantly, the reporters shuffled out of the room, grumbling and mumbling.

Abby turned to the two men. "I think that went well, don't you?"

Shearer nodded and Bridger said, "Better than last time."

Abby didn't rise to the bait. Instead, she slipped her arm around Bridger's, a sign that she was ready to leave.

Shearer put up one hand. "Almost forgot. Archives finally found Cory Austin's computer. We have some guys going over it. I suspect, though, that whatever we find may be duplicative of the cell phone information. Maybe not. Anyway, the phone evidence, along with what Shin and Vanessa told us, should at least get us past the indictment stage. Evidence is mounting, so good job."

Bridger smiled; his partner nodded. They said, in unison, "Our pleasure."

"Thanks again, you two," Capt. Shearer said. "Now go on out and celebrate."

Bridger moaned. He didn't need any more celebrating. His blossoming midsection was proof of that. What he did need – desperately – was some quality time on the piano at The Woodstocker. A little jazz jamming and his troubles would melt away. At least for a while.

231

Abby seemed to read his mind. She said, "I think I'm celebrated out. Malph awaits me. And Nelson DeMille."

The men looked at her, puzzled. She shook her head. Obviously, they were not readers. The partners of Eyes & Ears hooked arms and headed down the hallway.

CHAPTER 40

*"Men always talk about the most important things
to perfect strangers."*

– G.K. Chesterton

The next two days the detectives spent separately, reclaiming their private lives in their own personal ways. Abby finished re-reading "The Charm School" and started "Playing for Pizza" by John Grisham for the first time. Any other time, she preferred Grisham's legal thrillers, but by this point she was burnt out on mystery of any sort.

The morning after the news conference, Wednesday, had dawned gray, heavy and cold. A brisk breeze churned up the lake's surface. Autumn's presence had made itself known in a big way, seeming as though it might want to skip right to winter. Abby didn't venture outside even as far as her deck. Instead, she brewed pots of coffee and made bone-warming soups – rich chicken noodle, creamy curry vegetable and garlicky beef lentil – and wandered around her townhouse in a soft sea green track suit, UGGs and a delicious mixture of aromas.

Malph watched her from his corner bed with eyes that suggested he feared she might be losing her sanity. His mistress rarely spent long stretches in so calm a mood, or in such quiet pursuits. Malph would probably have preferred to hear her voice, even if it was just muttering to herself and not speaking to him about food or toys. Occasionally, these days, she made a call but mostly she lost herself inside the worlds of books.

Bridger returned to his own world, too, that of music, making spontaneous visits to The Woodstocker at odd hours, to the delight of the bar's owner. At home, he caught up on the latest movies that Netflix had to offer and phoned Abby three or four times, ostensibly to make sure that she didn't need anything. She assured him that she didn't.

The first morning, he offered to pick her up for coffee. She declined. He tried again Thursday but got the same answer. Ditto Friday. By Saturday, Bridger could stand it no longer. Instead of calling, he drove CON to Abby's lakeside cottage and pressed the intercom by her gate. As though anticipating this eventuality, Malph barked the instant it came to life, with a tone that suggested canine displeasure. Oddly, Bridger found that comforting; at least someone was acting like himself.

Abby buzzed him through and stood propped against her door jamb as Bridger walked along the path, carrying two Starbucks cups.

"Good morning."

"Morning yourself."

"I come bearing coffee."

"I have coffee."

Bridger handed one cup off to Abby. She stood there a few seconds, then said, "Thanks," and turned to go back inside. Bridger followed, reminding himself that she had never been a warm and fuzzy kind of person.

The two of them stood in her kitchen, leaning against opposite counters. Bridger noted how tidy everything was, unlike his houseboat which showed the detritus of his life over the past several days. A silence settled between them that carried an air of boredom mixed with curiosity. Two full minutes elapsed before Abby took a deep breath and asked, "So what's up?"

"Nothing. Just wanted to say hi."

"Hi."

Another minute passed. The only break in the quiet was an occasional sip, gulp or sniffle. Bridger, determined to jumpstart Abby's energy, finally asked, "Heard anything from Cari?"

"No."

"Me neither."

Maybe a reference to the Austin case wasn't the best strategy for boosting her spirits. Still, their relationship revolved around business, or mostly did. He shuffled his feet. "I've been going by the office to pick up the mail and check for new cases."

They had discussed this earlier and, since there was an old-fashioned mail slot in their door, they posted a sign beside it requesting that prospective clients deposit a card or note with a phone number through the slot, and promising to call as promptly as possible. Without a receptionist and with the likelihood for them to be out chasing leads or bad guys or just not wanting to hang out in an office with nothing to do, this had seemed like the best solution to the issue of potential walk-ins. Clients could also send emails, but Bridger and Abby were less likely to check that than their physical mail. Old habits.

"Uh-huh."

"Don't you want to know if we have any?"

"Any what?"

"Cases."

"Okay. Do we have any cases?"

"No." Bridger polished off the last of his coffee.

"Well, that was productive. Glad I asked."

Malph crept in to glare at Bridger, looking as though his attitude might soften considerably if a treat were to fall his way. "Sorry, guy. I've got nothing," he said, the double meaning not lost on him. Glancing at Abby, he noticed that she looked relaxed, contented and maybe a little tired. "Everything okay, Abs?"

"Yeah."

"Am I interrupting something?"

"Just a book."

Exasperated, Bridger studied the floor some more. Abigail Dalton could be one of the moodiest women he'd ever known, and he certainly didn't understand what put her into a funk. It happened, though, with fair regularity. There was no reason to take it personally, but Bridger couldn't help but worry. He peered across the small kitchen at Abby. "Are we good?"

She sighed. "Yeah, we're good."

His shoulders relaxed. "Okay. That's my Abs." Bridger gave her a big bear hug, then started for the door. Reaching for the knob, he half turned. "By the way, I'm going to be playing at The Woodstocker tomorrow night. Our old friend Jiggs Barone will be there, too, with his banjo. Should be a real good time. Casual, low key. Come by if you feel like it. We'll probably start around 8:00."

"Thanks. Can't promise anything, but I'll think about it."

Piano and banjo? Sounded like a lunatic combination to Abby but she knew she wouldn't miss it for anything less than an invasion from Mars. Music had replaced art as one of her favorite pastimes when her eyesight had taken a backseat to her hearing. Even she would admit, albeit grudgingly, that Bridger Flynn had talent on the ivories. Besides, there would be more than one reason to hit The Woodstocker tomorrow night if all worked according to plan.

She closed the door behind Bridger almost impatiently, threw the deadbolt and listened for the sturdy clank of the gate locking itself outside. At the sound, Malph snorted.

As soon as Abby was certain that her partner had indeed left, she settled herself at her desk and fired up her computer. The Austin case may be over, but there was another cause afoot and she had research to do. If anything could lift her spirits, handling this next matter topped the charts. First, though, she picked up her phone and punched in the number for Luigi's Pizza.

In the fifteen minutes it took for the delivery guy to bring her a garlic chicken smothered with sweet onions and mushrooms, she had found the website she wanted, delved into it four or five layers deep, and found the who behind the URL. She'd also found a little usable dirt mixed in with the bio. Abby relished owning knowledge, especially when it was as valuable as this. Now it was time to put all that she had learned to good use. She picked up her phone once again.

CHAPTER 41

"Every dogma has its day."

- Abraham Rotstein

Abby awoke earlier than usual on Sunday morning, feeling more refreshed and energized than at any time during the previous couple of weeks. A mounting sense of purpose had returned to her on Saturday and her Web surfing produced the kind of leverage she needed to make things happen. As a result, she could barely contain herself. She felt like the old Abigail Dalton. The weight of guilt over Bertha Peck's murder had begun to dissipate. She and Bridger had done their best, after all, and neither of them could have known that Lincoln Shin had beaten them to their witness. At least, in the end, they had caught their man. She could take some satisfaction from that, meager though it may be. But best to put the past behind her, for today held a new promise.

To pass some of the time in gainful pursuits, Abby decided to take Malph for a spin in the kayak, despite a persistent light drizzle. The dog seemed relieved, like he thought this felt more normal for his human. Abby's vigor had returned, grown even. Out on the lake, she attacked the paddling like her life depended on it, and maybe it did. Maybe she had something to prove to herself. After three days, she realized that dragging herself around the house with a long face had appealed to her for about half an hour. Then a soul-squelching lethargy set in, followed by a toxic tinge of self pity and depression, and finally a mental kick to her own rear end. Indulgent wallowing couldn't be healthy. Besides, she hated herself when she dragged her dog down into the doldrums with her.

So after donning thick leggings, a waterproof jacket and floppy rain cap, Abby and Malph cut cleanly through the mist, Malph posing as stocky masthead and randomly calling out to phantom presences that only he could see. Abby trusted him to ensure that they steered clear of obstacles. He hadn't failed her yet.

Forty minutes later, woman and dog returned to the cottage. Malph struggled his way out of the kayak while Abby remained in the cockpit, catching her breath.

Back inside and reinvigorated, she shed her paddle gear and ravenously attacked a large piece of cold pizza as she paced, mentally going over her plan once more. Late in the afternoon, she took a hot shower and poured herself a glass of chardonnay to calm her nerves. She might even have a second glass, she told herself, because of course someone else would be doing the driving. She did have a date, though, and he was due to arrive around 7:30. Every inch of her tingled with excitement. Guaranteed, this was going to be a wonderful night.

The gate bell announced her escort's arrival at 7:28. Abby let him in, then grabbed a scarf, wove it expertly around her neck, and selected a light raincoat. The Tri-Met shuttle – a popular public conveyance provided for Portland's disabled – would be pulling up within ten minutes at the outside. She gave her date a big hug, poured him a small glass of water, and drank the last of her wine. Malph turned circles on his bed, finally decided on a position, then laid there watching the two of them from under half closed eyelids. He probably wondered about the evening's events, considering the care his mistress had taken in choosing her clothing and fixing her hair. A tiny yelp escaped his jowls at the ringing of the gate buzzer again.

"Well, our chariot awaits." Abby pulled on her coat, snatched up her new purse, called out a good-bye to Malph and ushered her date out of the house ahead of her.

At The Woodstocker, Bridger perched on the piano bench as comfortably as he had once worn a uniform. Abby marveled at how that man could make everything in his life fit him so perfectly, even a stark piece of wood with four legs attached.

"Take Five" emanated from the Baldwin upright, Bridger lost in the melody. His eyes were closed, the expression on his face oozing exultation. It appeared that Jiggs Barone had yet to arrive. Abby and her date took their seats two small tables to the left of the piano, within easy view of Bridger. The pair ordered drinks, wine for her, a nonalcoholic mixture of some ingredients Abby had never heard of for him.

"Man, he sounds good."

Abby nodded.

"Real good."

"Uh-huh. This is therapy for him." Admiration flowed from her voice. Bridger had his jazz; she had her kayak. Those were the things that kept them on track. Whatever worked, she supposed.

"He never did this at home."

"He didn't have a piano at home."

"Maybe not, but he should have. He looks so happy, almost blissful."

Blissful? The word made Abby shudder; a little touchy-feely for her tastes. "Yeah, well, sometimes little things like finances get in the way. Compounded by double shifts, court dates and other types of life intrusions." Abby knew all about life intrusions. They were why she had a failed marriage and were the main reasons she never had children. The other reasons probably had something to do with her attitude. But none of that mattered tonight. This was Bridger's night. She reached over and squeezed her companion's hand, smiling. In doing so, she missed Bridger's look of shock morph into one of delight when he saw them there. In truth, it was less her distraction and more her disability that kept her from seeing it, though.

The piano bench scraped back, almost tipping over in Bridger's haste to get to his son.

"How…" He stopped himself. Unable to find the words, he simply threw his arms around Zach. Bridger held on a long moment, then let go, remembering their last encounter. He wiped at his eyes.

Abby remained seated, wanting to allow father and son the fullest extent of their reunion. She would have preferred it be private, but then again maybe this was exactly the right atmosphere for it. When she felt Bridger's big hand on her shoulder, she grasped it and squeezed.

"You – how did you…I mean, how…Wait. Do I even want to know?"

"Probably not," she replied, rising.

Bridger thrust an arm around her, pulling her into a group hug as he thrust his other arm around Zach. It might be a while before he let go of his son. Things would be strained between them for some time, maybe forever, but at least now they had a chance.

Zach appeared shell shocked, and Abby suspected the Children of Allah had been busily working on their form of brainwashing for the months they had him under their influence. She couldn't blame him for feeling confused, even overwhelmed. He'd begun the day at the cult compound outside of La Pine, endured a four-hour bus ride, ending at Abby's townhouse, and now sat in a bar on Portland's southeast side with his father playing jazz. His head must be spinning. Fresh out of what anyone would call an abusive situation, now back to the life he'd tried to escape. Well, friends, family and probably some mental health sessions figured large in his future for some time to come.

As if Bridger sensed he needed to back off and let Zach find his own way to relate to his father, he spread his hands and said, "Better get back to the piano. What do you want to hear? Let me play something special for this moment."

Zach sputtered, "Anything. Yeah, really, whatever. That last set was incredible."

There was clearly a lightness to Bridger's step that hadn't been there before as he made his way back to the bench. Abby and Zach sat down again to enjoy the next song. She closed her eyes and savored some of the chardonnay as Bridger launched into "Maybe Tonight" by Earl Klugh. Neither she nor Zach spoke, focused totally on the music. Next, Bridger segued into Bob James' "Mind Games" then moved on to "Kind of Blue" by Miles Davis and ended with a trio of songs by Chick Corea. When he quit, the room exploded into applause.

Abby hadn't noticed people filtering steadily in, she was so wrapped up in the rhythm and melody. Zach swiveled his head side to side, a look of surprise covering his face. Almost two dozen bodies had gathered around tables since Bridger had started playing.

Now he took an abbreviated bow and hurried over to their table again, signaling to a waiter on his way. Beside the piano, Jiggs Barone stepped up and adjusted the microphone, readying himself to play a few songs on his banjo.

"Nice job," Abby said.

Zach grinned, agreeing. "Yeah, Dad. That was really something!"

Abby excused herself, gesturing toward the ladies' room. She figured that the men could use some space.

Bridger and Zach spoke haltingly, Bridger straining to hear over the bar's crowd. Normally, he didn't care about talking, but tonight was different. Very different.

When Abby returned, she made a show of yawning, and raised her glass. It would be empty soon; she would be ready to leave. Ten minutes passed and Jiggs Barone wrapped up his short set. Before Abby could gather together her coat and purse, Jiggs was pulling a chair up to their table. Everyone shook hands and said hello, and Abby yawned again.

"Oh, dear. I should be going."

Bridger tried to protest, but Abby held firm. Instead, he thanked her with a sloppy peck on the cheek. "You don't know what this means to me, Abs."

"Oh, yes, I do. You've been moping around for weeks."

"No, I haven't."

"Bullshit. Moping. Big time moping."

"Well…"

"And don't call me Abs." She patted Zach on the back, waved good-bye to Jiggs and stood to leave. "Oh, by the way, I set up that meeting between Alan Garfield and Cari."

Bridger's eyebrows shot up and his jaw dropped. "Huh. You are an amazing woman. And you've been a very busy one since I left you yesterday."

"Damn straight. And now I'm going home to my dog."

Bridger nodded. "That's my Abs."

He escorted her to the door. "Really, Abby, thank you."

She looked him squarely in the eyes. "You've got your work cut out for you, you know. I did the easy part. I just got him here. You two…well, just make me glad I did."

"See you tomorrow for coffee?"

"Call me." She mimed a phone with her thumb and little finger, then grabbed the doorknob.

Bridger started back toward Zach and Jiggs, but stopped before his partner could escape entirely. He snapped his fingers. "Oh, by the way, Capt. Shearer called."

She froze. "What?"

"Yeah, seems he has another cold case for us."

Abby didn't bother to even look over her shoulder. She just made a gesture with her left hand that Bridger didn't need hearing aids to understand.

- - -

Acknowledgments & Disclaimers

Thanks to all of my friends and family for their support and encouragement, but special kudos go to Peggy Aitchison, who, in an apparent lapse of good judgment, agreed to be my reader/critique buddy extraordinaire. She is an incredible friend, one I've known since my court reporting days (before my husband even), and just happens to be the best critical thinker I have met. Thanks also to my husband Jim, who runs out to play golf almost daily, thus leaving me to write. He has stood by me through several murders, and helped keep me from killing my computer. And to Pam Oloyumaya, my long-distance feedback pal.

Now, for the other side of things. Several actual businesses and entities are mentioned in the story, like Darcelle's, Voodoo Doughnuts, Kornblatt's, Goose Hollow Inn, Salt & Straw, Leipzig Tavern, Portland Police Bureau, and a few more. Please realize that everything that goes on in these places in this story, well, I've made it all up. Only the names are real. None of the people exist. I've fashioned the characters out of thin air. And none of the happenings happened. The places are long-time and/or unique-to-Portland entities, so I wanted to include them. And let me say that Portland isn't perfect but it is a beautiful, wonderful city, and our special places like these make it even more of a draw. Thank you to Portland and its one-of-a-kind personality and people.

Cover Design by Kathy Jones, Portland, Oregon
Photo: A door somewhere in Dublin, Ireland
By Kathy Jones

About the Author

Kate Ayers spent much of her career as a court reporter in the Pacific Northwest, taking up the writing of mysteries in just the last ten years or so. She's the author of *A Murder of Crows* and *A Walk of Snipes*. Kate lives in Oregon with her husband of over three decades and her slightly imbalanced dog.

Visit her website: www.kateayers.com

Email her at kate@kateayers.com

Follow her on Facebook at Kate Ayers, Author

18794617R00138

Made in the USA
San Bernardino, CA
29 January 2015